STORIES OF GEORGE & OTHERS

A History of Joe Bloggs.

by

RON CRADDOCK

LLYFRAU
CAMBRIA

Published in the United Kingdom in 2013 by
Cambria Books; Carmarthenshire, Wales, United Kingdom

Copyright ©2013 Ron Craddock

ISBN : 978-0-9574894-8-6

Also by Ron Craddock – 'Around and About Membury.' 1999.

STORIES OF GEORGE & OTHERS.

The tale of George Gunner and others, in hope, in anguish ... and wallowing in bed. Told in two story strands, a continuing unfolding present day, and a counter-pointing, episodic past with a chronology that moves back in time.

An ancestry line, in reverse chronological order, appears on the very last page.

My many thanks to:-
Hilary, Celia, Michael, Carole, for reading and comment
... not forgetting the forbears
.. and Editor: Jenny Bryan.

CONTENTS.

A STORY OF GEORGE.

ONE ... Competitor.

THIS was to be a sweet moment. It was deserved. I had worked hard, pursuing the same activity again and again, regular exercise which made me fit and alert as befits a presentable late teenager. I was ahead near the end of the game, another point and I would be just one from victory. Practice makes perfect they say, and I was in a position to demonstrate that, and overcome an opponent of such high status, someone who had undertaken the same repetitive routine ... and had earned his reward – international honours. I was, for the first time, a potential winner against the international ... and news of that would circulate in the right circles.

But what a place for such drama to take place, the rank smell of sweat seemed to be permanently in the room. Yesterday's sweat, last week's sweat, an almost overpowering stink of sweat. The collective smell of many, active young men. The plane dark-green gloss-painted room had no windows, it was a basement. It was too small for really violent competition, there was insufficient room for moving back, away from a very forceful attack. There was room for just the table tennis table and nothing else. It seemed strange that such a game should be taking place in the YMCA but the venue, for some reason, had become a preferred practice place for many ranking international players.

Each of us gripped our bats firmly, me with my beloved Victor Barna bat, and my opponent, Harry Morton, with his favourite, the Johnny Leach. Both of us were in sweat-soaked clinging, lurid wine coloured shirts, and neat beige, tight cotton shorts. A shaded light hung over the playing arena, giving bright illumination to the green matt surface. The immediate surround of the table and the walls were in shadow. There was just the two of us in the room, there was no room for anything else. Other players were in the ante-room.

Battle stations were evident on my face which was crunched in tension, eyes unblinking, brain racing, body tensed for action because I was the underdog. Could that be a problem? Could I be too tight? Would muscular flexibility be impeded? Could anyone be relaxed and active, with muscles tensed for action? Could concentration be too intense? If I hesitated, did that undermine ability? I tried to dismiss everything but the moment.

I tossed the ball up, twisted my wrist to impart maximum spin, and fired the ball across the table. It came back with reciprocal spin, at speed. I blocked, and so did the international, keeping the ball low over the net. Each of us now played for a killing opportunity – drive, chop; drive, chop; drive, chop. Finally forehand smash. Harry Morton, older and more experienced, made his characteristic crouched movement, took a step, and thrashed his arm in a tight arc across his body. The ball flew clear of my back-hand. He was now even, I had lost a winning opportunity. That was why Harry was an international, he had that ability to concentrate completely and utterly on the immediate task.

I was angry. The tension in my body increased, my brain scattered thoughts in all directions. What tactic could I use? How could I secure a win? Keep the serve even lower … was it possible? More spin? Was that possible? A surprise, a fast serve into the body. Whoosh. Too fast. Too hard. It overshot. Harry Morton had the upper hand. His face was set, but expressionless. I next tried a serve that would drop low and only just over the net, one to contain any attacking effort. But the wily international tapped the ball back at a very acute angle and forced me into an unsafe, high return. Smash. Again. The game was lost.

I had never beaten Harry Morton in countless games, and it had become an aching ambition since I first met him in that sweaty, cell-like YMCA room. A string of defeats was counter-productive when Harry had the ear of the county selectors. If I could prove myself against him, I could get a mention to the selection committee and make the youth county team, 'That George Gunner is coming on … '. Harry Morton had nursed many young players into the youth team, and his opinion counted. A victory against Harry meant something and it was a result I ached for.

'Practice makes perfect', said the international. He was a small, reticent, cool man who could move like lightning.

'Yeah.' It was a dejected response. I wanted just one win against Harry Morton … but it seemed impossible. Why? It should have been manageable, once, with the number of games we had played. Was it a matter of practice? Maybe I wasn't fit enough? But I trained, did road running, drank little alcohol, ate the foods advised in a sports training manual I'd read. I'd even had coaching sessions at a World Champion's shop in Morden, Johnny Leach. So what was missing? Maybe I'd practised too long that day, it was getting late.

'There's always another time,' Harry said.

'I suppose so.'

'I used to despair. Almost cried once,' Harry said

I knew the feeling. 'Yeah,' I said again. I wasn't my usual self, normally I'm ready to laugh and cry. Well, maybe sulk, but only occasionally. I usually had a twinkle in the eye and a sense of fun.

'I still lose the odd game I shouldn't. It happens,' Harry said.

'Mmm,' I grunted.

Harry was trying to be sympathetic, but it was hard work. We each picked up our jumpers from under the playing table, and went into the ante-room to collect our outdoor clothes. We passed the next couple who had moved towards the playing room. "Bit hot in there?" one of them said.

"Wouldn't expect anything else," replied Harry.

The pair of us changed quickly into outdoor clothes and pitched out into the bottom end of post World War II Wimbledon Broadway, next to the church and almost opposite the Gaumont cinema, reeking of the 1930s. At the other end of the Broadway, past the station and up the hill was the High Street, of 'Wimbledon village'. In June it would have more than its share of parked cars, their occupants off to where the other tennis would be going on, at the 1877 venue officially titled 'The All England Lawn Tennis and Croquet Club'. In the late 1940s, America was dominant with a sequence of titles, singles and doubles.

TWO ... Home.

WE trundled off in the opposite direction to Wimbledon South tube station and split, Harry to somewhere over Colliers Wood way and me on the underground to Morden before a 93 bus journey and a mile long walk. Enough time to wallow in self pity over a defeat in a match that could have been a major opportunity. Home for a bit of mum's cooking to replenish the ravenous body of a burgeoning young man. Mum always had a good larder and dad put in the hours to get the wherewithal. They both carried out their family commitments with considered care. They had the odd disagreement but they rubbed along, conjoined by custom, convention, nature, call it what you will.

They would be in bed when I got back to tuck in to a dried up dinner in the kitchen, left in the faded heat of the gas oven - minced meat, mashed potatoes and cabbage (parental dictate carried out, 'You must eat your greens'), with spotted dick and custard for afters … not only dried up but almost cold. Well, it was only fuel, and it still went down very well, even with limbs wrapped round the legs of the small kitchen side table, and the edge of the copper boiler digging in my back, still mooning over a lost game of table tennis.

Mum did like all mums tended to do down the ages, cared for their little boys and girls, but my mum was very conscientious, unfailing in her cooking and washing. Dad was also diligent; no furtive visits to the pub, just the paid job then back home to work on the vegetable patch, repair the odd hole in a cooking pot, or add a cunningly sited supportive strut to the leg of a dubious chair. Everyone in the family mucked in to make life decent and tolerable. We children grew up with a good idea of cooking (... potatoes twenty minutes and don't forget the salt ...'), sewing ('... use a thimble!'), general repair work ('... don't use a screwdriver as a bradawl!'), even cement mixing ('... five of sand, one cement ...'), whatever was necessary to keep the show on the road. And what a talent mum had with the needle - reversing shirt collars, making curtains and cushion covers, stitching on assorted patches, darning, knitting jumpers and scarves with unpicked wool, nothing was beyond her desire to keep the whole household up to scratch.

It must have been in the blood, two generations or more of 'Dressmakers' preceded her. Added to that she had her early years in residential schooling within the system of Catholic Education, where the objective was to turn out assorted domestic staff for well placed Catholics, hence her skills also in cooking and washing. Dad too had been a residential Catholic schoolboy with, it later turned out, mum's brother. That had been the point of contact between them.

The home where the welcome repast was voraciously dealt with was a house in one of the huge London County Council Estates built in the late 1920/30s, an indication of an establishment with growing understanding that better housing for the under-privileged also resulted in a more comfortable social environment for all. The thinking behind the Garden City Suburbs, as they were known, was that of the late Victorian town planner, Ebenezer Howard, who had firm ideas about the quality of life and living space, for all. And so I was now able to go home, crossing the threshold of the Red Admiral polished front door step, to a hot bath with water hand-pumped upstairs from the solid fuel boiler below. Howard's influential ideas were evident at Letchworth and Welwyn, and after WWII, at Stevenage and Milton Keynes.

Amongst the LCC developments of varying sizes were two very, very large projects, one in Essex, in Dagenham, and one in Surrey, in Morden and Carshalton. Mitcham lavender fields had was chosen for the estate from the farm land of the Westminster clerical estate. Actual construction followed soon after the opening of the Morden Underground terminus in 1926. The Surrey project, the St. Helier Estate, was a huge rash of yellow, being built with the distinctive London stock bricks, duly flush pointed with lime mortar to maintain good weather protection. It all had the added advantage of input from a younger Landscape Gardener and town planner, Edward Mawson.

The estate provided a Community Hall for actor George Cole to exercise his early attempts at his craft, a hospital in which Prime Minister Sir John Major was born, a home for actor Eric Porter, and many, many assorted artists, sports stars, business figures who made good. In another of these estates the prolific and noted author, Peter Ackroyd was born. All attended the 'Secondary Modern Schools' built within the estates, and were able to benefit from opportunities offered by the enlightened 1944 Education Act of Rab. Butler, which was designed to provide better employment prospects for those down the social scale.

Our family had taken the opportunity of moving out of London to avoid the looming danger of war. A situation created by a deranged man who had somehow been able to deceive many of a sophisticated people to follow his malign lead. Maybe it was an example of how state control or more accurately, a secretive cabal of a few men, was able to manipulate a people to pursue destructive, juvenile ideas. Amazing to think that those same people had produced so much of the world's sublime music – Bach, Handel, Haydn, Mozart, Beethoven, Schubert ... but Mozart stood out.

THREE ... Hospital.

MOZART … Mozart … he died almost unnoticed with few, if any, at the funeral of a genius … it was the sound of Mozart … piano and orchestra … piano concerto by Mozart … 21, that's it. The march just before the piano comes in, then embellishment with a flourish. It's coming from one of those Walkmans or something. Where? Lots of white … a large room, and quiet activity … a low buzz, ipod things! A hospital ward!? Thoughts … about table tennis ... not beating Harry Morton the international ... going home dejected, very dejected.

I was dozy, warm and relaxed, but unfocussed. Then I remembered the pain in my chest. It seemed to possess me totally … I could hardly breath, sweat pouring out of me. I'd keeled over. Next there was a lot of fussing about, instructions. I was manhandled … the sound of swishing wheels, and an engine doing high revs., a siren, a mask clamped over my mouth, a jab … then the softness, comfort and – all the thoughts.

My head began to clear, disordered thoughts acquired a shape. A shape that seemed to indicate that the medication keeping major drama at bay must have finally lost the battle and the blood pressure had at last had its way. That final session of spring gardening had had a result. A result that suggested that there would be no more lifting and laying of paving slabs – just as the doc. had warned. Maybe I'd now have an incomplete stepping stone path, snaking through the lawn and past the shrub borders to my bottom-of-the-garden 'arbour'. Would it mean a more sedentary lifestyle? Just a bit of pottering around and then a long sit down to recover! Nice if the sun is shining, but in England, even Devon, one wouldn't be able to do it every day. Not like those old men in Mediterranean countries who spend the middle of the day sitting on a stool in the sun outside their little house - small trilby on head, stubbled chin, wizened face - respite between early morning and evening session on the vegetable plot. I admired their activity and health in advancing years. I'd let myself go a bit, in my middle age. Late middle, or middle middle, what exactly? I think I looked in reasonable nick, not overweight, no beat-up, raddled face. Indeed the steady look in the eyes and the pattern of lines indicated a thoughtful man, and one not averse to a bit of fun. In spite of that, in a hospital bed, I must have appeared as just another guy, like the rest of the ward. Certainly I now got breathless rather more quickly than I used to, and maybe I had to accept that I had a body that basically didn't work so well.

A voice interrupted the wallow ...

'Here, this is a good one, a bloke gets shot about every ten pages apparently. You men like that sort of thing.' The jolly book lady was doing her rounds with the book trolley and she had nobbled a patient in the next bed. She was a comfortable middle aged woman, probably worried about her waist line a bit.

'Not me. Have you got anything on the meaning of the universe?' the patient in the next bed asked with gravity. He looked the part, a rather drawn, long cadaverous face, and a widow's peak.

'What?!'

The patient was the Mozart listener with the ipod. He spoke in a serious, deep voice, 'Why are we all here?'

'I don't know anything about that, I just do the books.' She was taken aback and gave an answer she immediately felt didn't offer an idea of who she was. 'Books to, 'Educate, entertain and inform,'' she said, feeling that was the response that projected the real idea of herself.

'Ah well ...' He raised his hand in a gesture of disappointment, even despair.

The book lady was unclear about what was communicated and simply said, 'I see', not seeing at all. She walked off and behind her back, the patient winked at me, I smiled weakly in response.

I must have been in a serious state, seeing 'all my life before me'. Well, only a little bit of it, the failed table tennis bit. I looked round the ward. I now had to avail myself of hospital care, through the foresight of those who created the National Health Service back in 1948. That event must have been something of a health issue peak, using all the developments of centuries of trial and error, before eventually developing to the more organised research of recent times. How hospital treatment was gained and paid for had been a lottery, evolving as it did from charitable agencies. By the end of the nineteenth century a GP note or useful contact *might* facilitate attention at the 'Infirmary', which was supported by fund raising events, weekly subscriptions, door-to-door collections and *some* generous rich people; un-generous rich people remained un-generous rich people. There were some advantages in the twenty first century, and I was going to discover them. It was interesting that the birth of the National Health Service followed so closely after World War II. A war which had been the engine for many technological developments that had a wider benefit; benefits which would have appeared anyway, but within a different, longer, time span. And a great deal less painful one.

I thought I'd relax with the Mozart 21 my bedside neighbour had on the radio, but it didn't work. My thoughts scattered, my eyes fluttered, I felt absolutely exhausted. I wasn't sure whether the oxygen mask they clamped over my mouth made me feel that way, or I was simply clapped out. But with my last abstract, somnolent, idea I eased once again into unconsciousness. Back to my nostalgic reverie – walking backwards, maybe not to Christmas, but certainly going backwards ... to a time before my impactful table tennis defeat ... it was even a time before the emergence of the National Health Service.

FOUR ... War time and after.

THE young me was out of the ward, back in the St. Helier Estate during the tense days of World War II when I had been more concerned with laddish activities. A time when even sport had to be modified to fit the situation. It was a period when my father, a short stocky man with a sense of fun, was out at night on duty as an ARP warden, making his contribution to the war effort, helping to defend and protect his country, his wife and his family. It was a duty that was a bit of a come down for dad, who liked the idea of service to his king and country, but was medically unfit due to the work-related injury to his hand he suffered while working in the printing trade. All this was long before the twenty-first century days of Health & Safety, when he would have been encouraged to take advantage of opportunistic compensatory legal devices ... must keep the legal fraternity going.

There had been danger. When dad was out on patrol checking the black-out in 1940, a simple ARP tin helmet wouldn't have been much protection. I could hear shrapnel pinging down onto the house roofs in the dark night while I lay awake, worried in the blackness, in the bedroom I shared with my brother, Cyril, above the front room. But then the next day I would be out in the streets listening for news and signs of damage in the area so that I could collect the pieces of fallen shrapnel - six inch chunks of vicious, jagged metal that could have sliced off an arm or leg. Or head. Lethal ordnance dropped thousands of feet out of the black night sky. All of it went into a cardboard collecting box with other items – a heavy, lethal slug of cold steel, a slither of aluminium, burn-blackened bolts, the odd bit of tinny metal; bits of bomb and shell, and seemingly, a bit of an aircraft body. A treasure trove to share with my mates before playing war games in the debris of bombed houses a couple of hundred yards away, one of the boyish activities that preceded the Wimbledon table tennis dramas. A heap of bricks, a shattered window, the remains of a door, just the place for a top sniper, and no danger of getting injured, not for a lively young boy, in Resistance Army uniform of a rumpled shirt and grey, short trousers.

'I got you, you're dead,' I said.

'No I'm not, I was behind a pile of bricks when you said chgr.' ('Chgr.' is the noise made by a young boy to represent a gun firing. It's a fruity sort of 'clearing the throat' noise.)

'No I got you, because I heard where you was.'

'No, I shot you as I came out.'

I came back to him. 'Yeah, but 'cos you were running, you didn't shoot straight.'

'Yes I did because I'm marksman.'

'So am I. That's why I got you.'

In the interest of friendly international relations we decided to have the battle again, until we both succumbed to the shooting talents of each other, and then died with a lot of gasps and gurgles and tumbles and falls, followed by writhing in pain at some length. Then there was a bit of tongue lolling and eye rolling, and more indescribable noises … and finally silence.

'That was really good,' I breathed with some elation.

'Yeah,' the enemy replied.

That sort of action had been interspersed with cricket played in the road against the pig-bin used as a wicket on the corner green, a patch of grass that the town planners had included to relieve the un-relenting yellow London stock bricks of the housing. The aluminium tin bins were provided by the council to collect the leftovers to help fatten the pigs for bacon production as part of the war effort; bacon that acquired a distinct taste of potato peelings. The only problem with street cricket had been the double danger of running up and down the kerb between pig-bin wicket and bowler's end. The batsman could have been run out, and/or he could have tripped up the kerb. He also had to avoid the horse droppings of the rag-and-bone man if he had just been on his rounds. Bruised knees, scratched shins were all part of it. Later, street football was played with the same well-used tennis ball used for pig-bin cricket. Boys' street games were the sports academy to prepare for games of football on grass with a normal ball, and table tennis with internationals, two or three years after the war, when there was only rationing to worry about.

Further football education was at three o'clock on a Saturday afternoon, via a 93 bus (again) all the way to Putney, and a walk through Bishops Park to join the crowd heading for Craven Cottage, for Fulham Football Club - Ronnie Rooke, lightning centre forward in a shirt seemingly too large; Ernie Shepherd, darting down the left wing, and Joe Bacuzzi, English international full-back born of Italian parents. Their appearance preceded by clicking rusty turn-styles, snacks from the movable van, clambering up terraces to find a rust spotted bar to lean on, and standing on rutted, moss covered earthen steps, held in place only by battered wooden rises. At half-time, foul smelling corrugated iron lavatories. All of it - Heaven! It seemed basic, elemental. And it was. The players on £6 a week and living with their mum ... and they even had to have a 'proper' job to help make ends meet. But now, seating, reasonably clean toilets, purpose-built snack-bars ... wraps! Whatever happened to dog-rolls? And the cost! It's a changed world ... can't stop change. It's football millionaires now, but at least now talent is recognised, the master craftsmen known everywhere – Pele, Cryff, Maradona, Georgie Best, Lionel Messi ... and Mozart, he would be a millionaire today, and Beethoven, Rembrandt, Michaelangelo, artists and musicians who worked for the aristocracy and the church ... and a meagre living, getting scraps from their patrons, arrogant Counts, Bishops, self-obsessed Ladies ... and fawning hangers on, people who had an inflated idea of themselves. Too many, all lavishly decked out to be noticed ... as arrogant Counts, Bishops, and self-obsessed Ladies ... and nothing else. Unfortunately the real talent of the day may not always have seen their privileged employers for what they were – lucky buggers to be born in fortunate circumstances.

A STORY of JOHN and LUCY.
(George in hospital.)

ONE ... Parents.

MY parents, John and Lucy Gunner, didn't have any special talents, and they hadn't had it easy. There was just hard work alternating with stress, due to the problems of unemployment, especially in the 1920s and 1930s. But they may have been lucky too, with a certain idea of self discipline imposed during their early years of schooling. A century or so ago, a few years after the year 1900, dad then mum had both been subject to the influence of residential Catholic schooling. For dad, the learning process had somehow included exercising a talent for skipping and deaf-and-dumb language, which he took in his stride. In fact both parents had run away from school - to get home, or just to get away? Probably the latter. Maybe they felt they had been deserted? Or did they have a rebellious streak? Maybe evidence of that intransigence was initiated in these institutions when they had their first puff of Woodbine dog-ends in school lavs., before contributing to tobacco manufacturers' profits in later years. The strict and regimented daily life may have been resented, but the schooling engendered good attitudes for adult life.

The fact of the matter was that John's mother, Ethel Edith, couldn't cope. By 1905, aged 26, she had seen enough drama, at St. Adolphus Road, behind St. Mary's Catholic Church in Clapham, becoming a widow and single mother to four boys under seven. As a result, her oldest, Bert, the only one not born at St. Adolphus Road, was sent away to become a naval cadet. John, aged three, and his older brother, Sid, were sent away to a residential Catholic school in Mottingham, Kent, then West Grinstead, Sussex leaving the youngest, baby Len, at home with mum. Later, John and his brother Sid were transferred again, to the London Waterloo School for the older working boys where John had a few run-ins with the teaching staff, bunking off to sleep rough over the river on the London embankment in the odd horse cart or two. He got by with a bit of scrounging and the odd knock-off. But he had in-built cunning and was street-wise enough to avoid any blue-bottles. Ethel Edith, never worried. She had enough concerns of her own as, by then, she had remarried and started a new family. Anyway she was confident John would get by, 'John will always manage, he's a survivor.'

And John's wife, my mum, Lucy, had buzzed off too from her residential school, but in a fit of pique, as was her tendency from time to time. She paid a visit to an aunt, who lived near the school in Salisbury. The city was the place in which her father's family had resided before they moved to London in the hope of improving their lot. All the girls in the family had been subject to Catholic school discipline in Salisbury because of their mother's strong connection with influential people working in Catholic child welfare, a situation which had arisen as a result of the mystery background of Lucy's mother. It was a mystery she disregarded when she had married an Anglican.

Run-away Lucy would not have been able to manage the long journey home to her block of dingy Victorian flats just behind Waterloo Station, London, where she had been born ... and in school dress, so she was stuck with school and whatever it had to offer.

'I like history and gym,' she confessed to her aunt.

'Oh good.'

'That's in the mornings. But not the other stuff.'

'What other stuff Lucy?'

'Making the school viable, was what Sister called it – in the afternoon, washing vegetables for dinner, and school clothes, ironing. That's not proper school.'

'Might help you to get a job.'

'I don't want a job like that.'

'We all have to do horrible jobs ...'

'I hope I don't have to ...' Lucy said, and auntie didn't know what to say to that, so Lucy went on, 'And there's all that - having to do what you're told thing, "Yes, Sister, No Sister."'

'We all have to do that as well.'

'They go on, and on.' Lucy lifted her chin and looked snootily down her nose. 'Control Lucy Smith! Courtesy Lucy Smith!' she said in a hoity-toity voice.

Lucy had gathered an idea of what might lay ahead when she

saw that the older orphaned girls, just a couple of years before they went out into the world, would spend their time doing laundry work for local hotels in the bare-bricked rooms that had been tacked on to the main school building. The work had provided some income for the school to relieve the pressure on demands for charity funds from the Catholic community, and also conveniently prepared the girls for work - as servants in large Catholic households of privilege. Within her own family, Lucy had a bit of a reputation as a girl who tended to push the boundaries, but with this knowledge of her character the relatives had been able to coerce her back to school.

Schools had evolved somewhat during the nineteenth century. In the early 1800s the establishment saw schooling as being of minor importance for the majority. In contrast, the Catholic community was able to provide for its young with charitable funds, and benefited from the easing of antipathy towards the Catholic religion following the Emancipation Act of 1829. The beginning of education for all really started with the Forster Education Act of 1870 which provided for central funding and schooling until twelve years old, but it still took some time to be fully implemented. It had been necessary to overcome the resistance of those who obstructed ideas that may have enabled the lower classes to think for themselves, or question the teachings of the church - if the unskilled and labouring classes got too many ideas, they may not have accepted their allotted role in the scheme of things and reject the role of general dogsbody. Such a level of society was essential for the lifestyle of the privileged, and wealth makers. Mass education carried the additional danger that the lower classes might learn about things that were not safe for them to know. Unthinkable things may happen, they could even start a revolution.

TWO ... Salisbury.

IT sometimes crossed the mind of some of Lucy's older relatives that she may have been the one to start a revolution. Her energy and stoic character was perhaps shaped by being a young girl with three older sisters, and she had to be resilient not to get down trodden in a family of seven. The older ones had more life experience, were stronger, ahead in the pecking order. Two of them seemed to be rather clever, one good at the piano, the other learned effective use of the French language. Lucy's oldest sister was her senior by twelve years. Surviving that had been a growth experience for her.

Salisbury had been the home of her father's forbears for at least a hundred years, back to a time, before 1800, when one was in a serious version of the past, 'The good old days' – no decent roads to speak of, the early days of machine power; a time when the term, 'labour intensive', really meant it. 'Hand-made', was how it was done.

The grid pattern of medieval Salisbury, 1220, was laid out in the arrangement of streets and the market square, thus even three hundred years later John Leland could write, 'There be many fair Streates in the Cite Saresbyri, and especially the High Streate and Castle Streate ...', and four hundred years further on the history of City could still be discerned in Lucy's time - the churches, pubs, street names, plus of course the Cathedral with its soaring spire rising high above a red town. The Cathedral was the central reason for Salisbury's existence in the first place, a new town built to replace the wind-blasted old settlement to the north, Old Sarum, which had finally become a place in which the clerics decided <u>not</u> to live. A meadow at the confluence of five rivers was considered ideal, and some of the stones of the Old Sarum Cathedral were used for the building of the new Cathedral in New Sarum, the original name of Salisbury, 'the capital of the Plain, the head and heart of all the villages'.

Given the difficulty of travel and widespread poverty, it's likely that Lucy's paternal ancestors had lived in the city throughout the centuries, maybe right back to the building of the city. Both her father and grandfather had jobs in construction and it would surely have been possible that the tradition of son-follows-father went back up the generations. Some of Lucy's forbears over the centuries might have worked in the Cathedral, or visited it, to be awed by the creative energy offered to Jesus Christ, and moved by the rearing elegance of the spire. They must also have been impressed by the ingenuity invested in creating the oldest working clock in the world, made in the fourteenth century. A fourteenth century working clock, imagine.

THREE ... George meets Chas.

I BEGAN to come round again in hospital, getting to terms once more with where I was, and wondered if <u>my</u> face had looked at the oldest working clock in the world seven hundred years ago. Not the troubled face I had now, in a hospital bed. No, it would have been a younger forbear face although, whilst the face would have been younger, it may have looked older given the shorter life span, the harder life of those days. Certainly not like the well fed faces I'd seen in the supermarket only last week. I'd seen matching faces over three generations - a woman with her mum and daughter walking down the aisles. One only had to multiply that by ten for thirty generations, and there you were seven hundred years ago, the same face, and maybe looking at the oldest working clock in the world ... except it was new.

I looked round the ward and, yes, there was what I was thinking – a son visiting his father. I didn't need to be told of their connection, I could see it. Not peas in a pod, but evident similarities – some general connection of head shape, flesh and hair colour, something in the eyes ... they'd even managed to choose the same glasses. Same glasses?! Genetic choice?! Or an omnipotent fixer? A Fixer in cahoots with the Optician's Sales Department ... 'And look at this pair of glasses, you must have them, you can match your dad.'

'You with us again then, old chap?' I was puzzled for a moment before noticing a fellow patient was up and about looking for a diversion to fill the time. He'd notice that I looked vaguely engaged with the world.

I dropped the headset away from my ears, and my Mozart became just faint background music. 'I wouldn't desert my fellow inmates,' I said and gestured to the ward, 'All having had dramas of one sort of another. We have to show a bit of esprit de court, and pull together.' I humoured him.

The man looked round at the busy ward. He was a middle-aged, presentable man, not scraggy, not fat, not handsome, not ugly. Hair indicated that it had once been brushed straight back, but was now balding. Another version of John Public.

'I saw my mate Ted, he told me you enjoyed the bit of fun he had with the book woman. Bit of a joker he is.'

'Yeah,' I replied, 'Any excitement whilst I've been in dreamland?'

'This is a hospital, there's always excitement.'

'Major incident? Pile-up? Visiting royalty? Celebrity arrival?'

'The lot.'

'Oh … I'll go back to sleep.'

'Don't do that, my mate's gone off, been allowed out to the canteen.'

'Lucky fellah.'

'I thought, when the new bloke is awake, George Gunner …'

I flicked my head round at this.

'Name's on the end of the bed, complaint, BP, diet – they've got you logged in.'

'Of course.'

'Save you checking the end of my bed, I'm Chas Clark.'

'Chas. Right.'

'Yeah, I thought he looks like a man in need of a chat so … '

I embellished the words for him. '…he looks a bit of a gabbler so I'll just … '

'Are you?'

'I wouldn't have thought so.'

'So what will you be doing when you get out of here?'

'Having a look at what put me in here ... making a garden path.'

'Sounds like hard work.' Chas. had decent interviewing technique.

'Not really. I'm trying to make a peaceful spot ... place to sit, a place where you feel content, secure … home. Somewhere to survey nature, listen to the birds, and be at one with the world.'

'Sounds like fantasy.'

'Yeah, heaven on earth.'

'I tried to do things like that but there was always someone traipsing down the garden to spoil it.'

'You got a big family?' I asked.

'Not so much big, as busy. Always dropping by for a natter. If it's not that, there's someone who seems to want something - run out of peanut butter, the handle of the hammer's broken, the cleaner won't work, car wipers make a noise … it's amazing.' Chas didn't seem put out by the demands on his time.

'Takes all sorts.'

'You got a quiet life then?'

'I suppose so.'

'A wife and place in the country?' Chas. was persistent.

I felt the conversation was getting too private. 'That's the sort of thing.'

'Can't be bad.'

'It's not.'

Chas. Didn't let up. 'Boring then?'

'No.'

'How come?'

'Got a grandson, drops in for a chat.'

'Oh yeah?'

'He wants to be a star badminton player,' I said.

'I thought that was more of an Asian thing.'

'It was but our youngsters have been taking them on. Since I played my game, table tennis, there's been sponge rubber bats, penholder grips, improved footwear, laboratory researched training regimes, electrolyte liquid and so on and so on. Anyway, I didn't really have much success, and then I spent a lot of time wondering about it and rabbitting to my grandson, so he started to think my ponderings might help him. I suppose I've sort of become his ...' The effort of conversation seemed to be too demanding, or maybe it was the reference back to youthful table tennis. I lost the thread of what I was going to say.

'You OK?'

'Just a bit dozy.' I gave myself a moment. 'Trouble is, I've become a mentor for him, so I have to get on top of this,' I pointed to my chest, 'For him. It's important, and I have to admit for me too – so that he can do what I didn't.'

'So the talent jumped a generation?'

'Mmm?'

'*Grand*son, but not a son or daughter, the hand-eye co-ordination talent jumped a generation.'

'Who knows? How, why, did I get into the game? My dad didn't play seriously though he was a sporty type – football, cricket. Not that I would have thought he got much chance, it wasn't easy in the middle of London.'

Chas looked up to the ward ceiling pensively, 'Middle of London? That'd be about Paddington, St. Pancras even, right?'

I didn't quite follow his thinking but did see a link. 'Not quite, but there is a railway connection, Clapham Junction is just across the common.'

'One of the busiest stations in Europe. 180 trains per hour pass through. Did you know it's really in Battersea but it was called Clapham because when it was opened in 1863, Clapham then a bit more up-market. The reason it's so busy is because it's a hub for two mainlines, Victoria and Waterloo …. '

But he had triggered other things in my mind, I lost the enthusiastic ramblings of a railway fanatic with the mention of "busiest station", and I had my own train pictures in my head, trains noisily speeding through Clapham Junction Station, passengers unloading from standing trains. Hustle, bustle, my thoughts took me past Arding & Hobbs, through the geometry of back streets, and I was out of hospital and into Clapham proper, a Clapham of the past.

FOUR ... Clapham.

CLAPHAM could be said to be in the middle of London, given all the bricks and mortar spreading for miles on end, though it has the sizeable splodge of green Clapham Common. The district was where John Gunner, my dad, was born just after 1900, and where he lived on and off until he was nearly thirty. His comings and goings were dictated by an unsettled home life – other brothers away, a step-father, and new half siblings. But Clapham was always where John Gunner came home to. The place that had been home to his part of the Gunner family for a quarter of a century, other strands of the family had connections going back almost a hundred years.

At the time of King Edward VII, Great Britain was at its most powerful and top dog, but it didn't last long. Certain areas of Clapham were still quite fashionable, in spite of having fallen out of favour from their late eighteenth and nineteenth century peak, when it was the preferred abode for Victorian social reformers. Clapham somehow still managed to retain a village atmosphere with its attractive High Street, and it projected itself as having a distinctive character, even when it seemed so completely embraced by the bricks, mortar, tarmac, wood, glass of the London metropolis. Maybe it could present itself in that way because it was not, after all, so completely covered with man-made building - it had Clapham Common ... and three underground stations.

When John came home from his Sussex school it was only a short walk for him, and his mate, to reach the north end of the Common from his house, past St. Mary's Catholic Church and across from Clapham Common underground. It was an unexpected but welcome green space to counter all the urbanisation. The boys made for Long Pond where they could float their matchbox boats. They were just a couple more kids in darned pullovers, long baggy short trousers, and lengthy woolly socks bunched around their ankles. John was a typical young urban boy, noisy, lively, adventurous, but could be fonder of a prank than his mate. The boys gave up trying to race their lovingly, but quickly modelled boats against each other when they learned that without a current the crafts didn't go anywhere. They just wobbled erratically until they eventually got soaked, and sank. On one occasion fate dictated that an ant was caught on a floating matchbox-boat, and that gave them the idea of putting captured black beetles aboard. The joy then was to see the insects frantically swimming for their lives, which they did successfully - helped by the boy's shouts of encouragement. Swan Vestas was the best for those on board, Bryant & May seemed to sink more quickly.

Having raised the decibel level at Long Pond, they ran loudly round the bandstand so that they could enjoy disturbing all the pigeons and making them fly off in search of safety. Then they threw stones at the little fish in Eagle Pond. The result of all the boyish noise and energy was tetchy reaction from some of the ambling old timers seeking recuperative peace and quiet. The boys were given a severe ear bashing.

'You stop that you hooligans!' called a couple of old timers, interrupted in their gentle walk.

'What? I can't hear you granddad.'

'Don't you cheek me you monkey.'

At which point, John started jumping up and down, scratching under his arms, and uttering screeching, gasping noises. His mate joined in and they danced round each other, imagining tall equatorial trees in the jungle. Jaws jutted out, waddles, guttural noises, it was the full treatment.

'You stop that!' one old codger called and turned to the other, 'Little urchins.'

Feeling he was he was being asked to say something he feebly contributed, 'You should be ashamed of yourself.'

Even though the weather was mild they both wore drooping rain coats and battered hats. They looked like a couple of doss house hat stands.

'You want to come and play boats mister?!'

'If I get to you, I'll give you one hellava of a pasting.' The first old man waved his fist at them.

John and his mate taunted the old men but half turned away in case they were unexpectedly athletic. 'You and who's army?'

The old men became quite animated and almost incoherent. They shuffled from one foot to the other, waved sticks, arms stabbed the air. One nearly lost his hat. 'I'll get you … should be locked up … parents have no control these days …'

His partner added his definitive comment, his final statement. 'It's the same all over, no discipline anywhere.'

The boys just burst out laughing, 'You should be on the music hall mister.' Further communication finally broke down when they realised the old men were only just able to walk never mind run, so they ambled off.

'We know who you are,' the old men called after them, 'We're going to report you.'

The boys took no notice. They'd achieved their objective – making the old men behave like idiots.

Whilst all this was going on, John's mother, Ethel Edith, would have been standing at the bar of the Rose & Crown just opposite Clapham Common underground, having a quiet glass of stout and gossiping to one or more of her three younger sisters. It gave them a chance to discuss life and the world, without men getting in the way. Ethel Edith could tell them about the hard time life was giving her, though it didn't seem to impinge on her lively character.

It couldn't have been said that, "She was a looker," but she was one of those people who 'had a way with her'. She was good company.

Ethel Edith dressed as best she could, with large collared blouses, jumpers, skirts, all held tightly in with a wide belt to accentuate her figure, which went in and out in the right places, just a little. A soft hat with a small brim kept her hair in place and made her look neat and tidy. Ethel Edith had four children, was widowed, remarried, had three more children. She seemed to feel that life never went her way, but she still sailed happily on. From time to time the sisters were joined by one or other of their children, on a strategic visit to touch them for a bob or two whilst they were in relaxed mood.

There had been no shortage of Gunner family members gulping down the odd glass of beer in the area. Up the High Street towards Clapham North Underground, The Two Brewers had entertained John's granddad (yet another George) who lived nearby, and his uncle Walter who worked at the tram depot opposite. Minimum daylight penetrated the coloured ornamental patterns within the frosted glass window, so shading an unsavoury Britannia table at which they were sitting, its surface sticky with beer puddles and an over-filled ashtray. Over the years, the Clapham pubs and their brewers were very grateful for the residence of the Gunner family in the area.

'Funny how all the men in the family come here and the women go to the Rose & Crown,' George's worn face said, opening up a subject close to his heart. On his head he wore a curly brim bowler that was due for retirement like its owner.

'Well, we live at this end of the High Street and most of the women live at the other,' uncle Walter commented.

'More or less,' George replied. He was an old journeyman tailor and it told in his stoop, and screwed up eyes. His ragged, rumpled suit, adorned by the odd food stain, did not present a good image of his craft.

Walter knew how to keep his father chatting. 'It's for the best, anyway.'

'Men and women need a bit of space.' George sounded a bit of an authority. 'It keeps things on an even keel. Mind you Ethel Edith has got a mouth on her if you say the wrong thing.'

Walter laughed. 'Don't I know it?! Having an older sister who has … well, shall we say - an untidy life? a dramatic life? Whatever, she can be a bit rowdy when she gets going.' Walter looked as if he could handle that. There was an alert, intensity in the face that suggested he would be good to have on your side ... he was later to demonstrate it by winning a medal for bravery trying to stop a runaway tram.

'It's in the family. Your mother and I always seem to have something to squabble about. Was that down to her or me? Question of difference I suppose - a quiet young country girl, loses both her parents, is taken to Gravesend by big sister, becomes a Catholic, gets married at eighteen ... and there's me - town bloke with a dodgy childhood, not to mention a hand to mouth existence.' He shook his head at the complexities of life. 'Mind you she had it hard too out in the sticks, the youngest of thirteen children ... 13! *And* she was twenty eight years younger than the oldest ... 28! Was that a good thing or a bad thing do you reckon?'

'Made her a gentle I think.'

But George had his own line of thought. 'It was a pity she left me like she did, with all that we'd been through together.'

'Six kids for a start!' Walter said, still in his working clothes, trying to make light of it all.

'Six, amazing isn't it? Then she dies when we were all worried about the run up to the war, before the trenches and zeppelins. I felt bad about that, about not being ... complete, if you know what I mean.' Walter put a commiserating hand on the arm of his dad, who had started to look reflectively up at the ceiling, 'Her family had been Suffolk born for centuries ...' he said distantly '... and mine ...?'

He didn't expand, and left that history as a mystery.

FIVE ... Work.

JOHN GUNNER was oblivious to all this family indulgence, which continued for successive years during which time he led a disorganised lifestyle into which were interspersed home visits to Clapham, which always included nostalgic trips to the Long Pond and the bandstand on the Common. It was as if only there could contentment be found. John did eventually find a more normal existence when, strapped for cash, and foraying 'up north' over Waterloo Bridge to his old Embankment haunts, he crossed the Strand, and paused at the impressive columns of the Lyceum Theatre portico imagining it was a building in the sun, in Rome, ... or was it Greece?

A generation before, Sir Henry Irving had roundly projected Shakespeare into the grand interior, but now John could only see posters for, 'spectacular melodrama'. He walked round the corner to the Gaiety Theatre and went into a trance at the thought of its history of nightly dancing girls. He had a special passion for the girl who had won the annual, 'Miss Pears' soap contest and gone on to the stage. He stared at a picture of her outside but his fantasy of lascivious pleasure was spoilt by a group of gabbling young men who had arrived to just ogle at the pictures. So he trekked off past the Law Courts, steering well clear of a bobby who was standing outside and sallied down Fleet Street where he noticed a hand-written sign on a news stand down a side street. It was tied to the concertina iron security gates of a small half-shop establishment, 'Boy wanted.'

John went in past an untidy display of sample posters on the windows, and reams of papers, a composing stick, a typecase of emptied letter boxes and balls of screwed up paper dumped hurriedly on the window shelving. In the background was the noisy clank and clatter of machinery. John entered without expectation, more out of curiosity, even adventure, and came out after a short chat, having got a job in a small printing company. It was a shrewd move on the part of the man who engaged him, who must have been a bit of a psychologist. John, in spite of his wayward lifestyle, was a very conscientious person, an obey-the-rules man. Something no doubt instilled during his Catholic schooling, in spite of his recalcitrance.

John did indeed fulfil the hopes of his employer. From reliable dog's body, including a period as a delivery boy on a tricycle, he moved on to work as a machine minder in the very heart of the print industry - Fleet Street, the area of loud mechanical noise, inky hands, excited voices, fierce competition, dead-lines and men always in a rush. John was encouraged to take an interest in his surroundings, and gained insights into the craft to his subsequent benefit, although on the matter of personal safety, an excess of zealous commitment caused him to catch his thumb in the machinery and the digit remained disjointed thereafter. It later caused him to be rejected at World War II call-up, though the injury did not prevent him in the early 1920s becoming a typesetter at a more leisurely pace just off the famous street, in Fetter Lane, in a less glamorous branch of the craft, stationery printing. But it was a useful place to be when the General Strike happened, because his part of the industry became busy with the resultant mayhem.

Employment meant that John was able to lead a life of independence and after a short spell in men's lodgings at Rowton House in Newington Butts he moved nearer to his work, at New Cross. His landlady gave him a bit of a grilling before agreeing to let him a dim, sparse room – bed, wooden arm-chair with a busted spring and a dressing table, all well past their best days. On the floor was shiny linoleum, rather discoloured and worn by the door. It seemed she had rented out to print workers before, 'I don't want to see any inky hands,' she said demonstrating her idea of inky hands as if she was shelling peas.

'There's a bathroom just down the stairs.' Her arms gesticulated upstairs, and down.

There was something stolid about her, standing four square with a floral apron tied round her generous waist and neck. Her gestures suggested she could have a been a naval rating flagging morse signals.

'And you clean it afterwards.' The land-lady essayed the to and fro movement of cleaning.

'I will not have black smudges on my sheets.' The washing line outside was indicated.

John knew how to play the game, and he was courteously attentive in order to get out of the strict regime and the heavy snorers in the Rowton House lodgings.

In the outside world there were the excitements of New Cross Empire and greyhounds at New Cross Stadium where, remarkably, John generally ended his evenings on the credit side, just. He began to smarten up, dressed with a tie, jacket, waistcoat and hat. But sometimes the tidy image could be marred by his prohibitive smoking habit, acquired in late school days – the cigarette cupped furtively in the hand and held discreetly behind back. And of course there was 'the Den' for 'the Lions'. 'The Den' and 'the Lions' were Milwall football ground and its team for them north of the river … and the uninformed. All these venues were kept nicely ticking over by the Milwall dockers - and by John, called by his fellow workers, 'one of the south of the river lot'.

'Why don't you come north of the river and support a good team?' Tommy, one of John's workmates asked.

'What, West Ham? You must be joking.'

Of all the London football clubs, of which there were a dozen or more, the rivalry between Millwall and West Ham was, for many, the most passionate. It was tribal. It was as if the river was a national boundary and a trip across it was an invasion into enemy territory.

'I mean, what have you got down there? They haven't even bothered to put you on the underground,' Tommy said.

John knew he had a point, but had to defend his patch. 'All that noise. What do we want the underground for? Great big holes in the ground, what happens if it all caves in?'

Tommy was caught by the immediacy of John's reply and said shortly, 'Won't happen.'

'And who wants to have to look at Beckton Gasworks every day?'

'It's not in West Ham.'

John took no notice, he felt he was in a winning position. 'And where do you go for a holiday, Southend. Southend, I ask you!'

'What's wrong with it?'

'What's right with it?!' John came back. We've only got to go on a little jaunt down the Old Kent Road and there's Ramsgate, Margate, even Broadstairs if you fancy it? Proper places.'

John also thought of Clapham as a proper place. Even after leaving home, he went back on family visits and still went for walks on Clapham Common.

My mother, Lucy, did not pursue such an 'adventurous' young adult life as John but whereas he followed a chancy course, Lucy somewhat resentfully did what she had to do ... as indeed did the majority of people. She wasn't able to realise her young hopes of not having to earn a living doing the mundane jobs she had been coerced to learn at school. In the years afterwards she was confronted with a sequence of resented menial jobs that were essential to provide funds for food and shelter at the family home, a cramped third floor flat in Burdett Buildings, near Waterloo Station. (The buildings suffered bomb damage and a roof fire in December 1940. The target was obviously Waterloo Station. Chunks of the area were later demolished and developed. By the early 1960s Burdett Buildings were no more.)

Only for a short temporary period, as a seamstress in 1920s Bond Street, did Lucy feel her talents were being realised. She was happy in her first floor work-room sat at her Singer, scrabbling for threads, boxes of pins, and stepping around dress dummies. Lucy was neat and careful, and had a natural concern for an exemplary end product. The ability was in the blood, with at least two generations of dressmakers before her.

'Where did you learn to sew like that Lucy?' the couturier asked.

'At school, they were very keen on all the girls being really good. Any bad work meant that a girl had to work the vegetable garden or the kitchen.' Lucy's face lit up into a huge smile. 'I made a point of being good, very good. I used to add a bit of embroidery in my work to make it look nicer.'

The master dressmaker didn't need reminding of this additional ability, he had used it to his advantage. He was a nice old boy and been in the game for a long time. He was one of the old school and wore a wing collar with his tie. Tucked into his waist coat pocket was a fob watch and chain. A start in the East End had been embellished by opportunistic moves to eventually become a West End couturier.

'Where did you go to school?'

'Oh, all over. Salisbury, Yeovil, Westminster.'

'So you were away from home?'

'Yes, since I was about three or four ... except Westminster of course, I liked it there, just round from the Cathedral.'

In fact Lucy liked the whole of the West-end altogether, she felt alive in the busy atmosphere. Even just outside her first floor window, people bustled past all day and stopped at the tatty and stain suited news vendor who could be heard selling his wares, 'Evening News, Standard, Star !' Not that anyone unfamiliar with his voice could have deciphered what it was he was calling, it was just a sequence of jumbled syllables, growled repeatedly from somewhere near his battered ex-army boots. Lucy could see him too as she leant forward at the window where she sat to catch the light for her work.

'Do you walk all the way from Waterloo to get to work?' It seemed to the master dressmaker, Mr Stone, that a long walk of any sort asked too much of a person. A working life of sitting down and sewing was not conducive to exercise.

'It's the best way,' Lucy said, 'Walk over the river on Hungerford, see Scotland Yard, Big Ben, then Trafalgar Square and Piccadilly Circus, it's exciting. Dodging the omnibus, the trams, wending through teeming people, it's wonderful.'

'And you walk like that?' He gestured to her legs.

Lucy didn't quite understand the question. 'My shoes? I did shine them up before I left home.'

'No. That skirt is a bit short,' Mr Stone explained. He had daughters of his own and worried about that sort of thing.

'Oh no, everyone dresses like that. It's the fashion isn't it? And it's so much better when you're dancing, you can kick your legs about the way you have to …'

'Have to?'

'Oh yes, for the Charleston and that.'

Mr Stone was not convinced. 'Mmm,' he said, 'I prefer the routines they have in operetta.'

'You mean like the Folies Bergere girls?' Lucy blurted with youthful enthusiasm.

There was a trace of a smile on his face. 'Well, not quite,' he said.

It was still a time of expectation in working teenage years, and whilst Lucy didn't enjoy most of the work she had to do, she didn't really begrudge it because she knew her monetary contribution helped with the family finances as her father, my grandfather, was not able to undertake fully rewarding employment. He had been conscripted late in World War I when army numbers became depleted, and those of mature years were required to do their bit. And he did, returning with shell-shock. He spent the last years of his life with frequent bouts of uncontrollable shaking.

SIX ... George's concern.

AS if in sympathy I was shaking, or shivering, as I winced in my hospital bed. A nurse was passing at the same moment and her eye caught the movement. She stopped to assess me, and stood observing for some time. I gradually became steadier and my breathing began to be untroubled as I once again settled and returned to being an inert patient. The nurse wondered however whether there was still a little tension in my jaws.

The ward sister came over to the nurse, 'Everything alright?' She'd been around for a while and was instinctively alert.

'I was passing and noticed that he seemed to be distressed.'

'Do you think he is in pain?'

The nurse thought for a moment. 'No, it was a different sort of expression. It looked a bit like one of the faces I saw in a hospital documentary I saw on telly ... about Afganistan, post-traumatic distress disorder.'

'Do you think he's suffering from ... 'the sister started to say.

'Oh no, nothing like that. It was just the look.' There was a moment, before the nurse said, 'No, I think he's alright.'

The sister also had a keen look at me, before she said, 'OK then, but just keep a close eye on him.' She wheeled away, eyes expertly scanning the ward for anything else amiss.

The nurse gave me one last look for reassurance, and continued to the patient she had set out to see before I had commanded her attention.

There may indeed have been an easing of tension in my face. I was just one of two neat lines of hospital patients, each prostrate with his own conscious or unconscious expression, of anguish, placidity and anything between - apart from those recuperating by sitting or standing to share stories of this and that. Their medical condition probably. I was one of the inert ones, putting together my mental journey into the past.

SEVEN ... Marriage.

THE COMING together of mum and dad, John Gunner and Lucy Smith, did not remotely follow a normal course of events. During one of John's occasional visits home to Clapham his appearance coincided with that of his older brother, Sid, with whom he had been at the Catholic residential school. They had not seen much of each other because a year or two after leaving the school, Sid had spent five years in the army. He had grown to be a good looking, suited young man with sleeked back dark hair and an easy manner. He'd had periods of covert service in Ireland and the eastern Mediterranean and was demobilised in the early 1920s as a very good and experienced driver, thus in civvy street he became a chauffeur.

One day he had been mooching around the historic 'Cittie of Yorke', the pub on the south side of Gray's Inn, having recalled that the place was associated with ex-servicemen - and housed a veteran's club initiated by Arthur Haggard, brother of Rider. Whilst Sid was dithering about whether to go in, he looked disinterestedly at a bewigged figure hurrying to his chambers and his eyes caught a familiar face. He saw another man loitering. It was an old school mate from his Sussex school days, Stan Smith, cap at a rakish angle, mooching around as was his wont. Stan told Sid he'd come to see the club he'd heard about from his dad, but when he went into the pub he learned it had moved. Stan ended up taking Sid back home across the river.

Being a chauffeur meant that Sid didn't get much of a chance to use public transport and Stan took him on something of an adventure. They hopped on a tram at Holborn Station for a trip through the Kingsway tunnel which was only a short walk away. The clank and clatter of the vehicle as it rolled the rails and rounded the curves was a new experience for Sid. He found thought inducing diversions to add to the adventure. Advertisements such as Pears soap, with the privileged, laced collared 'Bubbles' boy, to contrast with Sid's virtually homeless childhood. 'Guiness is good for you', brought back memories of his troubled army life in Ireland, and Camp Coffee with its soldier outside an Egyptian desert tent prompted the memory of his uneasy tour in the Eastern

Mediterranean.

The other passengers did not seem to have anything in their heads. They were hard-faced working men, in all shapes and sizes, tatty and irritated by the rhythmic, noisy, swaying movement of the vehicle ... except one man, who must surely have been an old sailor, rumpled and weather beaten, happily puffing on his short clay workers pipe, unaffected by being lurched from side to side.

'Bloody tram! Sorry duck.' One of the workers disentangled himself from the young woman beside him. The tram lurched on. The woman gave the man a look that said, 'You did that on purpose.'

The old sailor, if that's what he was, looked up at the exchange and smiled to himself. It seemed as if he had observed and knew of all human machinations, and there was nothing to get excited about.

Thus it was when they reached the block of the over-crowded Victorian flats, almost next door to Lambeth North Underground Station, Sid met Stan's sister, one Lucy Smith, my mum. Sid and Lucy hit it off almost immediately, soon to fall into a routine. Following a little sup at The Horn in Kennington, they repaired to the adjacent gaudy Assembly Rooms where Lucy could demonstrate her gym school work with lively renditions of the Charleston and Black Bottom. The result was they got married, and at the appropriate time, had a son, my brother, Cyril. But Sid died within two years as a really young man, seemingly the result of querulous events during service in the army. It was believed a head injury, rumoured to have happened on some unrecorded duty, may have been the cause of the certified, 'cerebral tumour'.

Sid's brother, John, was there to support Lucy. He had the right caring character, maybe indicated by the fact that he really was a genuine belt and braces man, and had sensible ideas of safety. The result was that he played a similar role to that of Henry VIII. In the early 1930s he married his brother's widow. John helped, then courted, then married Lucy, in a rather different style to Henry. However, whilst both John and Henry were hard up, John had the more excusable situation - and a much more caring, indeed cherishing, character than Henry.

Perhaps John and Lucy had thoughts of betterment when they were together. Their ponderings would have been affected by the ideas circulating at that time, through conversation, or in the newspapers - the idea that things were changing. They had both been through World War I, a first and then a second Labour government, the General Strike, flappers and talkies, and the depression. Having got through all that, they anticipated a period of comparative calm. And behind the positive attitude of John and Lucy were some opinion formers who contended that over the years there had been a growing understanding within the establishment, that political responsibility embraced the idea that a trickle of grudging concessions for improving social structure for all, offered wider advantageous developments. Some also recognised that their self-interest was best served by a trouble free populace when those down the social scale were content.

Parliamentary Acts of social importance during the nineteenth century were often the side effects of the technological advances of the Industrial Revolution - restricting working hours for children and women in the mills, a growing concern for safety in the work-place, an increase in the franchise. These major reforms were a precedent for more of the same into the twentieth century. In 1908 came the arrival of social welfare with the Pensions Act to provide for the over 70s of 'good character' - seven shillings and sixpence (thirty seven and a half new pence) per week for a married couple. And, following a precedent set in Germany, the 1911 National Insurance Act for sickness and unemployment was enacted, so the franchise widening Acts of 1918 and 1930 were passed.

So now, emerging from the Wall Street Crash would, had to, provide opportunity and a change in the affairs of the country, even in the dark days of 1930s. Two years after their marriage John and Lucy were blessed with a son in their crowded, rented Victorian accommodation in Boundary Lane, down from the Elephant and off Camberwell Road. (Demolished late 1960s and replaced with a new estate.) It was indeed the old boundary between the parishes of St. Mary, Newington and St. Giles, Camberwell, later to become the boroughs of Southwark and Camberwell. The son was me. We had the pleasure of noises three times a day from the school playground opposite, and the engineering works next door. But it had mod-cons, a cinema at the end of the road and a pub a couple of doors from that. In the cramped living room, John, tie-less, collar-less, looked at his little boy, propped up by a cushion on the well used settee and still needing more time to make his first ten pounds on the scales, and said, 'I can see him now Lucy, flying down the left wing ... dribbles round the right back, steadies himself, kicks, lovely centre ... goal! Milwall win the cup. Again.' He flung his arms up in celebration. 'Come on the Lions!'

'I sometimes think you're going funny John,' smiled Lucy.

'Oh yeah? Do you think I should be on the stage?'

'I don't know, just give me a hand with his little woolly.'

John pushed a chair out of the way and carefully slipped the tiny arms into the sleeves whilst Lucy, all ready in outdoor coat and cloche hat and perched on the edge of the settee, held baby me forward.

'After we've done a bit of shopping on the stalls, do you think we'll have time for a quick one?' she suggested.

'More than that, we'll celebrate the goal that baby's scored, I think we'll have time to do the George and Dragon *and* the Albany Tap and ...'

'John!' said Lucy smiling through her admonishing voice. 'I'm ready.'

'Me too, two minutes.' John was busy fiddling with his collar stud. He cursed whoever had decided to make shirts with detachable collars. 'Well ... maybe three.'

John and Lucy maintained their spirit. As a new couple they reckoned they had a future and were buoyed by the idea that when you were young, anything was possible. Though they lacked social status and lived on the edge of subsistence, they had hopes. Hopes, it must be said, that were punctured intermittently by the economic gloom of the thirties and by the meagre benefits resulting from the new pensions and unemployment acts. They still managed to add to the family, and my sister, Carole, was born. In the early forties their presence was commanded by conscription to the factory for munitions work as part of the national war effort. Here their spirit was amalgamated with others on the shop floor to create a community spirit, which became a pocket within a larger, entire, national spirit, massaged by government and military agencies striving for victory. The war effort in the factory, in turn, was helped with comedy and music, courtesy of 'Worker's Playtime' and the like on the factory speaker system, all with distinctive, distorted crackle.

EIGHT ... George's hospital reflection.

THE CLEARER sound in a twenty first century hospital was a drifting and pleasant imposition of the Mozart 21 into my consciousness, even with the headset half on half off my head. The emotional character of the piece contrasted with my trip into the past, 'between the wars', when jazz was the thing alongside pockets of destructive human activities here and there in the world. The rapturous excitement of piano scales and arpeggios that decorated the main theme could be heard, then improvisation, reappearance of the theme, the scales and an end in fulfilling resolution. The music had become the means of re-establishing the surroundings of a hospital ward, and I was fulfilled by it, though still not sure whether I had been given some form of medication or was simply whoozey after my heart attack. I did appreciate in a cloudy sort of way that in spite of my situation, I must have been, probably was, lucky, in the way the chips fell. I felt maybe I was one of those people who generally seemed to generally make out.

I was able to look back on early retirement and rewarding work as the area public relations manager of large hotel chain. I meeted and greeted, I presented and chaired, I fixed and organised. I'd been fortunate to be there when the company expanded and took advantage of it. It also happened that my interest in creative things had a certain appeal to the hierarchy. Alongside busy sporting activity, I managed to fit in 'art' - the Old Vic., The Festival Hall, The Albert Hall, The National Gallery, The British Museum, The Victoria Albert Museum, etc. etc. etc. All visited and revisited. I think I was a bit of a culture vulture on the quiet. It all seemed to gain me brownie points. Again I was lucky because there was no evidence of interest in these things within my family. Maybe there wasn't time for my parents. They were Mr & Mrs John Public and making ends meet was occupation enough. I didn't have a parent or grandparent who knocked off the odd canvas, or symphony, or trod the boards.

And now I was in bed, in hospital. With blood pressure like mine it was inevitable, the red stuff working too hard and wearing out all those rubbery tubes, then clogging them up ... even though I had on the whole led a tolerably healthy life. There had been the odd indulgence, a firm's brandy dare, a pub crawl or two, exhausting week-ends of football matches <u>and</u> table tennis competitions, even with illness or injury. Overwork, late nights - something like it had been going on for years, centuries even. Hyperactivity, workaholic, burnout, call it what you will – Isambard Brunel, Marie Curie ... I was like countless others who were only fulfilled by being busy, with whatever their talent dictated.

But, unlike them, I'd been lucky enough to be born when I was, and able to enjoy the progress of the second half of the twentieth century, before the twenty first century disasters – IT crash, sub-prime crash, euro crash, 2011 and the riots, 2012 and the banks on the fiddle. These troubles were already eddying beneath the surface, set in train by an over-supportive society of the seventies, and a self-interested society of the eighties. Thanks to the dubious patter of the governments of the day. And beyond the government, an electorate too ready to believe political propaganda – 'You want to have lower taxes? AND, you want to have better schools, more police, improving health care? All together?' 'We can do it. Vote for us.' An impossible task, why believe it? Not that my family could have affected anything, John, my father, had not been eligible to vote until 1918. Another bit of luck, I could vote. With that feel-good realisation, my reflections closed, and the life of the ward finally imposed itself on me.

'I wanted to be a rock star.' It was an enthusiastic young patient.

'Oh yeah?'

'I thought, learn a few chords, practise a bit, and then find a pub that would give me a chance.'

'Just gotta have the neck to go for it,' his companion said.

'Exactly.'

'Funny, I had that idea too.' The companion was obviously on the same wavelength.

I looked up to see a couple of young men across the other side of the ward, one with his arm in a sling, the other on crutches. Both had spiky, unkempt greased hairstyles and such white faces they would have done justice to a soap powder ad. I tuned in to them more fully for a moment.

'My fingers got sore just doing scales.' 'The arm' was a bit on the podgy side.

'You have to play through it, don't you?'

'I know.'

'You'll go on won't you?' 'The leg' was rather lanky.

'Yeah, I suppose so.' He wasn't convincing.

'Practice makes perfect they say.'

'I know.' And the unfulfilled rock-star strummed an imaginary guitar with his good arm to demonstrate what he should have been doing. Then he kicked his legs, and bounced gingerly, careful not to shake his injured arm. 'It takes so much time.'

I wasn't interested, thoughts of suffrage engaged me. Dad had voted when he could, he made a point of it, because it seemed a lot of effort had been expended by a lot of people, and for a long time. The idea had been expressed many centuries before but it only became a really hot topic in the seventeenth century, with ideas of votes for all, after a civil war. And it took two hundred and fifty years for something of the objective to be achieved ... so John was able to vote as a young man in the 1920s. Previous generations had no say in how their lives would be managed ... unless they had a property or two, or connections to some dubious property owner, or an opportunistic liaison.

'How did you get on?' Failed rock-star said with potential envy.

'Well ...'

'What?'

'That's why I'm in here.'

'How d'you mean?'

'I did a few gigs,' lanky legs replied.

Podgy arm complimented him grudgingly. 'Good work!'

'Not really.'

'Oh?'

'That's how I did my leg. Stupid really. The stage was too small. I was doing my stuff and bouncing around like you do, and my foot got caught in a cable so I tried to shake it off, but it pulled down one of the speakers. The lead singer tried to dodge out of the way and knocked into me – bang. Off the stage.'

In the back of my mind, I reflected on where I was ... in hospital, courtesy of the National Health Service. Thoughts seemed to intrude into my drifting mind as if wanting to overlay one picture on another, like a painter who reuses an old canvas. Being within a hospital complex was almost like being in a separate, independent community - little was missing. The entrance was a walk through a shopping mall - newsagent, dry cleaning, chemist, baker, café - and upstairs, was the restaurant, and a church room. I compared that with what was available to my dad who had spent half his life without the benefit of such a free service, apart from when he was 'on the panel', the colloquialism for the insurance bit of Lloyd George's 1911 National Insurance Act; or the Friendly Society. When, in the 1930s funding for the scheme was cut, you had to pay for a visit to your GP and it was two shillings and six pence (old money) to have a chat with doc. Whilst twelve or thirteen pence (post 1971) seems like peanuts today, back in a time just before the National Health Service, we're talking about the equivalent of up to ten pounds a visit. Add medicine, dressings, etc. etc. and it became prohibitive. Even if registered 'on the panel', you still paid for drugs. All in the first half of twentieth century, when it was not exactly the healthiest of times for peoples who continued to struggle to live.

The two young men took their arm sling, crutches and heads of hair down the ward, and left me in comparative quiet. I'd wallowed in the past, but also wondered about the future, about grandson Peter and his hopes? The lad ached to succeed, and because of our time together, I was also bound up in his needs. The thought that maybe I wanted fulfilment through Peter flitted across my mind. Again. It was not a new thought, but had to be admitted. That Peter should succeed was important to me, but my desire was not to impose. It would be counter-productive and wrong for Peter. I dithered before dismissing these thoughts, deciding to allow my physical situation the space to take me where it wanted.

I drifted back to whatever world I had previously been in, aided by drugs and/or an undermined state of health. Whatever state my head was in, I felt warm and comfortable, tucked up in bed, and able to allow my mind to take off. Drift out of the hospital and go deeper into where-ever inside my noddle.

A STORY of FRED in LATE 1800s.

Grandfather Fred.

WHILST I had my early days in Morden, my father, John, had spent his in Clapham. My grandfather, Fred, only knew that place fleetingly, which was why John never really knew his own father. John had learned from his mother Ethel Edith, on the rare occasions that he had seen her (if not at home, maybe in the Rose & Crown opposite Clapham Common Underground), that his father had been a soldier, and died when he was still a baby. She told John that was the reason why he and his brother Sid had been sent to live at a charity school in the country and he had a step-father. It was the reason why I was born over a quarter of a century after my grandfather had died.

All in all, the chips had been stacked against Fred. He started life in 1863, in Denmark Court, a filthy, crammed alley off Golden Lane, in Cripplegate, London (now the site of the stage door entrance to Barbican Hall). There was one unsavoury toilet per tenement, a stand pipe per street, too many people, too much noise, too much stench, too much surrounding, dispiriting building, too much … too much awfulness everywhere. The reaction of Fred to these childhood odours was that he developed a life-long quirk of sniffing, especially at moments of tension. Some people blinked, some cleared their throats, some said 'Err.' Fred sniffed.

Cripplegate was well named, it has to be said. The whole place was crippled. It had been one of the old gates to the medieval walled city of London, built on the site of the northern entrance to the original ramparts of the Roman fort. Of the plague in 1665, Defoe wrote that Cripplegate was the parish with peak mortality in the old city area, an earlier indication of suspect health conditions. It was not apparently the place of begging cripples, but in the middle of the nineteenth century the inhabitants begged for respite from the foul, crippled living conditions. It was a stone's throw from Smithfield, the old site of the annual Bartholomew Fair, a meat market of inordinate size and sleaze, an area of even more repulsiveness. Cripplegate and Smithfield were all of a piece.

Fred spent his first few years within a struggling family which was Catholic, and Irish, the result of the relationship of his father,

James Gunner, and his partner Bridget Shaughnessy. Together with her next-door Shaughnessy relatives, they shared the degraded living conditions of an over-populated alley. Attitudes towards the Irish at the time were ambivalent, coloured by their abject poverty (which was not their choice), their rumoured doubtful commitment to work (but railway construction companies were very grateful for the navvy), and their bouts of inebriation (though given the life-style which they were obliged to pursue it was almost inevitable).

Fred, being the half Irishman he was, would have been affected by all of this. Indeed he often had conversations with his young mates that began, 'Here, you're a paddy ain't cha?' ... and he had to explain he was not, to which the next response generally was, 'Oh yeah, a bit of a mongrel eh?' followed by guffaws of laughter. Fred responded with a very po face, he liked mongrels.

It seemed as if Fred, who grew unsurprisingly to be a small thin man, had been subject to the schemes of some malign, mystic agency at birth. He lived through the degraded urban life of impoverished people in Victorian England, recorded in reports, and actually seen, in the pictures that became available following the introduction of photography after 1840. These journalistic writings and pictures of depravation were available together with the novels and paintings of 'society' earlier in the century, when impoverished people were living simultaneously alongside those social worthies but much less well represented. Fred's story embraced experiences of these conditions in Cripplegate, and the notorious Seven Dials district.

In between he spent his childhood days away from the great Wen were spent in Wakefield Street, Gravesend (the site now a supermarket). It was a very busy and popular town, being a prime entry point for immigrants and a major facility for river traffic, a place with no end of possibilities for waterside adventure, like sponging lifts from Watermen relatives on ferries across the estuary to Essex, and even to London. There was also the town pier to race around with cadging opportunities with relaxed town visitors, who had been encouraged to take a leisurely river trip, or the new railway out of London, thus by-passing the old stage coach journey through the infamous highwayman's territory of Blackheath. Visitors came in plentiful numbers to visit the camera obscura and the other amusements at the old windmill, plus the attractions of Rosherville

Gardens with its botanical exhibits. Fred's characteristic urchin's sniff proved useful, moving visitors in holiday mood to put coins into his out-stretched hand from time to time. On top of all that, the allure of Milton Army Barracks was only a few hundred yards away. Soldiers in uniform pitched out into the town to find Fred ready to accost them with, 'Was' it like in the army?' 'Have you killed anyone?' 'Was' it like?'

'It's like being at school, but worse. You have to do what you're told … or else!' they replied.

'Or else what?'

'Or else you're punished.'

'Yeah but you're all tough blokes ain't cha?'

'Have to be.'

'What do they do?'

And the soldiers would touch the side of their nose and then, with a wink at their girl friends, move on into one of the many town pubs, leaving Fred with ideas of heroic deeds and adventure in foreign lands.

By the time he was young man, Fred's bad angel had returned. His father had died, the family had moved back to London, to the disreputable Seven Dials district, and his mother died. So, maybe with memories of Milton Barracks still fresh, at the age of twenty five, Fred enlisted in the army in 1888 to escape both Seven Dials and the drudgery of work as a Sugar Boiler with its valves, condensers, vats, hot and sticky air. He calculated that at least the pay would be regular, but hadn't reckoned that three or four years later he would be in India, in sweaty Secunderabad, with its 100 degrees Fahrenheit heat in May, followed just a few weeks later by three months of monsoon.

After four and half years, Fred was transported home in 1896, transferred to the reserve, and later declared, 'unfit for service'. His situation was made harder by the general state of his health - an unhealthy deprived early life, army service, the climate in India, malaria and mercury treatment. It seemed a valid idea to direct a plea to the charity organisation, The Soldiers and Sailors Society, but more than a century ago, especially before the pension and unemployment acts, official charity was scarce. He died just after his 42nd birthday, within ten years of his pension-less discharge, whilst trying to get financial support from the Soldiers and Sailors Society, in Brompton. He had fathered four boys in seven years including of course my father, John, and thus created a situation that was rather difficult for his wife, Ethel Edith.

Fred died soon after the twentieth century began, probably from the malaria from which he had suffered due to service in India, though it has to be said that he also had a history of sexual diseases which the army treated in the Locks Hospitals in India. These Hospitals were created to handle cases arising from activities in the brothels officially provided for the British army's libido. The concern was to recover the health and effectiveness of the British soldier and avoid having an army with deteriorating and dubious health. Within ten years of Fred's death this same military force would be fighting World War I. Private Frederick Gunner had been given mercury treatment in hospital, a doubtful cure, and his decision to take the 'Queen's Shilling' could be said to have been unwise, and would seem to have been another part of the package engineered by the same fateful bad angel that dogged his life.

A STORY of JAMES & BRIDGET in VICTORIAN TIMES.
(George in bed.)

ONE ... The Shaughnessys.

FRED'S mother, Bridget Shaughnessy, was born in wet Galway, during the early period of a time when Ireland was a part of Great Britain. The Shaughnessy's lived the hard, frugal life that had been pursued in a similar way for centuries, probably thousands of years. The family, parents and siblings, escaped to the mainland in the 1840s. Bridget was a sturdy and resolute woman, in spite of her spare looking frame. The horrors of a tenanted smallholding in western Ireland living in a crumbling single-room stone and mud building, with a porous thatch roof, undermined her health. And the family were frequently undernourished due to the recurring blight on potato crops. Even this animal existence was denied the six of them when the landowner, keen to exploit his asset, ejected them, flattened the hovel and turned the land over to sheep.

Not that their landowner had done anything unusual. The fight to maintain living standards in declining financial circumstances was aggressively carried out down the ages. But the situation was exacerbated by absentee landlords who left their estate management in the hands of local agents who took advantage of their position to line their own pockets. Beyond that, there problem was a lack of understanding and support from the central government of Great Britain & Ireland. It was another item in the unhappy sequence of outsiders wanting to take control - raiding Vikings, William the Conqueror, Henry VIII's disagreement with the Pope, the settlement policy of Elizabeth I. Then there was the accession of Dutch Protestant, William III, clashing with James II and Catholicism, at the 1690 Battle of the Boyne.

In spite of newspapers and prominent politicians pleading the cause of the Irish, the government of Lord Russell and his responsible civil servant, Charles Trevelyan, proved unresponsive. The produce of Irish agricultural output was not diverted to the starving, suffering Irish, but transported for export and profit … to England. Trevelyan even had the idea that the potato blight was an act of God, sent to control population increase. Thus maybe a quarter of the total Irish population of eight million was lost, about a million to emigration and about a million to the of the angel of death.

But Bridget and her parents had the foresight to escape and join the huge exodus.

The journey across Ireland to Dublin was not easy, 150 miles of begged lifts from one town to another, bumped in countless carts offered by sympathetic and understanding, even envious, fellow countrymen. In between tiring, straggling treks on many rutted tracks, with the worry that, in that tense and vulnerable situation, maybe imagined, that there was danger of attack from any other equally desperate fellow countryman. Bridget's father, James, anticipated the emotional and physical demands of their escape and advised, 'No talking … to anybody. Keep even talk between us to a minimum.' He had carefully thought through the emotional onslaught the journey was to make, realising any diminution of resolve could, in the long run, prove disastrous. 'Dad can I…' was met with a punishing look, followed by unseen moist eyes. It was a journey of painful sights – begging old people with emaciated outstretched hands, agonisingly distraught mothers clothed in little more than an Irish shawl, and shoeless, skeletal children with huge frozen eyes. Even inert, probably dead, figures laying down beside the road. The Shaughnessys said not a word, but simply looked down to the straw and dirt upon which they sat, listening to the rattle, the laboured bump, clip-clop and grind of any rescuing cart, pulled by a horse that also was in doubtful health.

The ship from Dublin to Liverpool was overcrowded and miserably uncomfortable. There was sickness, fights for food, lack of sanitation and the heaving seas. Then it was Liverpool to Manchester, Manchester to London. Altogether it was a very demanding and remarkable journey. Not that it was unique, in Liverpool, Manchester and London there were ghettos of impoverished Irish immigrants who had made the same journey. Some had been resident long enough to become somewhat Anglified, though the core of them remained Irish. The English, and Scottish, were happy to exploit their need, and offered them unskilled jobs for low wages.

TWO ... Family support in hospital.

THE PAINFUL travails of mid nineteenth century Irish immigration were not lost to me in my twenty first century hospital bed. They engaged me in my unconscious world and I did like the idea that, as a grandson of Fred, I could consider myself as one eighth Irish. But around me in the ward other dramas were being enacted, and I gradually became aware of an adjacent ongoing scene - a patient and his surrounding family.

His wife, a rather dowdy middle aged woman, seemed really concerned about her husband, having considerable tension on her face and talking fifteen to the dozen, she had not even had time to take off her outdoor coat. She raised her spread upturned hands from time to time in a pleading gesture, and from her urgent, low mumbled but distressed monologue, every now and again one could hear her say, 'Oh No!'. The children of the pair, brought along to show support for dad were not involved. The teenage daughter wore the latest clothes and make-up as per the Teleshopping channel, and was busy on her mobile, standing and squeaking like a film cartoon mouse in response to news at the other end, which was evidently amazing - 'Is that true?!' 'Oh No!' said mum.

My old friend of the ward, Chas, was as usual wandering around in search of someone to talk to and looking at the family. Perhaps he was wondering whether he could rescue the patient with some sort of distraction, but then the daughter squealed into her mobile, and mum said, 'Oh no.', and the son looked as if he was not in a sociable mood.

The son was sitting on a hospital chair apart from the others to make room for the lap-top on his knees. He was in the right gear too - hooded jacket, jeans, trainers. The son had as much tension on his face as his mum, but the rage of his film cartoon cat was due to communication problems of advanced twenty first century technology – 'Stupid thing, how can you do that?!' he spouted at his electronic paraphernalia, which was momentarily in danger of a rocket launch through the nearby window. 'Oh No!' said mum. The only person who seemed relaxed in the midst of all this family communication was the patient, who gave Chas. a nod as he decided to pass on. The nod was saying 'What do you think of this lot?!'

A couple of beds away I was looking relaxed too, but it was an expression hiding feelings within my unconscious state. 'Oh No!' said mum. I was having more demanding times in mid Victorian London.

THREE ... James joins the Shaughnessys.

THE SHAUGHNESSYS exchanged 1840s pauperdom in remote Ireland for 1850s pauperdom in a London alley, and the London Bridget had a pot belly, probably due to a bread-loaded hunger-dealing diet, following on from her potato-loaded hunger-dealing diet in Ireland. It was through Bridget that the paternal line of the Gunner family became Catholic. Given their financial circumstances, she dressed in long, dark skirts and blouses which were changed only occasionally. Washing involved giving clothes a good soak in unsavoury water in the stone sink, then bashing them with a smoothed branch of beech wood. If a little dubious lye could be scrounged from a stall-holder by her father so much the better, but only if void of any noxious smell. When they first came he used to watch her and say, 'The water's no good for making poteen Bridget ... I to filter it and t'was awful.' He was a small man, lively and garrulous, given to periods of contemplative quiet but of uncertain mood, so Bridget was never sure which of his remarks were jokes. Lack of sun on a washing line across the courtyard housing made drying difficult and wind-blown dust and detritus added its contribution. Clothes were changed when possible, through hand-me-downs, acquired by uncertain means, or from the dead. Bridget's father had a way of getting things, and frequently came home with blouses, skirts and shoes, 'Here's the 'ting you were looking for Bridget.' The 'ting was sometimes in an unacceptable state and had to be 'mislaid' shortly afterwards. To present some semblance of tidiness, Bridget wore a shawl over her head ... and a decent apron – she always said, 'My apron's the only thing I can wash and change, so I will.'

Onto this downtrodden family had become attached James Gunner (my great grandfather), a rather untidy Journeyman Tailor with an untidy history. He was born in north east Hampshire and came to London with his father and family as a very young boy in the 1820s, and seems later to have become an apprentice to a Master Tailor in Walworth. His father had been seeking 'opportunity' but did the unwanted jobs of the exploited, before eventually making a move to the East End to become a publican, and James ended up in the City. At only 22 he married an older woman just three months after she became a widow. He had hooked up with Dinah Phyllis Fielder, nee Tyler, the daughter of a Gravesend Shoemaker, and her daughter. James and Dinah Phyllis then had three children, the last of whom died five weeks after her birth; Dinah Phyllis herself died just two days later. James was now left with two children and a step-daughter, but was able to foist the latter onto his brother, yet another George, a Landscape Painter up in Islington, leaving his own two children to remain with him. It <u>may</u> well have been these two children that later attracted Bridget Shaughnessy to James because she had, at that time, reached the critical age of thirty

Music provided respite and relief from hum-drum living. Bridget's father and brother were musicians and could offer a decent Irish jig as an attraction for neighbourly countrymen. The result was a dancing troupe amongst the lines of washing in the yard, and loud voices - 'Look out you oaf!' and, 'Mind my washing!' from sudden faces at doors and windows.

'It blew in me face, 'tis all wet,' was the standard muffled response with an impish grin.

James was in his element, he was a man who liked to always be on the move. 'This is like we used to do back in my village in Hampshire.'

'After the drinks James, was it?'

'This is Morris dancing!'

Bystanders looked on with amused curiosity. 'What's the handkerchief for?'

'That's a part of it,' James said and fluttered his handkerchief.

'Thought you had a runny nose.'

'It's traditional.'

'Looks like a horse dance.'

'I should be on the stage.' James was enjoying himself.

'T'would give people a laugh.'

James' efforts were indeed somewhat ragged in comparison with the evident Irishmen in the group, including some old-timers who were good and lively, but only to start, they then gradually faded, and dropped out, 'It makes me puffed, I'll tell you that'. They would totter away to lean against a house wall, rumpled but happy. The likes of such musical interludes followed the pattern of similar diversions enacted down the ages and made lowly environs bearable.

The adjacent Smithfield area was a usefully wide open space, convenient some centuries before for tournament jousting ... and executions, William Wallace the Scottish patriot, was one who met his gruesome end there in 1305, as did the rebel Wat Tyler, leader of the Peasant's Revolt in 1381, by means of the Mayor's dagger. In the changing religious affiliations of the sixteenth century, more lost their life, including swindlers and coin forgers who were put to death by being boiled in oil. Such occurrences in a long dramatic history made the area an attraction for visitors. But it may have been this very history that affected it, making it unloved, and uncared for. Smithfield was an over-crowded, dark, damp, dirty mess. It had been the destination for herds of animals that had tramped to London for a thousand years from the surrounding counties. Some herds had travelled from well beyond the counties nearby in an effort to find a reliable and rewarding market, but were exposed to the dangers of sheep and cattle thieves who were lying in wait. The establishing of the railways in the 1840s later rescued many a livestock drover when the network eventually reached Smithfield.

The market was a place of putrid air, with the hot, steaming bodies of animals exhuding noxious fumes as they were poked and bustled towards their final demise, and urgent conversion into assorted joints, shoulders, chops, bellies, heart, livers, tails, tongues, eyes, and end products - leather, sausage skins, rennet, lard, glue. Good little earners all. The activity was carried out within and without, as the crowd jostled, and smelled, and shouted with abandon. The whole could not fail to result in the under-foot condition of a soggy, mire of sludge.

There were times when this foul business did not provide the required diversion from the dispiriting hovels in which James and Bridget lived and they had to seek relief via the odd visit to the church of St. Bartholomew the Great, a twelfth century priory church founded alongside the hospital. It was a better expression of man's creativity. Not that Bridget saw it in that way, 'How could Henry VIII do that? Take over, take over ... ', she stressed the outrage, '... the Holy Catholic Church?!'

James didn't get very far in his response, 'Well, I heard that ... '

'Tis a terrible thing to do.'

'I think it was something to do with ... '

'Imagine what would happen if some Chieftan did that sort of thing in Galway, or in Dublin. '

James was quiet for a moment before he came in with his tactic to divert Bridget from the Holy Mother church. 'So you don't want to go in and see all those beautiful arches in the nave, and in the sanctuary, all built by those dedicated monks hundreds of years ago.'

Bridget hesitated. 'I know, 'tis really a lovely church. We'll go in and I'll 'tink I was in a time before Henry VIII.'

James thought the whole church business was a fuss about nothing, because life itself was a conundrum He just relaxed with a quiet victory.

For a period of about fifteen years (apart from a short break in Manchester), James and the family lived in the Cripplegate area, moving house from time to time, dictated by their meagre, sometimes non-existent, financial circumstances. Often their hungry, tired bodies would have to cram into a lodging house that reeked of age, with ten, fifteen even twenty people. Just beyond their run-down area, in contrast with Smithfield, was Clerkenwell, which had once been something of a fashionable place, visited by the Kings Henry II, Richard II, and by Shakespeare, and such celebrity might just have been generally known and of interest - alongside the history of horrors and assorted executions. But the short walk from their tenement to visit James' brother in Islington, took them past the Houseless Poor Asylum in Playhouse Yard where the gathering outside included haggard old women wearing patched shawls to cover their ragged clothing, and young boys without footwear playing stone-rolling in the street, and splashing in the puddles. It was a reminder to James and the Shaughnessys of where they were placed in the social hierarchy.

It was during the time that the Gunners/Shaughnessys lived in the area that the century's old malodorous, Smithfield shambles closed, following many, many years of protest. The prodigious activity of one and a half million sheep, and a quarter of a million cattle being herded every year into the market for slaughtering, and onward transportation … as meat products, was stopped. And the Gunner/Shaughnessy family lost an almost daily distraction. They could simply twiddle their thumbs. But the potent image of doomed, unaware herded animals remained.

FOUR ... George still in bed.

A YOUNG nurse in the hospital was looking at me with a concerned expression and said softly, 'Are you awake Mr Gunner?'

I didn't respond but her experience must have told her that something was going on.

'How are you feeling Mr Gunner?' The slip of a girl had sailed in smoothly to the side of the bed and gently put the question. She was neat and confident as nurses tend to be. When do they get a chance to be themselves?

I opened my eyes, looked round and blinked, my mind was struggling to interpret what I was seeing. I couldn't see poorly clad people in dingy homes ... or even stiff, over dressed men fawning before short, stocky, richly dressed woman. The situation fell into place. 'A bit ... sort of floaty,' I said.

'That's to be expected, you had a heart attack. We were very worried about you.'

'All I remember was the pain. It was like being hit with a sledge-hammer or something ... I could hardly breathe ... sweating like I'd done a marathon.'

'I can imagine. Well you're in the right place now.

'What happens next?

'Well, we've already gathered quite a lot of information. The doctor will be along to chat to you.'

'Is it all ominous?'

'No, everything's as normal.

'I'll wait with growing excitement.'

'That's the idea, rest now, and we'll bring you a nice cup of tea.

I vaguely noticed something happening down the ward. 'There's something going on,' I said gesturing.

'Oh he's in a safe place now,' the nurse said, nicely saying nothing really. I marked the moment, suspecting a drama of loss contrasted with the alert control of a young woman ... all in a day's work. The nurse glided away to the nurse's station as I was arrested by the vague sound of Bill Haley's 'Rock Around the Clock' from some radio or other. It impinged because it had been so long since I'd heard it, and before my memory provided an answer as the piece came to its end, ' ... rock around the clock toniiiiiight.' and any announcer's information was lost in a gabble of excited voices entwined into a melange of sound.

'... I was under for four hours...'

'... she had a mask on, just eyes showing, talk about full of eastern promise, then I went under ...'

It seemed like a cue, I faded again, the sound seemed to become distant, and the ward seemed to lose definition, out of focus Monet and in a drunken haze ... and on a rather foggy night. I started to breath with a slow, steady rhythm.

The ward carried on its activity, resting and emaciated patients lying flat out waiting - for whatever fate would bring. Here and there some patients had paired off to chat away the time, the newer patients exchanging details of their illness, or operation, but all were concerned with one question, 'When can I get out of here?' The National Health Service would have been happy to oblige but it had an established commitment to patient care which it preferred not to compromise.

I eased into momentary vague wakefulness, took a jaded look at the ward. It was a flashback to my old RAF billet back in Suez when I was on National Service, similar room size, similar layout of beds, spaces between, and similar clutter – chairs, books, newspapers, outdoor clothes. But Suez didn't have radio headsets, phone trolley or a library trolley. It was the same, but different. Outside was different too, it had been all sand outside. Over by the mess and the cinema an area of sand was compacted for the station sports arena. I'd taken a few wickets in the station cricket team, and played in the basket ball team there, managing to keep the sports going whilst still serving the monarch. I'd even appeared in the station revue show.

I hadn't quite lapsed into unconsciousness again, when thought of strategies about management of the intervening time struck me, I wondered if I would be allowed to get up, check out the rest room. I looked around for a likely source of information. The emaciated chap on the other side was flat on his back, mouth wide open, and fast asleep ... or was it a bit more than sleep?

I was noticed in my awakened state. 'Hello matey, how are you doing?' It was Chas.

'I think I'm OK.'

'You'll find out when you get up.'

'Yeah.' I searched for something to keep the conversation going. 'Are we all heart attacks?' I was now more or less fully alert.

'No, a mixed bag. But looking at some of them in here, you wonder if it's a waste of time,' Chas. said.

I laughed. 'Maybe I'm safer in bed then.'

'Bit boring.'

'I dunno, it's been interesting … I've been having … well dreams I suppose you'd call them."

'Beautiful eyes peeping over a mask in the operating theatre?'

I smiled in response. 'Whatever, it's all only electrical activity isn't it? Buzzing around in the brain, out of control.'

Chas. took that in. 'I don't trust lecky, I mean it was only just over a couple of hundred years ago it really made an impact, and now it's taking over. You get bamboozled – frequencies, waves, lasers, satellites, robots … where will it all end up?'

'I expect there's still more stuff to come. '

'Bound to be, but do they know what's going on out there?' He waved his arm vaguely up to the ceiling and the sky beyond. 'Quantum mechanics, particle physics, neutrons, protons, black holes, time, space, speed of light … how does it all fit?'

'Have to read your Stephen Hawkins?'

'Why?'

'A Brief History of Time.'

Chas was puzzled. 'I don't know about that but there's no limit, you've only got to look at the last twenty or thirty years.'

'My electrical activity has been looking much further back than that - about how people used to live … how most of us lived."

'I don't give it a thought.'

'I know what you mean. I never used to, but now, in here, you realise how lucky we are. Parents, grandparents, and all the people before, scratching a living. Yours too probably.'

'Could be.' Chas. didn't seem particularly interested.

I was pensive. 'Maybe it's not entirely dreams ... when stuff actually happened, so it all gets dragged up.' The remark seemed vague, even naïve, so I added, 'Sort of.'

'I don't worry about it.'

'Maybe it's a case of, 'seeing all my life before me'?

'As I said … ' Chas. didn't get any further, I corrected myself.

'All my live<u>S,</u> All my connections back to dot.'

'Yeah,' Chas. said in a disinterested way, it wasn't really his thing and he wanted out. 'You look as if you'd fancy another trip to your dreamland. I'll leave you to it.'

I was in the zone. 'The thing that comes screaming through is that, in a way, it's me. I was a printer and lived in New Cross. I lived in Cripplegate and served in India. I escaped the Irish famine ...' I had to pause at the seeming enormity, or madness, of the idea.

Chas. was looking for an exit line. 'Yes, it's amazing ... as I say, I'll leave you to it.'

I didn't take any notice. 'But when you think about it, it's not how it was, is it? It's my version of what they did ... and how they did it ... sort of ...' I stumbled to a stop.

Chas. saw an opportunity. 'It's all too much for me. I'm off.'

He wandered off and left me to find communion with my ghosts. The ward seemed to drift, people appeared to glide, noises sounded as if they were in a chamber. It was spacious, airy, other-worldliness. The ward merged into a vision of wispy indiscernible shapes and it wasn't long before surroundings were lost, it was like a real Scotch mist ... then I was oblivious to everything. I wasn't in the ward. I was elsewhere, back in the past. With relatives ... the Irish ones.

FIVE ... The English and Irish get together.

GREAT grandfather James Gunner had become a bit Irish because of his relationship with Bridget and with being part of the Irish community. The James Gunner of eighteen fifty was a small man, under average height, and puppy-like in his character, something that appealed to a certain kind of woman. He was happy to let his life be run that way, and take the consequences. James was one of those people who always seemed to be on the move, bustling around in his tatty, hanging jacket, baggy trousers, and shirt, which may well have been white once upon a time. He was on the boney side because of always being on the go. He didn't sit still, fiddled with things that were lying around, pushed his hair back, rubbed his eyes. Giving him a specific task was the best way of stopping him fidgeting and Bridget made a point of touting for work for him with any of the master tailors. Most of them used threats of scab labour from Holland in order to pay less than the magistrate's rate, so James and Bridget would sit on bare floorboards working into the night because James' children also had mouths to feed.

Together they scratched together small sums to contribute to the household budget. Bridget's father and brother, next door, both called James, were lucky to have their musical skills and could earn a few coins at the Penny Gaffs, entertainment venues created to provide distraction from the wretched lives of the down-trodden in the area. The Shaughnessy duo performed in what had once been the premises of a failed furniture maker who seemed only to have had time to put in a good surround of tongue and grooved walling before things turned pear shaped. The couple offered pipe and fiddle, with a jig and some lively patter, to an audience that made a ripe stench in the crowded room. But unpleasant odour was forgotten in moments of bawdy banter, mellow drunkenness, furtive groping, and in the joy of not engaging with the surroundings of Cripplegate. Sometimes almost forty odd people – haggard men, happy young children, prostitutes looking for a client, the disabled looking for companionship – packed into the welcome darkness. There was insufficient seating which gave rise to close packed standing in the small room and the opportunity for, as it were, a sample fondle before a deal could be struck and then sealed elsewhere. There was also a sprinkling of men who brought their supper with them, the most noticeable being the ones who dived into large pockets in voluminous coats, and stuffed hunks of bread into gaping mouths. One could guess that there was good reason for the large coat and large pocket.

The Gaff owner, a portly man who always wore a lurid waistcoat and hat whether indoors or out, introduced the entertainment in the strangulated sort of voice that comperes always use, 'And nyow for yawer delite and felishitashun, I give yuwoo, the singin', the dancin', the …'

'Get on with it !' boomed from the darkness.

'Let's have de Paddys on.' A gentler voice came with an Irish lilt.

Some members of the audience obviously knew the show included the Shaughnessys but first came an Italian clown who was also something of an acrobat. In having a visual entertainment the Gaff owner astutely offered an act of easy impact, void of any difficult accent, the intention being to settle any wayward, noisy or drunk people in the audience.   Then there was the Shaughnessys. Dad was the more out-going of the two and his mischievous face had its own winning way. He was a jigging fiddler and his son a dancing piper. They had built into their performance a routine of being in unison before falling out of step, then having amusing problems finding a way back. Dancing in amongst the washing lines had been useful rehearsal. It provided a laugh and always went down nicely with a reasonably well disposed audience, sprinkled with supportive fellow countrymen. The show ended with a Cockney storyteller enacting a range of Costermonger people, which inevitably included some rather ripe material. He offered a parade of quirky characters in mime, in convoluted Cockney, and in a gamut of loud but uncertain noises. It was a bustling sequence of odd balls - a wooden legged stallholder crying out his wares and a bystander gyrating his neck to see through crowds of people in order to avoid a stiff marching, shouting policeman. The policeman got knocked down by a drunken, mumbling tramp who was escaping a noisy and irate stall-holder raising his arms in rage. There may have been other people, it was difficult to tell, the general mayhem was enacted with such prodigious energy, involving so much eye popping, shuffling of shoulders and arms on auto-move, that the audience was stunned into comparative quiet.

Some of the audience may well have been avid Penny Gaff visitors and have just come from, or were about to go to, another one offering different fare. The back room of 'The Scouts Arms' round the corner in Little Britain, where James had once lived with his deceased wife, presented something called drama, or to be more exact a performance of a small group of men doing duologues and soliloquies with a bit of 'business'. The entertainment was split into two halves with a 'play' in each half and all thrown together with a minimum of props and 'costume'. Thus could be enjoyed curiously short and garbled versions of 'The Escape of Jack Sheppard' and/or 'The Daring of Dick Turpin' and/or a recent murder case - 'Maria Marten and the Red Barn' and/or even a half hour rendition of 'Hamlet'.

This entertainment, such as it was, had been a useful distraction for James and Bridget, who were able to get the odd free pass. But their domestic situation, with James' two children, was desperately over-crowded. Their bare shared tenement had to serve as both living and work space for the odd bit of in-house, bottom-end-of-the market tailoring work that James did manage to get. Their decrepit room of ageing lathe and plaster walls, dotted with holes, was not without ornament, there was after all, a cracked, blue vase on the mantle-shelf, a wall barometer that didn't work, and bellows which were barely usable because of a split in the leather. All items were well meant acquisitions of Bridget's father.

By 1860, James Gunner and Bridget had decided it was a life that needed to change. She had learned through the Irish 'bush telegraph', that there was an employment opportunity in Manchester where the cotton industry was vibrant and more importantly, pay was possible. She could also find some form of habitation within the Irish community. James was reluctant as he would still have been awash with Irishness, and Manchester was to him the equivalent of the moon.

The transport problem was compounded by trying to scrounge lifts in broad Hampshire intermingled with Bridget's broad Galway (and vice versa), and exchanged with broad Bedfordshire, or broad Warwickshire, or broad Staffordshire. Everyone resorted to finger pointing - to each other, to the north with pleading face, plus gestures of two tired walking fingers, followed by the beam of happiness of being jogged along in a cart, pulled by a trotting horse. It seemed their performance had a winning way, the response was an amused smile, and transport.

As it turned out Manchester was no better, the jobs were not easier to come by and the housing was equally dreadful. The same situation as London prevailed – the idea that a man-made big city offered a better chance of getting money from work than the rural spaces of nature, but, as everyone seemed to have the same thought, the job prospects were not good. The one advantage in Manchester for Bridget was the proportionally larger Irish community which offered the influence of the old country at a homelier level. But the life of Bridget, James and family was not enhanced, quite the contrary. They lost the child they had brought to Manchester to Scarlet Fever, Bridget's health suffered and she had been unable to work. James found no work simply because people spent so little on clothes of any sort. The family became depressed, and the prospect of the workhouse loomed. Life went on in its drab way, as in London, with the future uncertain.

SIX ... Dealing with the poverty stricken.

ON paper, to some influential figure, the idea of the workhouse may have seemed a good and practical solution to the problem of homelessness and unemployment, as well as an opportunity to deal with malingerers. The workhouse was to provide sustenance plus shelter, and offer work for those in need. The work-shy simply would not be housed or fed if they chose to pursue their own selfish lifestyle. For women who were to give birth it was often the best place to be, away from a dirty hovel at a managed facility and some staff with rudimentary medical knowledge.

Under the Poor Law Act, in 1834, a huge scheme was devised to initiate the construction of over 600 large buildings in what seemed to be an architectural confusion of grand house and prison. Boards of Guardians, being representatives of parishes within designated areas, were created to administer the system, making appointments of workhouse management. The character of each workhouse depended on the person in overall charge and it was agreed that ex-army men would be the best Workhouse Masters, someone who could bring order to a large institution. As a result workhouses so run tended to become regimented, unlovely places.

The 'Workhouse Act' (Strictly, The Poor Law Amendment Act, 1834.) was designed to completely overhaul the Poor Laws that existed for dealing with the needy. But it was not easy, there were the old, the sick, those unable to find work, and the malingerers. It had been a problem for centuries, and changes were made repeatedly over time in response to demands created by the constantly changing, and increasing, population. In the process the new Act overthrew an ad hoc locally funded relief system that had been financed, and administered, at parochial level for 300 years or so, and replaced it with a centralised system, but still paid for by reluctant local rate-payers, but with nationwide control.

For over two centuries the poor had been dealt with under the Poor Law Acts of 1601, initiated during the last days of the reign of Elizabeth I. These Acts recognised the right of the poor to support from the land, the entity, into which they had been born. In effect the land, as it were, owed each English born person a living. It was a right which dated back to the medieval church when land was considered to be held in trust for the poor. This _idea_ was projected onto the 'Workhouse Act' and so any misuse of the workhouse system was potentially a denial of rights which had been held by the poor for many hundreds of years. What evolved was that those who were financially able in each parish community should support the poor - the old, sick and unable – through 'out-door relief'. This commitment to subsidise the needy through the payment of rates continued under the 1834 'Workhouse Act' with 'in-house relief', but on a countrywide scale rather than through a multitude of parish administered units. Those same rate-payers were now obliged to a less direct administrative system and were enabled to agitate against what they saw as an onerous financial obligation imposed upon their carefully acquired propertied place in society. The obligation of a local parish community charge became lost in the national dimension. The appearance of a government controlled workhouse was a significant moment in history.

SEVEN ... George and Doctor.

NEARLY two hundred years after the Workhouse Act, the National Health Service provided shelter and care of a different kind for James and Bridget's great grandson, George, in his hospital bed. It is an institution that interestingly, partially developed from the workhouse system. The 1834 Workhouse Act was finally killed off by the 1948 National Health Act and many workhouse buildings were converted into hospitals of one sort of another. Some have even become blocks of privately owned flats.

Twenty first century me was in my National Health Hospital and having my promised cup of tea. I was impatient to get out of the hospital, so I urged my release with every member of the staff who came near my bed. I bent the ear of the nurse who brought my cup of tea, but with experienced, professional expertise she diverted me with, 'Don't let it get cold.' and, 'Best to keep your blankets well up.' So I now spoke jokingly to one of the nearby cleaners, 'Aren't you fed up with clearing around this bed, don't you think it be would better if I moved out?' The rather mumsy nurse assistant said, 'Oh no luv, I'd miss it. I look forward to it, seeing you trying to wangle your way out.'

'Me? Would I?'

'You and every one else luv.' She turned at the babble of voices that followed the sound of the opening and closing of the ward door which had let in an echoey cacophony of noise from elsewhere in the hospital. She then nodded to me and said with an amused smile, 'I think you're about to get the chance of testing your powers of persuasion.'

I could see a small Asian doctor, gowned and smiling his way towards me, stethoscope dangling round his neck, the badge of office. It was evident that news of my intermittent consciousness had got to the man with a say in my freedom. The doctor reached my bed.

'Hello Mr Gunner, how are you, I'm Sanjit Patel.'

'Hello, doctor. I suppose I'm not allowed to say 'I'm ready to go am I?'

'I'm afraid not. We were a bit worried about you when you first came in. The paramedics had to give you Oxygen in the ambulance, and resuscitation.'

'Yes, I vaguely remember something going on.'

'I think you're more stable now, but we'd like to give you some mote tests, see what's going on.'

'So I'm in here for a bit?'

'A little bit.'

The accompanying nurse chipped in with a reinforcing back-up, 'It's best that you are in a place where there's expert help on hand.'

I was disappointed. 'Yes, I can see that.'

The doctor continued, 'You'll be out soon enough, but the idea is to take things very, very easy.'

I just responded with a sick smile.

The nurse chipped in, 'Your wife will be coming in later. We had a bit of difficulty tracking her down, she was visiting your grandson.'

'I know.'

'Apparently your grandson is keen to come too.'

I smiled at that. 'Good,' I said.

'Your wife said you're not to worry about anything, she'll sort it all out.'

'That sounds like her,' I added, 'I don't mean that sarcastically, I mean she'll be sensibly organised.'

The nurse smiled. 'All things considered, it seems you're well set up.'

I reflected on that for a moment. 'I find things generally work out for the good.'

'Excellent,' the doctor said, 'The main thing is to keep your pecker up.'

I wondered what 'pecker' was in Hindi before I said, 'There's a chap I can kill time with, he's watching football on TV at the moment.'

'Oh yes Chas, he'll keep you occupied,' the nurse said. There was a trace of a smile on her face as she turned to look at Doctor Patel. It seemed the humour was shared.

He embellished the nurse's words. 'He's got a mate, Ted they're a bit of a double act.'

The response made me wonder if I should learn a bit more about my fellow patients, maybe they would be rather tiresome, but doctor and nurse were away to their next job. It was of desultory interest, I had more important things to consider. I slid down the bed to contemplate my situation – what really was my state of health? Would I have to curtail my activities? 'You must take it easy.' What did that mean, sitting down all day?! Living inside my head?! And there was always the matter of the medic's careful patient management – did they tell one how it really was? Exchanges were relaxed, but was that just cover … like the way the nurse earlier came out with, 'He's in a safe place.' What did she mean? I wondered how many, if any, of my forbears had had heart attacks. Did I have some genetic condition? They must have been subject to stress, done physical labour … on an indifferent diet … in bad weather … and in sub-standard accommodation … and … and … I lost the thread of where the thought was going but decided I was a lucky boy, warm and comfortable in a nice hospital, one of the first workhouse conversions done by the National Health Service, re-opened by the king no less, and subject since then to up-date improvements ad infinitum.

The thought got lost and confused in the miscellany of my environment, the mish mash of ward voices, movements, assorted bangings, electronic sounds, and very distant car traffic. I slipped gently into that world which is a sleeping wakefulness, or an awakened sleepiness, and the aural mess eased into a reverberating babble of voices, seemingly bounced around hard walls and mixed with rustling, shuffling feet. Then, intruding in this melee of sound could be discerned some horses clip-clopping to a stop, accompanied by grinding steel wheels, to recall sounds of the past. 'Here we are,' a voice said. A horse shook its mane, and its tangle of straps, brasses and a bit clanked me into the past.

EIGHT ... Workhouse.

BRIDGET was in that past, and in all the mayhem of the Gunner/Shaughnessy lives, she had somehow managed to become pregnant. And she had her confinement in an 1860s workhouse, (on the site of Manchester's extended Victoria Station) which James and Bridget had been happy to find was indeed a safer, cleaner space than in their own dirty and over-crowded, shared room. That was after they had experienced the rigours of the workhouse acceptance and settling procedure. First they were entered in the Admission & Discharge Book, but only after a slightly fractious debate about their eligibility due to their short period as residents in Manchester. James and Bridget were just a couple of the dozen that were admitted, replacing a similar number who had moved out that week, people hopeful of work, and money, winter being well over.

They were told, 'You're lucky with your timing, the inners and outers give us a few gaps at this time of the year.'

It appeared that the house attendant could read something on their depressed, drawn faces because he went on, 'Most of them will be back when the work dries up after harvest.' A Scottish accent seemed to give an edge to the words.

James managed to just say, 'Oh.' in response.

The house attendant didn't appear to be happy in his work. He had a long lugubrious face and wore a dark uniform. In fairness, it would be reasonable to point out that maybe anyone in that situation would not be a barrel of laughs, checking in 'inmates' does not give much opportunity for levity.

James and Bridget were noted as 'Journeyman Tailor and wife', stripped down and fumigated, given a pauper's clothing then tagged with inmate numbers. James was not allowed to remain with Bridget, men and women were kept in separate areas of the building, with no exceptions. They were put into their respective 'Able-bodied' sections being considered able to undertake workhouse tasks.

Each section consisted of a large Day Room with a small iron grate in the centre which was only lit if the evening got chilly. This was the place where the men gathered, sitting on benches, leaning on tables and chuntering about the problems of getting work, finding food and getting a bed. James spoke of his hard life only to learn that he was considered lucky. There was access to the Work Yard and Exercise Yard with private walled corner for a toilet - a neat, well made hole in the bricked ground. Upstairs was the respective dormitory with rows of beds of wooden pallets and another small iron grate. The workhouse was not generous with candles and nights were spent in a darkness relieved only by the illumination of the fading fire in the grate. All interiors had white-washed brick walls which was a help for those placed furthest from the windows because, given the large rooms, any fading daylight did just manage to reach the last beds. James was lucky enough to be half way along the row which meant he had the benefit of a bit of late spring light and a bit of heat. However given the lack of illumination, a tiring work day and the repetitive daily routine, James succumbed to tiredness and boredom and spent as much time as possible in his uncomfortable bed. These arrangements were much the same for the Old & Infirm of both sexes.

On his first night, as he sat heavily on the bed to recuperate his worn body, James anticipated oblivion, but the man next to him said, 'Can you tug off me boots lad?'

James complied silently. The man seemed a ragged but solid individual of no special significance.

'I've got a pain here you see,' he pointed to his stomach, 'It hurts when I bend over.'

'Bad luck,' James commiserated.

'It was a bit. But I got the other lad. I laid him out flat.' The man's face wore a satisfied grin. 'I done good, I got a good fee for the fight, and I bet a bit on meself as well y'see.'

Now that James had engaged with him he could see in the gloom that the man had a gap in his teeth and had a half-closed eye. He had the impression that he was maybe a bit old for the fight game.

'A bit o' prize fighting. That's how I get by in the bad times.' The fighter said as he wriggled about on the bed trying to find a comfortable position. There was the odd, 'Ooo.' and, 'Ahh.' as he tested assorted places.

James settled himself down flat out and stared up into the darkness. 'How did it come to this?' he wondered, and vaguely recalled the space and peace in Hampshire when he was a boy, then his years in London for which he had few feelings.

'I shouldn't have fought that last lad though,' punctured the night.

James never discovered the significance of, 'that last lad'. He had no interest, being too overcome by the circumstances of his own life, and avoided the fighter thereafter.

The work demanded of the Able-Bodied inmates, was not dissimilar to that done in prisons - oakum picking, breaking stones, and gardening on the vegetable patch. James was once again lucky, or clever, in being assigned to the vegetable garden, though that was not entirely advantageous when it was rainy. Able-Bodied women also could be required to do gardening, alongside the washing chores. Bridget too was quick thinking and able to play up her expectant condition so she was assigned to the easier chores. The workhouse matron had a softer disposition because of her own troublesome birth experiences. Most of the rest of the female Able-Bodied were not so considerate towards Bridget though, their attitude in the main was, 'Don't make such a fuss, we've all been through that.' However the younger, motherless girls, were more sympathetic, having listened more than once to horror stories of birth dramas. Bridget, having manipulated her situation for lighter work demand, found she had time on her hands in which to compare her boring, daily routine with her previous life of deprivation in rural famine Ireland. She was unable to decide which was worse.

Bridget as an expectant mother was on a 'Class 5' diet while James, along with other inmates was on a less nutritious, cheaper, 'Class 2' diet. It was difficult to discern the difference though, the diets simply included variable amounts of vegetables and meats, with pickled bacon, but little or no fruit, and a lot of potatoes, bread and cheese. There was also a generous ration of dubious liquids for most meals – gruel for one, soup for another, and broth for a third.

James and Bridget had joined a community of 650 people, about 60 % being men, and about two thirds over 60. The occupations noted were various but in the female wing more than a few were recorded as 'Prostitute'. As each workhouse attempted to be as self sufficient as possible, night-soil workers were also chosen from amongst the inmates.

Whatever had been the hope, or self-deception, of the authorities for the workhouse, it was not a place to find ease. Indeed the hard hearted of some of those in authority held on to the idea that a lack of ease was exactly what was desired, and the workhouse should be a place that was so unpleasant that no-one would *want* to go there. The idea that there could be people like James and Bridget, who could not find work, had no money, and no place to live, appeared to have been inconceivable to them. So inmates were treated like penned animals in a workhouse. The thought never extended to the question of what would happen to the 600 or so expensive, prison-like fortresses, should the stance of deterrence became so effective that people rejected entry into the workhouse, and the buildings became empty.

As soon as they were able, James and Bridget, with healthy new baby, decided to give up on Manchester and return to London. The experience of their stay made them feel that living in London closer to family would be better than enduring the influx of post-harvest returnees. They were let out into the wide world and waved on their way by a couple of workhouse attendants who were massaging their bleak lives in the pub next door to the workhouse. One was the house attendant who had booked in their entrance, and he smiled cheerily. It seemed that as soon as he got outside, life got better. 'Had enough of our weather up here?' he said.

Bridget was also cheery. 'You mean the showers we've had? You should try Galway weather, that's serious rain.'

'I'd put my Western Isles weather against yours any day.' The accent seemed to thicken with the mention of his home country.

James chipped in, 'You can keep your weather the pair of you, I'll settle for London.' Outside the workhouse, even London seemed to be a nice place.

'Aye well … ' the attendant said and let a raised hand say the rest – you don't know what it's like to live in God's own country.

Bridget and James understood the national sentiment.

'Enjoy your ale,' Bridget said. The pair of them waved and started their trudge south.

Having a new baby in tow proved an advantage and they found the journey less uncomfortable and quicker, with people showing consideration for their plight. They returned to the Golden Lane area of London … and the life-style from which they had tried to escape. But something positive had happened, following the healthy birth in the workhouse, Bridget now had another child in London. This was the unfortunate Fred, my grandfather, the soldier who went to India.

In view of Bridget's loss of her first three children, it seemed that her body had become healthier in spite of everything. Change must have been in the air. The old Smithfield market, unused whilst they were in Manchester, was being developed with a new market building providing a covered area half a mile long, complete with the new steam railway providing a cattle-train depot. But the family return to London did not last long, in the mid 1860s they were once again on the move, this time to busy Gravesend. So they did not see the final completion of the new Smithfield meat market when it re-opened in 1868.

The Gunner family managed to stay in Gravesend for ten years or more, during which time their impoverished and peripatetic life-style caused them to debate whether they should have emigrated, to America or even Australia, where workers were needed, and passages could be subsidised by the host employer. There was the added attraction of being able to find food readily available off the land, but they decided that such a move was too late life for them. Things began to pick up a bit as James got work from time to time (Bridget had nagged him, 'You must tidy up the way you dress. You're supposed to be a tailor.') It wasn't too long before James became amenable to his surroundings, with the Thames a short, pleasant walk away to the distractions of the busy dockside and a nice pub at the end of the jetty.

'I've become very fond of Gravesend,' he said in his last years, by which time he had managed to add a bit more flesh to his previously scraggy frame. 'It can be crowded like London but I don't feel so hemmed in.'

'I miss the Irish people,' Bridget commented.

James gave her a sideways look. 'I don't find that too bad.'

'I know. You found them too much in London. I find it too much without them here.'

James was reflective though. 'Amazing what we've got through.'

'Because we're tough.'

'I wonder if we'll get a medal when we go up there,' he pointed up.

'Bound to, 'Long Service and Good Conduct', they call it over in Milton Barracks don't they?'

Not long after that exchange James died, happily it seemed, away from the great Wen, and Bridget was able to return to London and St. Giles, where the Irish community had been established for a hundred years or more. The family lived for two or three years, in the famous, or should one say infamous, Seven Dials, in Great St. Andrew's St. (now Monmouth Street, the address a pricey boutique). There, Bridget died having been got at by the cold February, London weather, and Fred soon escaped to join the army.

At the north end of this street had once been the place where condemned criminals were given a last drink of ale as they were progressed in an ox-cart from Newgate Prison to Tyburn gallows (a site now known as Marble Arch at the west end of Oxford Street), complete with coffin and following parson. The doomed were encouraged to provide some sort of merry occasion for watching spectators, an act by which to be remembered. Some prepared a rehearsed performance. The sombre/merry occasion climaxed at the old village of Tyburn, with many opportunists exploiting the heightened mood of the event with sales of food, drink and trinkets. Even though the whole macabre show had stopped in the century before Bridget lived in Seven Dials, when Newgate Prison was rebuilt (and public executions took place outside the new building), lurid stories were still told in the Beer Houses of Great St. Andrews Street, intermingled with the following tales of debauchery in the good old days of the 'Gin Palaces'. Some of the dubious neighbours with whom Bridget and Fred mixed had a life not so distant from that of those who had taken that final, fateful journey up the road, on the way to Tyburn.

Seven Dials may have been an even more dispirited and degrading place than Cripplegate/Smithfield – dark, close-packed, stinking alleys with beggars, robbers, vagrants, all the riff-raff of the day, dressed in tatters. Alongside - amazingly, shoeless children in rags, somehow offering young faces in which could be seen a life of hope and expectation. Evidence that life goes on regardless of circumstances in spite of a squalid young life that would have to overcome the memory of winter nights clasping another, maybe unknown, body for warmth on a floor crammed with other bodies, or hot summer nights spent trying to find space to be clear of other unsavoury bodies ... wet days walking through foul detritus.

As was Cripplegate to Smithfield, so was Seven Dials to Covent

Garden, a place to find diversion, convivial social meetings, shops aplenty - bones, old iron, smelly pipes, bird-fanciers, rabbits - dead and alive, dubious fruit, the previous day's stinking salted fish, music, petition writers ... but it was best as a daytime diversion only, it was not advisable to be away from home territory during the hours of shadowy night-time gaslight.

All this had been a considerable part of the life experience of the Gunner family, the forbears of George Gunner, Area Public Relations Manager of the Wayside Friary Hotel chain – 'Welcome to Good Food and Comfort.' …

NINE ... Pam visits George.

THREE generations on from James, Bridget, Seven Dials, hunger and deprivation, was me, in hospital, my face puckered in anguish, my mind embedded with ideas of poverty-stricken Victorian life. But after a second or two the expression eased and relaxed into a noticeably more contented expression.

'I think he's asleep.' A female voice had finally broken the general quiet. I blinked, and looked around to get a handle on where I was ... London or Ireland? Somewhere else? Where? My situation began to come back to me – heart-attack, ambulance, hospital.

A familiar woman was beside my bed with a good looking teenage lad. Feminine art was on display - tastefully dressed, make-up of discreet colour, and unshowy but effective ornament – rings, necklace, ear-rings, the picture of a tolerable life-style. The pair had been sitting beside the bed for almost an hour waiting for something to happen to my inert body. Apart from the odd sigh and grunt, here and there, and the occasional repositioning of the body, there had been no useful communication.

'I think he's awake. Are you with us George?'

'Hello Pam, good to see you.'

'Am I allowed to hug you?'

'Climb in if you like.' I held the bedclothes back.

Pam glanced at the lanky boy beside her before she said with an amused smile, 'It would spoil my make-up.' She leant forward and gave me a very tight hug. 'I was so worried about you when I heard from the hospital. 'Hospital', sounded so scary.'

'I didn't know much about it. Stab of pain. Zonk. In bed, and here.'

'So, what's the news?' Pam said.

'They've done a blood test, and ECG. I've had Aspirin, and treatment called thrombolysis.'

'Oh yes,' Pam said knowingly.

'Of course, you girls are in to all that sort of stuff.' I added with a smile, 'Sounded dodgy to me ... the cardiologist is checking an angiogram.'

'We talked about all that after our last parish council meeting.'

'I might have known you and your mates would know all about it.'

'Just bit of dye put in and circulating to see what's what. X-ray?'

'Maybe, but keeping me in suspense.' I turned to my grandson, 'Exciting eh Peter?'

'As long as you come out in one piece … a fully functioning piece.' Whilst he was tall, he was not thin, but well built and had that air of health that comes from a well exercised body.

'Pam will make sure of that, won't you Pam.'

'I'm already on the case. Been speaking to Maureen and Nancy, they've been through all this with their other half.'

'I won't worry any more then.'

'Will you go for angioplasty?'

'We'll see.'

'By pass?'

'Ditto, but probably not.'

Pam went into organised mode. 'I got all the info., the full story of how, why and what. You've got to rest up my boy.'

'That's my girl,' I said.

'You've got to stop …' Pam didn't finish.

'… lifting things, bags of cement, paving stones, bricks, pebbles, grains of sand …'

'Don't be silly. You know what I mean.'

'You're on my side aren't you Peter. Come on we can make it two against one.'

'Could do, but look at the opposition grand-dad,' he replied nodding his head towards Pam

Pam ploughed on. 'It seems you'll have to change one or two things now George. Careful diet, careful exercise … and so on.'

'You sound like the medics. Pam.'

'Well you do push yourself … always doing things you shouldn't.'

'Only live once.'

'So best to be careful George, think things through, find other ways of enjoying life.'

'Like the parish council?'

'Exactly, you'd be very good.'

'Maybe, but I wouldn't enjoy it.'

'There's other things, the flower group, or …'

'Yes, I do know what goes on in the village. You go to your meetings. I'll contemplate my next moves in the garden.'

Pam's face immediately showed concern and I corrected myself. '… contemplate how someone else will make the next moves in the garden.'

Pam turned to young Peter. 'Don't you think granddad should take it easy Peter?'

The teenager was aware he was being asked to take sides and he also knew I still had useful knowledge, advice and support to offer him in his quest to make an impact in the world of badminton. Peter seemed older than seventeen years because his body had filled out with, even at his age, many years of training and exercise. Indeed it could reasonably said that the person he was, was partly due to me and the time we had spent together in the gym and on the track, and simply talking about fitness, talent, mental attitude. I was aware that I wanted to fulfil old sporting goals through my grandson, and we talked about that too, it was a matter which enabled Peter to perhaps acquire a greater understanding of the complexities of being a committed sportsman. Fortunately for us all, my son Hugh, Peter's father, kept a careful watch on us to monitor any potentially over obsessive ingredient in either of us. Hugh had no ambition in that direction and found fulfilment in a good balance of home and professional life. All of us knew that if the matter was not carefully controlled it would founder. In this respect Hugh was almost the key figure, able to be objective. At this point in time he was abroad with his job, a well-paid position in civil engineering in a consultancy capacity. I could never quite fathom what exactly he did, but it didn't seem to involve much actual work, i.e. sitting down (or standing up) and doing something. Time jetting off to somewhere or other also counted as work apparently. It was all based on a good appropriate, degree, judiciously selected experience, and commitment. There seemed to be lots of reading, and lots of talking … and meetings, of course. Either way, when Hugh wasn't abroad he was 'working at home', which seemed to allow ample time for playing around with his huge collection of rock band music, on all formats, old and new.

Peter carefully chose his words to sooth Pam but at the same time get across to me that he wanted my support in his badminton ambitions.

'Well of course, when you've been unwell, or had an injury, you have to be careful, take it easy. But if you go too far, that could be even less healthy. The body goes flabby, resolve goes, I suppose even the immune system goes, so it seems to me ...'

Pam interrupted. 'I can see how it seems to you. You're all the same you men.'

I chipped in, 'Vive la difference. Eh Peter?'

Peter smiled. He was very close to me after the hour upon hour we'd spent together.

I continued, 'Has me being in here, got in the way of your training?'

Peter wasn't entirely sure of the best reply, but said, 'It did a bit.'

'... but you can see I'm alright and you'll keep at it?'

'Yes.'

'You have to keep in tip-top condition, body ... and mind.' I stabbed a finger at my head. 'That's what I got all wrong when I was your age.'

Peter was engaged. 'I'm getting much better, my concentration is definitely improving. I can focus completely on the moment. Eliminate what's just-past, not anticipate what's-next, just be in now.'

Pam was aware she was being cut out of the conversation. 'Oh, you men!'

'That's us,' I said. Peter responded with a smile, he'd experienced this sort of thing before, more than once.

Pam stood up from the bedside chair, 'Well, we came about an hour or more ago and ...'

'I've got a meeting to go to.' I finished the sentence.

'I have actually, it's the flower club.'

'You go. I need to get all the rest I can, because I must get down to the gym tomorrow, I've got to get back to fitness ... I could do with an hour on the weights ... and there's a little five miler we could do Peter, shall we say about ten o'clock, I heard the forecast is good.'

Pam was alarmed. 'You can't do that! I'll speak to the doctors. I'll ... '

I laughed. 'Gotcha!

Pam relaxed. 'Oh, you…'

'You go off. I'm safe here aren't I? Not in danger. Just resting. Having quite a good time actually, gently dozing. Sort of re-living the past,' I corrected myself, 'All my pasts.'

'Alright then.' Pam didn't pursue the matter, she'd lived with my quirks for long enough. She leaned across the bed to give me a peck. Peter stood by watching.

'Good to see you granddad. I can get back to normal now.'

I said, 'You do that. See you later Pam.'

'Of course.'

The two visitors trundled off down the ward and I could hear them talking as they walked. 'Are you driving or am I?'

'Do you think it would be OK to visit granddad again?'

'Of course, do him good. He'll get fed up in no time, being in bed all day.'

'Well, I'll …' Peter didn't get a chance to finish.

'But no getting into all your physical jerks stuff together.'

'Of course not. Whatever you think about hard training, not going beyond what the body can handle is also part of what you have to do … or not do if it's necessary.'

As their voices faded I slid back with my arms behind my head on the pillow and looked up at the ceiling. Pam's outwardly relaxed behaviour could have been hiding real concern about my condition. I certainly felt washed out all the time. Everyone could have been taking it easy with me. I caught a bit of movement of something on the ceiling. It was a fly. How could they walk upside down on the ceiling? And there was a spider, I remembered seeing it before, it hadn't moved. How could they do all that? Did blood go into their little head … like an upside down man. What went on in their little brains … or did they function by sort of auto device … and there's mosquitoes … and gnats and … The fly came back for a moment, then went off. My eyes drifted across the ceiling to the spider … where? Gone? White, all of it. The ceiling must have been redecorated, it was so white. My eyes cast about with growing disinterest. The fly had gone, the spider had gone. There was just nothing. My eye lids fluttered, and then closed

A STORY of GEORGE & ANN, in the LATE REGENCY period.
(The patient still in bed.)

ONE ... 'Early' George.

I WAS in the ward and yet, in a way, I wasn't in the ward. But I could be seen, in bed, in a hospital that had an array of the latest gizmos, all 'free at the point of delivery' above the bed - air line, suction line, angle poise light, radio facility. Just across the ward was a nurse's trolley with BP equipment, catheter, canula, syringes and drawers of drugs. Not something that my father, John, could have been experienced between-the-wars when he would have had to pay to visit his GP. Or my grandfather, Fred, born into degraded and unhygienic Victorian London, with even fewer medical facilities; or my great grandfather, James, an unskilled country boy, who was overawed by early Victorian urban living, and experienced the workhouse. None of them could have imagined the twenty first century medical climate as anything other than fantasy ... if at all.

Yet another George was father to great grandfather James. 'Early' George (my great, great grandfather), was born in Hampshire over two hundred years ago at the back at the end of the eighteenth century, a time when advances in medical science had not seriously started and healthcare was almost unknown. Individuals, especially women, who had specialist and unusual knowledge of plants, of potions and cures, were the nearest to health carers, but were treated with suspicion, and even seen as witches. In that time of slow change, harassing these women was not unknown. The burning of women accused of witchcraft in the previous century remained an item of intense interest. But the creative energy of the Industrial Revolution went beyond the engineering and mechanical, medical matters had begun to attract wider attention too.

The time of 'early' George Gunner's birth, was one of social unrest. In France, a turbulent underclass had been aroused, and revolution ensued in 1789. The vacillating but over-privileged monarch was executed in 1793 and a bloody contest for power followed. It affected Britain, the upper echelons took fright and countered any ideas of social change with oppressive measures.

England had its revolution almost 150 years before, when the rights of the people were similarly pitted against those of the ruler – those whom Oliver Cromwell came to lead, against King Charles I. It also resulted in the execution of the monarch, in 1649, and a subsequent contest for power between factions within a monarchical opposition – an uncomfortable alliance of army, parliament and church. An unsettled 'representative' Commonwealth government appeared in the years following the Regicide so the English Revolution was incomplete, even with the enacted Bill of Rights of 1689. The unrest remained into 'early' George's time.

The desire for social improvement had firmed up by the end of the eighteenth century, and pressure for change came from a growing number within lower the levels of society, alongside a modicum of liberals amongst property-owners and gentlemen. The movement coincided with the changes in the socio-economic circumstances that resulted from advances in manufacture and technology. The under-privileged were no longer passive or ignorant, formal meetings were held and pamphlets were produced - developments of which the ruling establishment did not approve.

With all this change, and the unsettled economic conditions that followed the Napoleonic Wars, 'early' George decided to leave his life as a Gamekeeper at the comparatively new Georgian House at Hinton Ampner in 1820s Hampshire. He'd heard about the endless opportunities that seemed to exist in London. Not that Hinton Ampner was without excitement. It had been a Tudor House once, but was demolished because it had become haunted.

'Early' George had decided that a life of scrabbling at the soil did not fit the 'new world'. He had done most of the jobs on the land – stone picking as a boy and throwing them to scare off crows, then he'd ploughed, hedged and sowed. He'd delivered calves and sheared sheep and whilst there was indeed some intrinsic reward in being surrounded by nature, there was also some unsatisfying element. He decided it was time for him to also change.

TWO ... Brompton.

EARLY George arrived in London with his small family and stayed with his cousin, Robert, in Brompton, the artist's quarter. Brompton at the time of George IV, was a village cluster, not so completely enmeshed by the big metropolis. With smart Knightsbridge to the north, it had grown from a hamlet between Chelsea and Kensington and was about to be overawed by Thomas Cubitt's grand buildings in Belgravia. Soon after he arrived 'early' George did catch a glimpse of the king on his way to his favourite haunt, Kew Palace, as he drove from the hundred year old Buckingham House, recently revamped by John Nash, and soon to be renamed Buckingham Palace. The occasion for early George, amounted to one of the excitements he had heard about, and he anticipated many more.

But first he had to deal with the language, or more exactly, the accent. He had little difficulty in understanding what was said to him, but the problem was the people to whom he spoke couldn't always follow what he had to say. As his ears became attuned, he modified his speech a little, and eventually got on splendidly. His easy going character and manner with people enabled him to land a job, first as an ostler in the stable then as cellar man, at the Red Lion in Brompton. He also offered his employer a physical presence if the odd drinker became rowdy or got out of hand. If such a situation occurred, early George suddenly appeared nonchalantly, but hugely, and somehow menacingly, by the barrels. All in all, London was a good place to have gone to, and early George happily added more children to his family. That however, was not such a good development as the increased size of his family caused relations with cousin Robert to become strained.

Early George decided to broach the subject of moving on. He surprised Robert one day by arriving at his workplace, a small dyeing business he ran with his brothers just off Church Street, on the Kensington and Brompton borders. Cousin Robert understood immediately that George wanted a confidential conversation. His cramped mews yard business entrance, with a three foot counter, sample table, cloth hangings and stirring rods, was not the place so

Robert led the way to the interior. He was a small man, but well built, alert, and guarded, anxious not to appear vulnerable. Even his dress seemed to be a defence tactic – an overall from his neck to his knees, so that all one could see was a rumpled neckerchief tucked into a floppy collar, and coarse stockings. Robert rubbed his dye stained hands down his overall as they exchanged small talk walking through the painted brick store room. One wall was lined with labelled boxes offering a range of dyeing materials - onion skins, lichen, funghi and the like, essentials for Robert's main market, the cheaper end. Some smaller boxes contained indigo, saffron and such for the occasional more expensive job. The two men avoided the puddles of the vat room but not the odours of the fixing room, even with its sash windows open. The stale urine, vinegar, and the potash made a noxious smell. The pair got to the drying room and settled in a corner on a couple of three legged stools made available for a moment's respite for the vat stirrers. The room still hung with moisture that held pungent odours, though less distasteful than the fixing room.

'Look Robert, I think my brood are getting a bit too much for you. We've both increased our families and it has become a bit crowded. I think it's time for us to move on.'

Robert protested but not entirely convincingly. 'We can manage George, especially now your girls have found work east.'

'No, it's your place. And it's not only the number of us, your older ones are beginning to need a bit of space of their own, so you need the room.'

'That's true but … '

'Don't' worry about it. We Gunners are used to looking for places to live. Look at my granddad, lost his home towards the end of his life because his place just happened to be on a bit of land that was sold by a senile land owner. Or to be more exact, because he happened to be on a bit of land *controlled* by the grasping son of the senile land owner. And he happened to be one of those pushy, grubbing, money men ... said too many squat hovels had been built over the years.'

'I can imagine, too nice for his own good your granddad. Do you remember in history, the old kings – Richard the Lionheart, Henry the Navigator? Our family used to call your granddad, 'William the Good'.

'He was. So he was exploited.'

'What actually happened?' Robert said looking down at his hands, rubbing at the blotches of dye.

'The son only wanted to clear the land, granddad's place with it, so that he could rent it out as pasture for sheep - and a good return. Granddad tried to fight it but the investigation into the thing involved a lot of curling, faded old documents and only proved that all rights were properly legal and the family home was gone. At least that's what was said and decided.'

Robert was sceptical. 'I wonder, you know what the legal lot are like … he was probably in with your land owner.'

'It's all beyond me. Anyway, that wasn't the end of the story. Because of all the enclosures, there was no work. The only work the family could get at the time was as labourers clearing their own house off their own plot.'

'My God, what a world,' Robert responded with feeling. He picked at the dye under his finger nails.

'Gran and granddad crowded in with one of their girls, Eleanor, back in Hants.'

'That must have been a bit of a squeeze.'

'It was but, in one way, it turned out to be an advantage. Gran and granddad were getting a bit past it and moving in meant that they had support available.'

Robert shook his head and smiled. 'Funny old thing, life.'

Early George smacked his hands happily. 'Exactly, and he made out in the end, somehow. And so will we, we always do.'

THREE ... Mile End.

EARLY George was not without contacts further east because his eldest children had all found work in Islington. Encouraged by them, and accompanied by his quiet wife, Ann, the couple ventured across the metropolis in the late 1820s. They endured a short spell reacquainting themselves with sleeping on the floor at the Bedford Arms in Walworth with early George doing the work no one else wanted to do. Then he found more amenable employment just outside the City. His relaxed manner but resolute, tough streak, cultivated in a working life contesting the elements, meant these attributes, alongside his pub know-how, was a bonus for any similar enterprise, and The Old Globe, in Mile End Road (now a Ladbrokes betting shop) gained the benefit of his experience. Early George had arrived shortly after the pub was rebuilt following a fire. The incumbent publican found a couple of years continued rumours about his role in the event so intolerable he moved to a farm in East Anglia somewhere. Reports in the local newspapers had confusing eye witness reports about a fight, and an oil light, but what happened was a mystery. The main point was that it all occurred when there was pressure to tighten licensing regulations. Early George finished up as the publican and, with passing time, became a man free of parental responsibilities when the last of his children flew the nest.

Most of the children were not far away, in Islington, where yet another George, son and Landscape Painter, lived with his head in the clouds. The females of the family had both found residential domestic work in a Solicitor's household, as a tutor-nurse and a nurse-maid and, it seemed, they were almost imprisoned by their employer who filled their lives with demands. Early George's other son, James, had lost a wife Dinah Phyllis and lived with partner Bridget Shaughnessy in nearby Cripplegate.

Early George's wife, Ann Crockford as was, also grew up to country life but on the farm of a kindly farmer. She was a small, unsmiling person inclined towards a sedentary lifestyle. Thus, she always appeared to be doing things that required sitting down – shelling peas, scraping potatoes or apples, darning, sewing, rag rug making which she had learned about in The Old Globe from one of the immigrants down from the north. Early George thought it was her reaction to the life to which fate had led her, and from which she had chosen to almost disengage on a social basis. The rug-making job of 'Prodding', as it was called, seemed to occupy most of Ann's time, she spent hour upon hour cutting up rags, then endlessly prodding bits of material tightly through old sacking scrounged from Mile End stallholders. The floors of their living room and bedroom were entirely covered.

Ann did indeed have difficulty with London life, or more exactly East End life. She was not so unhappy in Brompton, with its different clientele, where she could get a glimpse of grass, shrubs and trees, to remind her of her country days. But Mile End seemed to offer nothing but the growl of steel cart wheels, clip-clop of horses, and costermongers trying to out-shout each other. Squabbling children, howling babies and rowing couples filled the few quieter moments. Their relationship became distant after the children left. Behind early George's warm façade was an unsettled and sombre domesticity, a situation their children preferred to avoid even though they were only a couple of miles distant.

The lives of Early George and Ann settled into a mainly uneventful routine. But on one occasion, in the early hours, after another long, noisy and busy day, as they tumbled in to bed, George said, 'Thanks.'

Ann replied, '… have to do something.' It seemed her pursed lips and small mouth fairly represented her reticence.

There was a long pause during which they listened to the bed creaking as they positioned bodies and arranged bedding. 'Makes a change from rag rug making,' George thought, but punctured the jumble of noises with, 'Sorry,' and gestured to the room as a means of indicating the pub., even life itself.

Then Ann said, 'I'm sorry I don't come down to serve more often.'

'Well, I know you don't like it.'

'It's a bit different from back home.' Ann still thought of her young life back at the farm in Hampshire as home.

'Things change I'm afraid.'

Ann felt a need to communicate that she understood but only managed regret, '… unfortunately.'

'A big change for us.' George was tolerably happy with his

change.

'... sometimes you just have to do what you have to do.'

'I'm afraid so.'

'But it's the same for everyone.' Ann turned over to sleep ... and indicate the end of the conversation.

George was still in reflective mode. 'Yes, you've only got to see our customers.'

'So we have to live on as best as we can,' Ann said and gave a final tidying tug of the bedclothes and George too slid down in the bed. She doused the earthenware oil lamp and George understood that conversation really was over. He soon caught a whiff of the lavender that Ann insisted be added to the dubious oil mix obtained from the market. He appreciated Ann's remarks, it had all been a bit of a struggle and it was nice to know it was shared, even if reluctantly. George knew that Ann was not happy but there was not much he could do about it. In the circumstances he did well by his customers, offering an ear for their problems. All the pair had for their solace was, beer for George, and rag rug making for Ann.

The East End, and the pub worked for George, he became quite a hit in Mile End. The sound of his slow, gentle Hampshire burr made him stand out in the mangled vowels, muffled consonants and dubious aitches, of the East End. He looked the part as he stood behind his rough and ready planking bar with varied earthenware jugs and tankards on its surface. But it wasn't his speech that enabled Early George him to make such an impact, so much as his good humour. He took the joshing of his country ways in good part and was liked for it. And his burly size was a help, it projected an idea of authority. His physical farm work had made him fit and his country experiences were a help too, he'd been kicked and charged at a few times by some rather large animals, so any odd East Ender was nothing to worry about.

FOUR ... Bar talk.

THE regulars at the Old Globe in Mile End Road all felt at ease as they leant on the bar or against the wood panelled wall, and nattered about their problems – shortage of money, foulness of drainage, irritation of insects, short life of candles, scant sources of firewood and dozens of tit-bits that pressed for satisfactory management ... all the while soothing away the pains of their existence with the product of the house. But the thing that most came up was the changing times. The new farm mechanisation was a hot topic.

George was often on hand to supply a useful bit of information, which he'd scooped up from the miscellany of personal stories he'd heard, and he could deal with some of those matters; it was another thing that helped George enjoy his London life. It hadn't been quite what he'd expected but it did seem better than grubbing in country dirt. There was wind and rain. It was too cold in the winter and too hot in the summer, plus exhausting work at harvest time and ploughing time, then none at all. Altogether, country life could not be said to be one to which one should aspire. Urban life, where one had shelter in the warm (though in the summer London could get sticky and smelly) was an improvement, and anyway there was always a drop of beer to ease any discomfort at the end of the day.

The other talk that cropped up was of course about changing times.

'I bet you're happy to be out of the old country games George', a small scrap of man said. He was inordinately undersized and had difficulty finding clothes to fit him, all his garments hung in folds.

'I'm not sure they've got so much trouble in Hants, the serious stuff is going on down in Kent,' George replied.

'You can understand it though can't you?' another man said.

George knew about the issue fully, he'd experience some of it directly through his grand-dad. 'Losing the waste and commons is a big blow, but the thing that's turned it, is these new machines coming on the farm. It's putting men out of work.'

Shorty chipped in again. 'The bloke who's doing all this smashing up, that Captain Swing, who is he?'

'One of my customers told me, nobody knows,' a stall-holder chipped in.

George had more to say. 'Had a chap in here last week who said a man in his village was so desperate he stole sheep.'

'Oh no, that's dangerous.'

'It was. He was ordered to the gallows and felt so hopeless he didn't care.'

There was a moment of respectful quiet. 'All they want is fair dos,' George added.

'But is making trouble the way to get it?'

There was another pause whilst the men pondered an answer. It was a chance for a man dressed in greasy clothes to get involved. He'd been puffing contentedly on his clay pipe listening.

'They got moving machines all over now, carriages goin' on rails,' he said.

'No!'

'I've been workin' with a wheelwright … making wheels you know,' he added informatively. 'It's what they call an allied trade. Means I've got the experience … '

'Go on ...' One of the drinkers was suitable impressed.

'Yeah, they're operatin' wiv' steam up norf', in Manchester, on railway lines, like for mines.' He used his clay pipe to indicate north.

'They're always doing that sort thing, that northern lot. But I thought it was in Newcastle, somewhere like that.' Shorty was in on the act again.

And a cab man chipped in. '…as far as I'm concerned, it's more competition, I've had to deal with some people using rivers and canals and now you say there's these new rail things.' He still wore his heavy cloak, which was a necessary garment when outdoors all hours of the day ... and night. He seldom took it off, it was too much trouble, he was done up in a ball. 'Anyway this rail business is all up norf, nothin' to do with us. You heard about this new police idea? Should be good.'

'No. Jus' making the parish constables an' watchmen into one.' Greasy said it in a way suggesting there was nothing more to be said, and put his clay pipe back in his mouth.

'They're going to call them 'watchtables'', Shorty said with a straight face.

Greasy was on to it, 'And they are going to be in charge of all the watch thieving that's about.'

'I didn't hear about that bit,' the cabman said.

Shorty saw Greasy's face and started to laugh. Greasy was already bouncing with laughter and hot tobacco jumped out of his pipe. He frantically jumped out of the way and brushed down his clothes.

The cabman had wanted his say and his item of red hot news had been ridiculed, so he tried to appear unaffected, 'Who's idea was it then?'

'It's Parliament,' Greasy explained, reloading his pipe.

'Oh!' was a general response. That explained it all. And they all laughed. Except the cab-man.

A burly, unsavoury solo drinker sat on a stool nearby had overheard and also laughed. Another one was giggling more than was necessary as he looked with empty eyes at a young girl, his tired face showing through a relaxed, ale fed world. His thin daughter sat on the edge of a bench looking back at him with tensed uncertainty.

George too had joined in the fun. His changing working life in London had given him a change of character … or maybe it was because he was a publican rather than just being in London. He even dressed better than in his country days, wearing a shirt with a collar and a waistcoat with buttons. One was missing but it was an improvement. The final touch was a kerchief round his neck. But whilst he changed his dress, he had never lost his attachment to the country. The plain lime-plaster walls of his pub were decorated with an ox yoke, a scythe, sheep bells, and three gin traps which early George had tried to fashion into an ornamental feature. These items dominated the notices and announcements - property sales, public warning signs (punishments prominent), an advertisement for a Methodist preacher and even a torn old poster for Edmund Kean in Shakespeare's Richard III.

Ann entered from the street into what had become a male preserve, carrying her latest acquisition of sacking for her Prodding. As early George came from behind the bar to greet her, the burly unsavoury drinker said sarcastically, 'Making a new dress missus?'

George was across in a flash, 'What's it to you?' and placed himself in space ready for any physical development, like an animal prepared to defend his territory.

The speaker quickly assessed the situation, calculated a

potential tangle with George, and said, 'Just having a laugh.'

'We have other fellahs come here and do jokes,' George said.

'Oh, I'll try somewhere else then.' He stood up and made for the door. The exchanges were watched by the giggling drinker and his tense, thin daughter. Their expressions did not change. Ann was equally inscrutable but she did say, 'Thanks.'

Apart from such occasional, heated events, early George's social intercourse expanded greatly over time and he talked about many more things than what the weather would do to the crops, helping the cows and ewes that were having birthing difficulties or the working lifespan of a horse. He became interested in matters beyond the hand to mouth. There were the king's trips out to Kew, Jewish ghettos, prostitutes, the immigrants of all nationalities, heating with coal, ships bringing goods to the docks, and buildings, and buildings, and buildings - the overwhelming experience of Early George's new life. When activity eased off, and noise abated, it seemed bricks, mortar and the new tarmac, were a never ending imposition. The contrast with his somewhat sparse Hampshire home village life seemed unreal.

FIVE ... Nurse talk.

THE hospital where I, the living George Gunner, was lying flat out in bed and unaware was not sparse, but it was almost as busy as early nineteenth century Mile End. The comings and goings at the end of morning visiting time were overlapping with preparation for the lunchtime routine with its tidying of patients and things, it could have matched the bustle of early George's time - coffee trolley out, patient's trolley in, drugs trolley across, gastro analysis trolley going to the next job, cleaner's trolley meandering, trolley for cooling fan lost. Such movement took me back to earlier outside scenes of rolling vehicles, ramshackle carts of all shapes and sizes criss-crossing Mile End market. 'Wheelies' all. The raised voices of departing visitors, footsteps, staff coming back to 'active duty' with medication to distribute, all accompanied by chatter. That could have been compared with the cacophony of the Mile End ... apart from the clip-clop of horses. And the chatter was professional.

'I couldn't find a vein anywhere,' a young nurse said.

'What did you do?' replied her friend.

'Well I hesitated, and the old girl must have guessed it was my first time so she said, 'Stick it in there, that's the place everyone seems to like', and she held out her arm and pointed, then said, 'I promise I won't scream.'

'You must have felt dreadful.'

'Not really, I didn't have to hide that I was a new nurse.'

'I can see that.'

'When I stuck the sticking plaster on the vein afterwards, she said, 'We'd be in trouble without you girls.'

'That was nice.'

'It offsets some of the other stuff,' the nurse said grimly, not explaining 'other stuff'.

The chat was also part of ward life. There still the odd disposable cup to be dealt with - drunk or binned; the mobile 'phone to be sorted - spoken to or stopped; and even one or two people, just simply sitting. But I remained flat out, inscrutable, my head not in the hospital, it was still in Mile End.

SIX ... The customers.

MILE END itself had always been on the busy side. The road was the main eastern way out of London for travellers to Colchester back to Roman times, and was the route the Essex peasant rebels took in 1381 for the poll tax protest. At some time, probably in the medieval period, the place got its name for being a mile from the Aldgate entrance to the city. So, with 1,500 or more years of travelling activity, and all the potential of passing trade, it was not surprising to find a pub in the Mile End Road. In early George's time, the area bustled with immigrants of all sorts, British and foreign, Whitechapel to the west, Stepney to the south, Bethnal Green to the north. A pocket of Huguenot silk weavers had settled nearby in Roman Road a century before, just one of the itinerant groups in need of diversion, perhaps oblivion, at the end of a working day, and they mixed with those from the new homes built for skilled workers, the odd hundred yards or so north of the pub. They all preferred to enjoy a beer elsewhere than inside their own uncertain living conditions. The never ending crowds and their energetic bustle had been a new experience for early George.

The mix of customers provided early George with variety over the years. The general area was known for its clothing industry - weavers, silk workers and tailors but early George also had the custom of costermongers and bricklayers. There had also been a bare-knuckle fighter, a fire-eater who performed outside (sometimes the trick went wrong once, he burned his mouth and couldn't eat), an agricultural labourer who became a poet, and the nearby Huguenots who used the ale house to do their book readings to each other and so provide a sort of free penny gaff from time to time. There was even a doll's eye maker, a man enthusiastic about his craft, who seemed to have sold hundreds over a long career. He was dapper in a rundown sort of way - frock coat, rumpled waistcoat and a shirt with high collar that had seen better days, but he wore them with confidence. He smiled a lot and even on his first visit he had put his hat and cane carefully on the table to do his patter. He also made human eyes and showed early George his waist-high display case.

He opened the case and the publican flinched at the sight of two hundred closely packed eyes. 'Everybody does that, but the false eye gets worn out you see, because of the tears, it acts like acid, roughens it up. Then you need a new one. I have to have a selection.'

George was looking anywhere but the display case, or the eye-maker. 'Very interesting.'

But the eye-man was into his pitch, he took up his cane and pointed to a particular eye. 'Here, you see, this is a lady's eye. It sparkles more than a gentleman's.'

Ever courteous, George looked blinkingly at all the eyes, and looked away. 'Yes, it does seem different.'

'I saw one of my lady customers last week, married three years, husband doesn't know she's got a false eye. Marvellous. The colour match is the secret you see, essential … and the fit, tight over the ball.' He cupped a hand over his eye to replicate the idea. 'And then there are the servants, lose an eye, they're finished, never be employed again. So you can see the work is also a charity.'

'Yes, I imagine it can be.'

'I've got lots of stories I could tell you.'

'Don't forget your ale,' George said strategically.

The eye maker laughed. 'Of course, that's what I'm here for.' He started to carefully close his display case and just before his wares were lost to sight, he said to them, 'Bye, bye!' He grinned up at early George who responded with a well mannered but uncertain smile.

SEVEN ... Joe Friend.

AFTER a few years of his publican life, early George even became interested in a subject that was of particular concern to one of his patrons, the brother-in-law of his first son George, the Landscape painter in Islington. Painter George had married Mary Anne Friend, and she had a brother, Joe, who had been an avid reader since childhood. Joe was categorised by some as a social agitator, and he certainly had the confidence, plus the knowledge, to make his presence felt ... or to put it more correctly, to be heard, a characteristic perhaps formed by his background. Mary Ann and Joe were born in a Stepney hovel, the children of a docker.

For some reason he couldn't explain, Joe Friend enjoyed books ... when he could get hold of material. He first discovered the thrill of gothic novels, but best of all he became engaged by social pamphleteering, and the Corresponding Societies of forty years before. He amassed a mess of knowledge and soaked it all up to become a rather well read man, in spite of his life of subsistence, scratching a living as a builder's labourer in the Mile End. Joe was just a rumpled, ordinary rather tatty young man of average height and weight but that apparent inconspicuousness belied his character. The unusually deep furrow in his forehead stood out beneath his prematurely bald dome suggesting a contemplative man. But his animated face and demeanour had an intensity that indicated a man of energy and quick action. In his strange miscellany of reading he found one item that almost obsessed him, a prayer recommended by a vicar on villager labourers in their church at some time earlier in the seventeen hundreds:-

'Oh God, I believe that for just & wise reasons thou hast allotted to mankind very different states and circumstances of life, & that all the temporal evils which have at any time happened unto me, are designed by thee for my benefit: therefore, though thou hast thought fit to place me in a mean condition, to deprive me of many conveniences of life, & to exercise me in a state of poverty, yet thou hast hitherto preserved & supported me by thy good providence.....'

That was God, and Jesus. It seemed to indicate to Joe that he was stuck with his place in the scheme of things, and looking around him at the other customers in The Old Globe, it did indeed seem to be the case. There did not seem to be much chance of change. Would it be the same for his children, his grand-children? It was this puzzle that made him restless, that made him a mouthy man at public meetings. Was God misunderstood? But the prayer seemed clear. Joe appreciated that this sort of thinking was not peculiar to him, it had been going on for hundreds of years, but it was something he took up with early George during the quieter mid afternoon periods, and early George listened with courteous, interest. His country life also had been lowly, one of struggle, but he had discovered himself in lively London.

As a young woman Ann had been attracted by early George's enterprising and adventurous spirit. How else could a farm labourer become an East End landlord? But she had not found the journey thereafter so exciting. However, time and the aging process settled their relationship and, by 1840, Ann had fallen into the ways of a publican's wife, by simply 'making the best of it', because, 'life goes on'. Early George and Ann had by then became something of a 'double act', they had melded and mellowed over the years to become a publican version of a 'Darby & Joan' couple. Ann had come to the conclusion that 'making the best' was a sort of achievement, as was 'going on', which indicated continuity. Even the fact of having a family was a satisfaction. Ann wore a smile from time to time with her mop hat, and could be seen standing behind the bar rather than sitting elsewhere shelling peas or making rag rugs, and she became a genuine listener to Joe's well worn tirades. However as the years passed the converted Ann, like George, found the long energy sapping days could sometimes be demanding.

On one occasion, Joe was in full flow and one of the local drinkers intervened, 'No, you can't do that sort of thing …' His appearance at the inn had indicated that winter and fog was on the way. He was the local lamplighter and stood with his pole like a guardsman, the pole scraping the ceiling. He liked a jug before he did his rounds.

Joe was on about the need for change, again, and turned to the Leerie. 'Why's that?'

'You gotta have someone running things, someone to organise it all.' He was a lively sort of fellow, quick speaking and given to clearing his throat a lot.

'Oh yeah. Who's that?'

'The nobs. Lords and such.' He sounded local, yet not quite.

'Why?'

'They know about these things.' The lamplighter cleared his throat.

'Do they?'

''Course.'

'How'd that come about?'

George had been trying to recognise the accent, and then the gentle Irish impinged.

'They were born to it, you know.'

'Oh really?' Joe said nodding in apparent agreement. 'So they have responsibility for everything ... all the people ... how they live?'

'Exactly.'

'And they live in their smart houses and we're over here living in Mile End and the like?' Joe gestured airily to the sky, to everywhere.

The Leerie hadn't thought things through, he cleared his throat. 'Well ... I suppose so.'

'And do nothing.'

'It takes time I suppose.'

'So who's gonna speed it up a bit?'

'I dunno.'

'Us!' Joe said emphatically and loudly, pointing to himself.

The Leerie was silenced by the passion of his response and his lamplighter's pole twitched a little. The meaning of what Joe had said could be seen slowly dawning on his face. He cleared his throat. After a moment of quiet satisfaction achieved by his fervour, Joe turned back to Early George and Ann who had heard Joe's arguments many times and taken advantage of the diversion with the bystander to drift into a standing sleep. But the fervour of Joe's last remark had aroused them and George instinctively said, 'Exactly,' just in time and looked at Ann who said, 'That's right,' with her new smile. Neither knew really what was exact, or right, but Joe seemed satisfied.

Joe's intensity would not be quelled and his words burrowed into George's head. He had insisted that he was only speaking out in the same way that people had done for years. And George remembered that his father had once or twice spoken to him in a similar way when he was growing up. In his London, Mile End pub life, he had almost forgotten his previous Hampshire country existence, and using his young energy and resourcefulness to work beside his father, Albert. His grandfather, William, who was more of a thinking man, pointed out that their family was just a sequence of farm workers – himself, son Albert, grandson, George - and he too had puzzled over how their life came to be shaped.

Later still, when Early George had been persuaded by Ann to move back to greener Brompton, he still reflected on his discussions with son-in-law Joe Friend. By then a less frenetic life-style allowed him time to think back to those farming days when some of the men for whom he had laboured on the farm hardly acknowledged his existence, and yet he had doffed his cap to them as they passed as a gesture of respect to their social status. Early George came to agree with his brother-in-law. The circumstances of one's birth, the where, and to whom ... did affect later lifestyle. Ann had never got involved in those prolonged Mile End conversations but felt that the conclusion they reached was not entirely correct. She had noticed that people in Brompton could be talented, and achieve rank, position, regardless of where they were born. George never resolved the issue before he finally, gently, faded away in the Red Lion in Brompton where he'd started his working life in London.

EIGHT ... George reflects.

EARLY George could never have imagined that his great, great grandson would later become a person of authority, a man with a responsible position and underlings to whom *he* could give instructions, and even have the power of dismissal. In fact, back in his Hampshire days as a farm labourer, early George would have actually felt constrained to doff his cap to this descendant. Even Joe had tried to persuade him that he shouldn't be deferential to anybody simply because they had a polished presence, but George's rural lifestyle of showing respect always lurked within him. And now here was me, twenty first century George, shown the sort of respect that would have been given to a farmer or a parson, even a squire, just because I was a patient in a hospital. I had become the beneficiary of the actions of people down in previous years who had pressed for change, social, political and economic change ... plus health change. I was happy not to be subject to the healthcare available to early George, or more exactly the healthcare *not* available to my great, great, grandfather.

The George of two hundred years later, me, lay in bed, eyes closed, breath slow and relaxed. I wasn't fully compos mentis, maybe because I had lived, in a way, through some unsettling comatose experiences. And I had an incomplete idea of what prompted this development. I'd heard bits and pieces from parents, from aunts and uncles, from cousins whose hand-me-down stories had added embellishments, something not so dissimilar to dramas and documentaries on TV and film. This miscellany of information occasionally triggered me to dig for more detail. The resultant outcome appeared to be - day dreams in hospital. Or was it? Something like it *did* happen, and it was out there, up there ... somewhere, sometime. Still? With the mystery of black holes, time travel, parallel universes, quantum physics ... there were things still to be discovered. Whilst I had difficulty in embracing the more degrading details of the story that I was a part of, I still held on to the idea that I'd been blessed by 'Lady Luck'. I mused on the idea that my good fortune was due to the dollop of hard times already 'paid for' by my family.

The interleaving of thoughts and ideas had been disturbing, it was as if the bottom of a river had been unsettled by passing pleasure boats – clear, cloudy, muddy. But I emerged from this mental meandering realising it was a bit more complicated than a jolly jaunt round the old grey cells. Time and place of birth was critical … or was it? Was it down to genes? Nature or nurture? There were histories of achievers, based on generations of living within an informed social milieu, and generations of non-achievers living in a social orbit having only basic living. But there were people in both these social groups who broke the mould … broke both moulds. There were pit-boys who became cabinet ministers and old Etonians who slept on the streets. … that must be down to individual character, not circumstance of birth or genes … something different.

'You asleep old son?' Chas. wanted to fill his time again.

I opened my eyes and smiled. 'More or less awake, and debating with myself on the mysteries of life.'

'You still at that?!' Chas. said.

'I might be finding myself.'

'Shouldn't do that, not in your condition.'

'I dunno. Just the time, stuck in bed with nothing to do,' I replied.

'Just been watching some football, lousy match. Too much shirt pulling, pushing over, arms swung at faces, trippings up, it spoils the game.'

I was happy for a moment of distraction. 'I know what you mean, it's not like it used to be.'

Chas agreed. 'Certainly not like the version I played.'

'Life changes,' I said reflectively.

'Need a lot more sendings off.'

'Take a chunk of their money. That'll cut it out."

'No, they need to fully bring in more than goal-line TV … why do they resist it?'

'They've got all these old buffers …' that's as far as I got.

'I mean, you think about it, they've done it with rugby, they've got Hawk-eye at Wimbledon, they've even got cameras inside cricket stumps. On a different tack, there's these TV expose programmes, cameras hidden away. Then there's police surveillance, speed cameras, street CCTV, spy satellites … I mean.'

'That's right …' was all that I could manage. Chas was in full flow, it appeared he not only did trains, and quantum physics, but sport and espionage too. I tried to wind it all up. 'It'll change when the spectator gets fed up and takes his money elsewhere.'

That caused Chas to reflect for a moment. 'That would be interesting, test their marketing skills … but when it comes down to it, you want the old days, it was better then.' And he was off. He was a bit of a memory man on who-won-what too. The subject of cups was introduced – World Cup, F.A. Cup, European Cup …

I caught the catalogue of place names Manchester, Liverpool, Nottingham, Aston Villa; then came Chelsea, Tottenham, Arsenal … by which time I had my own catalogue of place names.

A STORY of WILLIAM & LIZZIE before INDUSTRIALISATION.
(George has visitors)

ONE ... Crondall.

MY jigsaw thoughts juxtaposed Morden and Clapham and Salisbury and Cripplegate and Seven Dials, and Manchester and Galway, and Mile End, and ended in the peace and quiet of Hampshire ... where it seems likely the whole story started. Hampshire two and a half centuries ago, about the middle of the eighteenth century, would have offered an outside ambience in which a restful quiet could be heard. Not silence, but a qualified quiet in which nature had a part to play – birds, and more distantly, sheep, the croak of pheasant, and farm life in open country. A sound-scape that was not disturbed by man-made mechanical noise ... and not a building in sight.

A world also, it seems, when a lifestyle was touched, even embraced by satisfying nature. A world before the smothering hug of urbanisation, the expression of growth, with its machines, canals, roads, railways, plus an infrastructure to accommodate it all. Man's restless and creative energy with all the attendant social complexities that facilitate expansion.

It was all indeed a long time ago, in the 'mists of time', back through the sequence of urbanised Gunners via Early George who, in his London, Mile End pub., had almost forgotten his Hampshire country existence, a couple of generations before. It was an earlier lifestyle with his father, Albert, and aged grandfather, William.

William Gunner was a lowly, but contemplative, man of the land, a humble Hampshire labourer, who could have been seen working in a field of grain near a village named Crondall. It was a place which before Saxon days was a chalk-pit, three miles north west of Farnham. The field was a lush stream-side meadow which had probably provided hay for centuries. William had a satisfied look on his face having seen a mouse-coloured roe-deer jump into sight from a thicket of oak and holly and immediately bound away into the more accustomed shade of the woods beyond the stream at the edge of the field. He was sinewy man of average height for the day, with a thinning hairline, and a craggy, lined face that had been scrunched up against the sun and rain over many years. He wore a short, night-gown-of-a smock and floppy, domed and brimmed hat with long hair straggling underneath. The elegance of movement of the deer combined with the spectacular leaping warmed William, life to life. Then he heard a pair of blackbirds singing to each other. He was totally captivated by a moment in which it seemed all his senses were utterly sated - sight, smell, sound, touch.

'Oi William!' The watching farm owner, Robert Moseby, interrupted his reverie, he knew that William, in spite of his abilities on the farm, could occasionally be distracted by his surroundings. The farmer was on the tall side, over six feet, and though the other side of fifty, his eyesight remained very good. Indeed some of his workers contended that his eyesight actually improved over the years … or he had eyes at the back of his head. Robert Moseby could be seen across the heads of other labourers working in the field, waving his stick, long coat billowing, and carefully placed hat with the brim cunningly shading his eyes. It was a busy time of the year and he was on his way to the sheep fields to check on the shearing. It was this diligence – a family trait that had enabled him to become a successful landowner, with expanding property.

The Gunner family had worked for the Moseby family for a couple of generations. The story handed down within the family was that some time ago, the Gunner son of the time had built a mixed mud-brick, paling and stone home on waste land of some titled family. Then one of farmer Moseby's forbears acquired the mud-brick building as part of a plot of waste land, which had been sold to cover fines imposed during Cromwell's day. According to excited village gossip, the titled land owner had a womanising and wastrel son who inherited the land. He was a gambler and spendthift, and one version even included some sort of fight. It depended upon which story one heard. The chronology was unfathomable but whatever the truth, the Gunners became beholden to the Mosebys for a home which had really started as a squat. It became a Gunner family copy-hold property.

William resumed his methodical scything, right arm stretched, left arm crooked, controlling angle and height of the implement, not too close in order to avoid catching an unseen stone, but low enough to get all the goodness of the essential winter animal feed. He kept a sharp eye out for the safety of any field mouse that may have been on the move. His rhythmic, steady work was disturbed by another distant, call. 'William! William!'

He looked up, a young woman was jumping up and down across the field and was waving and pointing to a field stile. This was Lizzie, bringing foursie refreshment. William waved back and gestured to the remaining section of field to be cut. She held up a bag and a small urn and pointed once again to the stile.

'Yes. Yes,' William said almost to himself and held up his arm in acknowledgement, then waved back, smiling. Lizzie continued her walk along the rutted and bumpy path. She was his lady-love.

William carried on working happily with just enough concentration to do the task and be safe – thanks to years of experience. He was in fact just one of a team in the field with scything and gathering going on all around him. There were other scythe men nearby, and the female stackers, but William somehow remained separate, because he wasn't a particularly gregarious person at work … though on the odd occasion, at the village inn, he could be different. A snatch of conversation in the wind drifted William's way, to add to the regular swish of his scythe.

'How are you fixed tonight Sarah?'

'Never you mind.'

'Go on, only takes five minutes.'

'No, I've told you before.'

'Go on, over in the rick.'

'No, you cheeky sod.'

'You're beautiful, you are Sarah.'

'You're only saying that …'

'Why am I 'only saying that'?'

'You know ... and I know what you're up to.'

'I'm not up to anything.'

'Yes you are. You're all the same you men.'

'Exactly, different from women, that's why I thought … '

'Stop it, you! Let me get on with me job.'

A man's distant voice could then be heard across the field. 'Better luck next time Tom.'

Tom pleaded to the world, 'What am I go to do?'

Another distant male voice, from another direction informed him. 'Same as the rest of us.'

The exchange didn't really impinge on William, he'd heard variations of it so many times before. The three-quarter men and gavel girls demonstrating the rising sap in young humankind to match surrounding nature.

Another exchange drifted in the gentle breeze. "You off to see the cucking stool carried out later on Tom, it should be fun.'

'Not half, I reckon women should be kept in their place … can't have them always lamming their husband.'

Tom replied. 'Will she stop?'

'I should think so. It depends on whether she likes being strapped half naked into a chair and paraded round the village.'

'Who wants to look at 'Nagging Nellie' like that ?!'

'Old Amos would for a start.' The two voices erupted into laughter.

It crossed William's mind that this exchange was for the benefit of the desired Sarah, wherever she was.

TWO ... William and Lizzie.

WILLIAM had always liked Crondall, even though it was the centre of a collection of hamlet tythings and manors that had made up the Saxon Hundred of Crundell (the original spelling for Crondall), and it was not as big as Alton, because that took nearly all the Winchester and Southampton traffic and the fewer people and carts in Crondall suited William's pensive temperament.

It was known to have been a place of habitation back beyond Roman times, evidenced by finds over the years of Neolithic flints before Roman pottery, medieval ornaments and venerable buildings – the Norman Barley Motte and Bailey, abandoned as a result of the Black Death, The Court, the village inn, and the Norman church, built on a Saxon site, of sturdy stone, with powerful pillars and arches. There was no evidence of wall paintings, dressings, and ornaments that had once featured. They had been banished by the changes wrought by Henry VIII and Oliver Cromwell, but there was an unlikely red brick tower. The old one had become unsafe when it couldn't support the weight of its bells, and was rebuilt of red brick during the late Interregnum. Given the uncertain and changeable character of the established church at that time it was suggested that there was some Puritan idea behind the replacement to mismatch building materials and style to demonstrate a change of Christianity. A church display case had a memento of that civil unrest, a cannon ball, evidence of the occupation by the Parliamentary Army. The village also boasted the splendid new house of a West Indian Planter.

The whole had grown in size over the years. Crondall was no longer a straightish street with a few houses tacked along the sides. It had better kept tracks and proper houses off the main street and additional clumps of buildings here and there – ram shackle sheds, byres, sties, and the like, to provide protection from the weather for food and livelihood. Even the once wooded surround was now extensive productive land.

William, with the rest of his work party, had almost completed scything the assigned field, and most of them were now at foursies. William was sitting on the foot rest of a stile erected at a break in a hedge of hawthorn and rampant brambles, which embraced his scythe, its glinting blade burnished by William's precious Ardennes grit whet-stone, bought at Farnham Fair some years before. The stile was on a well used route to the next village and a good place for eating the where-withal to succour the rest of the work day. William's teeth sank into a crust of bread, and the crumbs scattered down his smock into his lap. His other hand held a good hunk of cheese, teeth marks evident.

William found bread an irresistible food, and appreciated the work of the portly village baker, Ralph Ford, who dozed regularly in the pub, having been up at three a.m. in order to mix yeast into well kneaded dough, a process repeated before going into his brick oven for the light, open and crusty treat he made. The baker said his secret was the yeast he got from the village pub, but William believed it was the caringly made product, without the chalk, alum, bone ashes and the like found in urban bread. An isolated village was no place for undesirable practices, word got around. If there was such a thing as an artist-baker, Ralph Ford was it.

'You are a messy thing William.' Lizzie scolded with a smile.

'I know,' he said grinning and had a pull at his pot of cider. He needed it, it was one of those warm early summer days, bright sun, blue skies and just the odd soft bubble of cloud.

William and Lizzie were walking out. Lizzie was a lively young lady in her mid twenties, another lean, virile person shaped by a hard working outdoor life. She had the sort of grin beneath her soft cloth bonnet that could warm any company and something in her eyes suggested mischief and fun. Her features were enhanced by the sunshine on a pastel yellow sleeved blouse buttoned up to the neck, and the faun shawl over her shoulders. The inevitable apron, hid her ankle length wine coloured skirt, held a huge pocket of apples, and chunks of cheese. A few years back, she had returned to the village with her parents, from Abbotts Ann, near Andover, because they all had residence rights through their Settlement Claim, of a proven Crondall birth. Lizzie's itinerant grandparents had died in Abbots Ann.

'What shall we do tonight?' she asked as she brushed crumbs clear of him. The beady-eyed pigeons waddling along the footpath would soon tidy up when they had gone. 'We could meet up with the others, and then … '

'I don't know, I promised dad I would fix the wheel-barrow

before Pentecost.' William brushed away a blue-bottle that had decided there might be something of interest around his head.

'You can do that later. There's always time when days get longer.'

'True.' William was not exactly loquacious. That didn't worry young Lizzie, he was capable and could <u>do</u> things. She felt safe with him, protected.

'Look at that buzzard,' William said suddenly. The bird was gliding down gracefully from a fading up-current of wind, eyeing all the activity below and the opportunity for a meal. The diversion was an indication of other things on William's mind. Lizzie looked up as a matter of courtesy. 'Yes,' she said. But she didn't touch on their social activities again. She would wait for a more propitious moment. William seemed to go into himself

It may be that his contemplative nature embraced a touch of the melancholia and whether it was that or an adult responsibility thing Lizzie was unsure. But there was no doubting that William spent a lot of time concerned for their future, feeling that their blameless and simple life was being undermined by agencies he couldn't fathom.

After a while Lizzie decided that it was necessary to puncture the silence. 'You're still worried about this land and house thing aren't you?'

'Of course,' William said, 'It's puzzling. I can't work it out. On the one hand you hear that the country has had a growing population for years and it's difficult to feed everybody. On the other there's this idea of putting more land into food production, and ….'

'Sounds sensible,' Lizzie interrupted.

'Ah, but they want to do that by having the landed property lot buy up the commons and wastes.'

'Oh.' Lizzie immediately understood the significance, and conversation came to a halt.

Over by the next field Mother Runfold was waddling her way, late and careful, along a cart track in the lane with a basket of fourses for her boy, Caleb. There was something purposeful in the movement. She had that side to side sway of a person carrying too much body-weight, the slow, regular rhythm that was almost an elegant dance step. A dance to her doted boy. He would be fed regardless of effort, weather or distance. Mother Runfold's life had changed when her husband disappeared from the village, and her subsequent efforts to care for her children had become a bit sporadic ... except for Caleb, her first born and the one whose arrival was the subject of village whisperings. Mother Runfold was resolute in ensuring that her family rights were duly recorded in parish records, claim for outdoor relief beyond dispute, and meagre entitlements paid. She kept the village worthies up to the mark because she was never intimidated by vestry calls, especially if confronted by the more self indulgent middling sort, who were cowed by her pugnacious square jaw, wire-like iron grey hair and challenging manner. Even the vicar had learned *not* to make any condemnatory comments on her standards of behaviour. It was an item of puzzlement in the village how Caleb came to be in the first place. She beamed when she saw her precious boy.

William felt the need to explain a bit more. 'At the inn last week, Amos said it's all down to Parliament and these Enclosure Acts that they've done, so common lands and the waste lands are disappearing.'

'Where will we get our winter fuel, grazing for sheep and goats, foraging for pigs?' Lizzie responded

'Exactly. Allotments will go too.'

'Have I got this right?' Lizzie asked, 'The property owners buy land to produce the food that is needed, and at the same time we lose the chance to grow our own food.'

'Yes ... you see? It gives me a headache trying to make sense of it.' He seemed to have talked himself into silence, but then another thought struck him. '... *and* they have to borrow money from these bank places ... more new ones all the time. Borrow money! How does that work?'

Lizzie didn't have any answers but thought it was necessary to divert him from his sombre pre-occupation. 'Nice bit of cheese today. That's Cathy's cows.' She waved her arms about her head to whisk away some dandelion seed heads that had blown across her face.

'Yes,' William said, not having taken in the comment, 'I mean, we're alright now, but what about next year, five years time?'

'I suppose we'll have to manage, we always do.'

William chewed on that line of thought, but then reverted to his starting point. 'No. What will happen, seems right ... and yet it doesn't work out right. Something's funny.' The implication was that somehow he, and his fellow workers, would lose out to 'them', the property and land-owners … and people who borrowed money.

Lizzie patted his hand in a comforting way. 'Things always work out in the end.'

William just grunted.

Sparrows were chirruping loudly in a nearby hedge, the energy of their exchanges suggested communication of a more happy kind.

'You'll see,' Lizzie added, her big, open eyes offering ideas of unquenchable spirit. She was not an easy woman to deflate.

But William remained doubtful, if he couldn't inherit the cottage. Where would his children live? How could the next George Gunner come into the world? There had been George Gunners for more than a hundred years.

THREE ... Ward crisis.

THE twenty first century George Gunner, I, had a furrowed brow, and shut eyes, experiencing William and Lizzie's problem in a non-conscious mystery world, whilst wallowing in the comfort of a National Health Service hospital bed. But the changing expressions on my face indicated that I felt the dilemma of William and Lizzie with a similar intensity and I had an equal concern for the development and outcome of their relationship whilst on my labyrinthine journey.

Around me in the ward there was also a crisis, 'Anyone know where Derek Griffiths is?' This could be heard in the short lull in a busy daily schedule of goings on. There weren't that many between the delivery and clearing of meals and visiting times. Any pause seemed non-existent as the clear up overlapped the appearance of a concessionary visitor. There was still some activity, and in technicolour. Doctors in bright green, nurses in bright blue and cerise. Light blue was a specialist, cleaning staff in pink, clerical staff in white, porters in yellow. And it was a gizmo freak's paradise, a workshop of plastic and aluminium, with screens all over the place. Most equipment seemed to be telescopic, with lights poking out of walls, chair arms popping up, X-ray trolleys with thrusting antennae (looking more like electric chairs), other monitoring apparatus and equipment trolleys with bits that jutted out. A joy for the whizzy anorak wonk but, from a pause for thought, emerges '1984'. 'Has Derek Griffiths arrived?' wafted around the ward of the old converted Victorian Workhouse, its clad walls hiding all the cables, pipes and services that facilitated the functioning of the twenty first century medical paraphernalia. Hidden above the lowered ceiling, and still embedded in the very solid brick structure, was the odd cast-iron plate of the old roof structure, mementos of its past.

A rumpled little old man in a dangling raincoat with a stuffed, bulging plastic bag, stood before a senior nurse. She liked her food.

'Are you Derek Griffiths?' she asked brusquely.

'Yes, I was sent to the women's wing.'

'But you're a man.'

'I know,' said the dangling raincoat and plastic bag, looking forlorn. The complete story was lost when a yellow overall wheeled another patient in. 'Mind your backs.'

In spite of the little dramas being enacted in the ward, the period between the afternoon-visitors-followed-by-tea, and, evening-meal-plus-evening-visitors was a time of reasonable quiet. Maybe this comparative calm was the means that facilitated the twenty first century George, me, to fully re-engage with difficult questions of the past, back in the eighteenth century.

FOUR ... Enclosure.

WILLIAM could never have known of the complexity of the back-ground to his dilemma. Rights to land was an issue confused by hundreds of years of history, back to William the Conqueror who had made himself holder of all the land, directly or indirectly. That arrangement had gradually changed over time, as state coffers became depleted (wars were expensive!) and support from the Barons was necessary, then the merchants, the middle men, got a look in. Feudalism, manorialism came and went. Some land ownership changed hands many times down the centuries, even though unused, and some holdings got bigger, some got smaller. But alongside this activity, usage of some commons and wastes remained the time-honoured right of village and villagers. However, over time little pockets of village land here and there moved into private hands and with it, the right of common usage by villagers was lost. Land was 'Enclosed'.

By the eighteenth century a more potent acquisitive streak had developed in a growing propertied class, and rights of land usage of commons and wastes by villages and villagers became a purchase target of those with wealth. Those with social status used their influence to access authorities, and Acts of Enclosure became the means to achieve their objective. Some people could lose their homes if they had been squatting. In some cases such acquisitions could compromise the matter of Settlement Rights, the right to live in a village into which one was born. The whole situation really _was_ difficult to disentangle, and further complicated by the varying size of plots, from hundreds of acres, to one or two, or three. Whilst down those same centuries the odd enclosures here and there had indeed occurred within a manor or parish, the issue was now increasingly in the hands of the central authority, Parliament.

On top of everything else, the church had a big say because it was such a large landowner. Some in the church thought of land ownership as the right of everyone, simply because to be born on the land of the country conferred a right to a little part of it.

After all was said and done, the process of purchase of common land was against the interests of the labouring class, but it came down to a matter of rights, versus usage – common usage versus cost effective usage ... by an applicant the with means to exploit land more effectively. So the legal fraternity became involved. Commissioners were engaged, lawyers appeared before them, assorted others claimed expenses, and all the costs charged to the process itself. Result - some of the common land was sold simply to cover costs involved in investigating and resolving each Act of Enclosure. It was an additional consequence, and the village public still lost its facility, and the commons and wastes still ended up with the expanding landowner.

William kept abreast of these local goings-on at occasional meetings with his cronies in the tap room of the Plume of Feathers, a nice old pub dating back to before the days of Good Queen Bess. It had once been a wattle and daub hall-house, and its century old red brick walls sat well within its timber box frame. The inviting, homely effect inside was only marred by the stocks which remained outside. The head banging ceiling beams were darkened by years of smoke from a multitude of clay pipes and winter log fires. It was one of the many places in which Oliver Cromwell was supposed to have slept, one of so many that he must have been more of a tourist than an army general.

It didn't take long for passionate, then joking, chatter to fill the air above the rough, heavy tables and chairs, which were made to withstand careless treatment. The exchange of news and who had heard what, and what was going on here and there, was sometimes relegated in interest as the villagers enjoyed more of the beverage of the house.

One man was looking carefully at a jug of ale being brought to him and he rolled his lips together in anticipation several times, and made his whiskers tremble. Involuntarily he fiddled with the lucky hare's foot he kept wrapped round his neck. The bystanders watched him, he was not a local.

'You won't get a better brew than this for miles around,' the publican said and plonked a rough earthenware jug down. He wiped his hands on his blotched apron, spread over a well-rounded stomach. The blotches were evidence of his secondary occupation, the odd bit of slaughtering he did in one of his old animal pens.

The new face took a swig, and looked content. He was a visiting relative of Francis Stevens, the crusty handed basket maker from

Pankridge Cottage. His tongue wetted his lips once more, it was after all a warm day.

'That's my special.' Self-satisfaction grew on the face of the publican.

'Next, the publican will tell you it was his prize ale that put a stop to farm brew wages in the area,' said the relative. He was very tall and had to duck his head between the overhead beams as he moved around.

'Tis true, no one can compete with the best.' The publican could be said to be a positive man.

'A very drinkable ale with a nice balance of sweetness, lightly touched with bitterness, and a fresh smell of sugar, barley and hops.' This was William, projecting grandly and with a mischievous smile for once, and enjoying the evening. He was familiar with the publican's line of patter.

'Sounds like mine host speaking,' one of the other labourers commented underneath his wide brimmed straw hat.

'Well said William,' the publican nodded, side-burns wobbling.

'Won't get you any free drinks,' another labourer mumbled.

The new face uttered, 'Mmm,' in a satisfied way after another pull at his jug. He rolled his lips together and fiddled with his lucky hare's foot again, a contented man, as was William, his non-working face now homely and approachable.

It was in the Plume of Feathers that villagers also learned what was going on elsewhere when coach travellers who dropped in from a cross country journey to Odiham or Basingstoke when branching off the London to Portsmouth route. They needed respite from the sway, jog and rattle caused by the deep criss-crossing ruts churned up by the wide wheels of heavy farm traffic. The news of the day was filtered through from the bar to the tap room, and by this means the labourers were kept up to date with the ongoing battles with the French and the victory in Quebec of General Wolfe in 1859. This was closely followed by the succession of George III, his marriage to Charlotte of Mecklenburg-Streitz (they first set eyes on each other the day before the wedding) and the first of their fifteen children. Then followed squabbles over how the country should be run, and difficulties with the American colonies where people had the idea that being taxed without any say was irregular. The scandal gossip was of course about the dissolute behaviour of the new King's brothers.

There were times when William was so enamoured of the beverage that he could, on occasion, forget his troubles. It was perhaps only his delight in the brew made on the premises that offered relief from his preoccupations. Simple, fundamental experience of living gave him satisfaction, like a crusty hunk of bread, a decent slab of cheese, a good jug of ale ... and Lizzie. He didn't ask much of life, because he was a person who just had no need of it. His was a simple life, which was supposed to be exemplary, because he didn't covet money, he was gentle, and he did what the commandments said. So if everyone did the same, well ... it was a puzzle.

FIVE ... Dilemma.

WILLIAM gave serious thought to the church because such an ancient building, 700 maybe 800 years old, prominently sited in the middle of the village must have **meant** something. There were churches in all villages, hundreds and hundreds of them, offering guidance and understanding about life through the teachings of Jesus, telling of what he said and did for hundreds of years. He was exemplary. William only had to go to church on Sunday and listen, properly, to Parson White, a gentle man with a soft voice, and wearing reassuring clerical garb ... he could have the answers.

William did go to church the next Sunday with Lizzie but the pluralist Vicar had turned up for one of his rare visits to replace his underling, Parson White, because it was Harvest Festival. He was an upright, booming man who spoke with the air of a conquering king to match the massive Norman pillars. The Vicar talked for a very long time about, 'the abundance of God', but William lost the thread of what he was talking about. It seemed William should carry out his duties and obligations as diligently as possible and give thanks. The bible reading, then prayers, was experienced with decreasing interest, his eyes closed. Lizzie had to nudge him. The ornamental Norman masonry provided a pleasing distraction before he found himself staring sleepily at the back of a woman's head, looking at the grains of dandruff in the dark, dry hair beneath the brim of her Sunday hat. It was Eleanor Cooper who lived near the village pump. William tried to calculate whether the pattern of those flecks of dead skin matched any constellation in the night sky. It did seem that the innumerable grey dots could be a good match on a clear night sky but it was difficult finding a recognisable pattern. His calculations were interrupted when music started.

It was a welcome interlude even given that the village musicians, workers from the Itchel Estate, were not at their best that day. The recorder player lost his fingering and the lead fiddle player as in the devil of a hurry. The fact was they were too good, they were over-booked and a busy week had ended with Saturday night jollifications. William heard even Lizzie snigger. The uncertain sound was then lost on William as his attention returned once again to the Vicar who had a face of thunder as he looked up to the west gallery and the musicians. William suddenly realised, forcibly, that the Vicar was really 'one of them', those at the front of the congregation. Socially, he consorted with the squire, the major land-owners of the parish, and the Bishop, and even the Deputy Lieutenant of the county when he came.

As they walked back home past the village green Lizzie listened with sympathy to William's 'goings on' about land, about the church, about life, and he appreciated her passive support. The squire trotted past them on his horse and William touched his hat and made a noise of acknowledgement that sounded like a burp. When they were passing the malt house in Dippenhall, Lizzie pointed to it and said, 'The Lathams have got on, people do you know William. His dad used to be the muck collector.'

'I know,' William said with an edge in his voice.

'Old Mr Latham used to work all hours of the day and night.'

'That's old news.'

'He had a really expensive coffin.'

'So?'

'… just saying.'

'That fat Tubby Latham tricked me into using our cart for collecting tiles over in Farnham for his hanging repairs. Made me late for shearing ... and he didn't pay enough.'

Lizzie knew the event. 'He paid what you said.'

'Yes, but ...' William growled but didn't add anything and the yapping Latham's dog barked at him.

In a way their relationship functioned through her acceptance of his dark moods, and he was sensitive enough to appreciate this in her. Each had sufficient respect and care for the other to allow him, and her, to be themselves.

'I think we should try the Baptist chapel place,' William said suddenly.

'Where's that?' Lizzie asked.

'Fleet.'

'A long way.'

'Not too long.'

'Maybe.' Lizzie was debating.

'It's more on our level.'

'I don't think there are levels in the Bible.'

'It's not the Bible though, it's a building.'

'A sort of church.' Lizzie challenged.

'Chapel,' William came back.

'Do you mind if I don't come?' Lizzie asked.

'Of course not.'

'I'll go to our church.'

William took that in, before becoming protective. 'Will you have someone to go with?'

'I'll find some willing peasant,' Lizzie said with a cheeky smile.

'No doubt,' William smiled, he knew how effective her bubbly personality was. Not everyone saw his warmth and basic goodness, but Lizzie did. The tolerance in their relationship was what made it strong, her father had observed.

When William got to the chapel he did feel more comfortable with the people but didn't really get anything more useful from all the talk. It seemed helpful but all he wanted was to lead his own quiet life - have a family with Lizzie, supported by a good days work for a fair reward, just as his father had done before him. William imagined that such a life had been the pattern for generations, and wanted only to continue it.

Lizzie's family had a similar history, she could also recall a sequence of past uneventful lives, but for her this was not a problem, she simply got on with things because she found life had a way of resolving any difficulties … or so she thought, not realising that her own innate life management skills were the real means. She was not so convinced of William's life-without-change and was devoid of his gloom. Her only preoccupation was getting him to, as it were, plunge in.

William decided to confront the problem. On a bright early English summer Sunday afternoon, with sun shining and blue sky, the sort of day that eliminates everything except the joy of being alive, William wandered to Dora's Hill, 'his' hillock near his home, his hideaway where he went to be alone. It had been 'William's place' since he was about eight years old. It was where he used to play 'highway robbers' with his mates. William was Dick Turpin on Bagshot Heath, it didn't matter at that time that being on a hill without a track was not highway robber territory. The site offered wonderful views and Farnham Castle could be seen in the distance, but the hill was not visited so often by the grown up William. Some of the bushes of his childhood, the blackthorns, the hazels, hawthorns, beech, had become small trees. On this occasion however he had settled there to find peace and quiet to lie back and think in the relaxing weather and surroundings. He even had a skylark trilling above him as it spiralled upwards.

William was seduced by all that was around, he wallowed in it, and was only half awake when the nagging thing reappeared. It almost imperceptibly over awed his sense of his surroundings. The niceties of feelings were lost to the dark mood, and he was transported to fields where he was working in lowering storm clouds, pelting wind and rain. The storm blew him into his sparse home, where his old father sat at a bare table grumbling incoherently about his aching body. There was a loud crack of sound and they were blown outside looking at the ruined hovel. The light began to quickly lift and the hovel merged into a view of a tree, William sheltering under it with his arms around Lizzie who smiled as she gently chivvied him about the passing time. The picture continued to brighten to become luminous and William appeared in a huge elaborately decorated golden palace where he was pleading to some grandly dressed man with a beautiful silver wig and intense staring eyes. The majestic figure was sitting on a chair that seemed to be nothing but carved gold ornamentation. William was pleading, '… not have a house … marry Lizzie …'The resplendent man had an aura, he seemed to shimmer, and was magnificent in his multi-coloured jewel encrusted cloak and furs, but he seemed not to hear. William pleaded mightily, because the man seemed to be a God-like figure … maybe he was God. William was insistent, '… commons and wastes … rights … marry Lizzie … 'The man, or God, started to listen, he seemed to become sympathetic, and nodded. Thinking he was perhaps getting through William pressed his case. '… me, together with Lizzie, and have a family …' William was still pleading with the majesty when he heard crisp footsteps echoing in a stone hall, then the sound of rustle of silk and satin. He saw a beautiful woman, who must have been a painting brought to life. William next heard the majesty say, 'Ah, my angel.' before the angel (if that's what she was) actually spoke. 'George, George, you must help these young people, they need it.'

'God will provide,' the majesty replied.

'We need all our good, honest workers,' said the angel.

'And because of that, they will succeed.'

'How do you know?'

'I know,' said the majesty with conviction.

'George … I think you do.'

'And what about me Charlotte, will I succeed?' There was a salacious chuckle in the majesty's voice.

William heard a scuffle of movement, 'No George, George someone might see. George, not here. We must wait to play. George, George!' There was the sound of hurrying footsteps.

SIX ... Peter returns.

IT was Chas calling as he came across the hospital ward. 'George, George, you've got visitors, well visitor.' Chas. got to the end of the bed. 'It looks like your grandson walking down the ward.'

I came down from my windy hill, dismissed the progenitive royal couple, collected my thoughts together, and returned to my current prostrate situation, just as Peter got to my bedside.

'Hello granddad.'

I turned to Chas. 'Thanks.' Then to Peter. 'Hi Peter.'

'I'm just on my way to the Leisure Centre.'

'Good.'

'Is grannie Pam OK?'

'Of course, she flies around as if there's no tomorrow.'

'That's my girl.'

'She was really worried about you.'

I lifted my arms in a gesture as if to say, '… these things happen.'

Peter didn't know what I meant, it was not within his standard social intercourse, so I said, 'Now what have you been up to?'

He replied, 'That's the question I should be asking you.'

'I keep a look out.'

'Oh yeah?' Peter said questioningly, he knew I had not always been sensible about my health as I became older.

'I've been doing extended horizontal exercises … in the bed position. And I'm exercising myself, with sustained sleeping exercises.'

Peter had never fathomed my way of expressing things, so he just replied, 'Sounds interesting.'

I needed to expand on this. 'A trip into the distant past, with the aid of this …' I pointed to my head. '…and by shut-eye. It seems a dodgy condition, plus drugs and bed, has dredged up some interesting stuff.' As Peter understandably showed no sign of knowing what I was talking about, I let it go, 'What about you?'

'The physical stuff's going well,' Peter tried to make light of the situation. 'But I need some of those head exercises … whatever they are.'

'Preparation, concentration, we've been over it many times.'

'It's not easy.'

'Of course it isn't, that's why few become, in today's language, stars – Federer, Ashkenazi, Messi, Nureyev, Schumacher, Leonardo, and countless others, in all activities, they go on and on with their art, their craft, they're obsessives.'

Peter looked slightly crestfallen, the demands to make out as a top badminton player seems endless.

I noticed. 'They looked like that too. It's a huge task. Huge. And the spirit drops at what's ahead. But that's what <u>has</u> to be endured, and it's not undertaken by ordinary people. Are you extraordinary?'

Peter's face said it all, he was doubtful.

I was not deflected, if Peter wanted to be successful in competitive sport, relentless engagement in the task was essential. 'And as you get better, you see what more needs to be done. And at that point is the test, can you go on? You get to the next stage and another looms. And another. And another. And you have to go through them all. Amazingly, for some, they lap it up.'

'Obsession,' Peter said.

'Yes, and when the time comes, they are void of tension, in the zone. All of them, top sportsmen, musicians, performers … prepared, utterly focussed.'

'The head part.'

'Maybe the main part.'

There was a difficult pause in our conversation, between us there was an uncomfortable truth that what was said, had to be said. It would have been wrong for me not to say what I did, and Peter knew that but he didn't want to hear that there were yet more mountains to climb.

'Silly really, I knew you would say something like that, yet …'

'You hoped I'd give you a short cut?'

Peter just laughed. 'Back to the task then.'

I patted his arm. 'That's my boy. You <u>can</u> do it I've seen what is possible in you.'

'Thanks granddad. In a way, I just needed a prod.'

'What about your diet?'

'No deviation from what we agreed.'

'Have you looked at those videos of your game?'

'Yeah.'

'More than once?'

'Enough. I have straightened out my footwork, my timing.'

I pondered on that for a moment, was 'enough', enough? I decided not to press the point at this stage. 'One more thing, atmos. - get into the habit of monitoring temperature and humidity when you play, if you really do make a go of it you could be playing in a great variety of conditions. Check how the shuttlecock flies as a matter of routine, every place. Even the Leisure Centre here.'

'Right.'

'You're on the right track, don't let up.'

There was a lull in conversation, Peter didn't know what to say. I did. 'The Leisure Centre calls.'

'True. I'll go whilst I'm fired up. I'll do it for you.'

I was touched. Peter turned and strode resolutely down the ward and I pensively watched him go. Seeing the ward brought home to me the circumstance of my present situation. I really was still very tired. Drifting, detached thoughts prompted me to look around to see the general whiteness, again … white walls, white ceilings, bedclothes, uniforms. I seemed transfixed by white. Whiteness everywhere, even the assorted items of equipment seemed mainly white. They overwhelmed the blobs of occasional colour, the faces, clothes, lurid books and small specks of miscellany … and then all of it seemed to merge into wadding.

A STORY of MARY & THOMAS
in the CIVIL WAR.
(George gets out.)

ONE ... Nature.

THE patchy whiteness changed. It had bright blobs. The patches became clouds, teased by a gentle wind, lit by summer sun. Clouds flickered, dark and light. Young Mary Gunner took in the varying light level as she lay back in the grass. Her eyes fluttered and she was breathing deeply, her broken gulps sucking in recuperative air. Her shoulders heaved, but she wore a smile of contentment. For a moment there was just stillness, before she moved and her hands reached to hold those of the man beside her. They both looked up to the sky, two young people, silent and sated. Thus they lay inert for some moments, their almost naked bodies caressed and cooled by the soft wind. Mary, her breasts had the artistic curve of a Goya painting, but the addition of a triangle of pubic hair. He had a powerful, virile body, and flaccid member. They were happy and proud to leave their bodies exposed to the air. Both had removed only the items of clothing necessary to enact the urgent task at hand. Breeches down, skirt up and chests made bare in order to divest hindering garments. They remained quiet for a further moment, eyes bright, faces buoyant, their young hair entwined, each with long flowing locks; his thick and dark, hers lighter and even more luxuriant.

'That was simply the most glorious experience of my life,' he said.

Mary giggled in agreement.

'Didn't I say it would be wonderful out in the open, here on this part of the estate?'

'I know.' Mary replied, 'It's true. But only when the weather is good.'

They lay unspeaking for a little longer, relishing their experience, enjoying their life. Then they began to re-dress, shuffling on shirt sleeve, blouse sleeve … pulling up, pulling down, pulling on

128

… tugging stockings, tidying hair, and brushing off assorted bits of grass, leaves and smudges of dirt, then adding doublet coat, and bodice. And finally apron. They had arranged their tryst for the unfrequented edge of the estate, where the land had untended grass and straggly bushes, and they had been careful to ensure that there were no deer chasing young men from the village in the vicinity. The only witness to their coupling was the man's horse, nibbling happily at lush, green oak saplings nearby, and young starlings, chattering vigorously in a windbreak of tangled young beech trees. But the birds were more interested in whether to try out the flying world for the first time.

The house, the man's home, was visible some distance away across the deer park and framed between the fronds of fern and low hanging elm branches. The man lived in a nice country pile, a manor house that had been in the family, the Germains, for a hundred years or more. It had a comparatively new wing added to what had originally been a monastery, but was unrecognisable after three or four centuries. A half dismembered oak hadn't been cleared from the working area, and was being used as a source of weathered wood by the estate carpenter. A bit of newer turreting suggested an effort to maintain historical character. Beyond the estate, to one side, Crondall village could be seen, home for many with some sort of obligation to the Germains. The man was John Junior, future owner of all that could be seen.

He was self sufficient and self confident, his social position generally giving him leadership of any circumstances with which he was confronted. Being young, well built, he was an altogether personable man. And Mary Gunner was the sort of young girl who would have been attractive to any man. Not beautiful but appealing because of her positive and outgoing nature which showed in her lively face. With this fundamental characteristic she could enliven any situation, and whilst she was clever enough to carefully manage most circumstances, there was the odd occasion when her zest led her astray … perhaps for instance in her dalliance with the young man-of-the house.

John Junior once again initiated conversation. 'I wish we could do something about your bed when we get a chance to use it. It would be so much more enjoyable. Look what happened last week when I fell off the stupid thing.'

'Couldn't you speak to your father?' Mary asked.

'Then he'd know wouldn't he? Or he'd guess. I reckon he knows what goes on anyway. I sometimes wonder if he isn't up to this sort of thing himself. Do *you* know?'

Mary was discreet. 'How would I know? I just do my job, keep my place.'

'Don't you talk to the other servants?'

'Of course, but it's about work. Keeping the house tidy, putting things away after they are used. Keeping things clean, keeping everyone's wardrobe the right way. There's washing to deal with. Food is a big thing - getting it, preparing it, cooking it. There's always something to do with the animals in the yard. Keeping the fires going in the winter …'

This really wasn't what he wanted to hear. 'But you must talk about something else.'

'How, it's such a big house.'

'Not as big as some.'

'Forty eight rooms is big enough.'

'Yes, all right Mary, I understand.' John Junior knew that this young woman was a very capable person. It was why someone in his position was nevertheless attracted to her.

There was slight lull in their conversation and Mary felt obliged to ease the moment, 'I liked it too.'

'Oh good. I think you're absolutely wonderful Mary.'

'Thankyou sir.' Mary said, and her partner was not quite sure whether she was being sincere or may have been twitting him. He looked at her for a moment and he confessed his thoughts, 'You make me go all stiff,' he said.

Mary responded with the feminine awareness of the centuries. 'I guessed.'

Mary had been fulfilling tasks beyond the call of duty following her reaction, or more exactly non-reaction, to the occasion when the young master quietly crept up behind her, put his hand up her skirts and fondled her whilst holding her tightly with his other arm. She had been taken aback for a moment, and was additionally anxious to discourage him with due deference, but he was so effective with his affront that she failed to indicate her rejection of his actions with sufficient intensity. Indeed, contrast to what the other young female staff had said, it had been an altogether rather exciting experience.

The first time had been in the guest bedroom a few months previous when Mary was making beds after guests had left. The young master must have been waiting for his opportunity. Thus had begun a regular compliance of his needs (and, in fairness, hers) with John Junior having explained that there was no possibility of pregnancy because he had been told by a friend that when women convulsed energetically and disturbed all body parts it frustrated child-birth ... and Mary had indeed been extremely energetic, so was safe. The gratifying period lasted for six months before, unsurprisingly, Mary became pregnant.

This same six month period was a time of considerable upheaval in the household, the fractious relationship between the King and Parliament in the 1640s was a cloud over the place. John Junior was inveigled to join the Royalist Army of Charles I with his father, Sir John Germain. Both felt obliged, but reluctant, to offer their services as befitted their station, so they had to organise a muster for the King's cause. Meanwhile Mary treated her situation as 'one of those things', the name of the father remained unknown and later appeared in the parish records as - Thomas Gunner, 'base-born'.

At the time, because of her inability to resist the demands of nature, Mary's future seemed under threat but the Germains were good Christian people and had a caring position to uphold in church and community. Whilst there were rumblings about what should happen to Mary, Sir John felt it was his place to show Christian charity. He was sympathetic to women, having been widowed some years before by his wife's demise in childbirth, and any touch of masculine arrogance had mellowed. His stance with Mary was to act upon the forgiving examples in the Bible (which he frequently used to justify his seemingly inexplicably tolerant attitude) and the whole matter became accepted and dealt with as if it was one of life's small, ongoing incidents ... though hardly small to individuals involved. It wasn't exactly an unusual occurrence even in the best of families, though one didn't speak about it, and thus it *seemed* very unusual, but everyone *knew* otherwise. Sir John's thinking was quite simple, '... this is the sort of thing that goes on between the staff ...'

However the Squire, being a figure of prominence and influence, did feel a need to explain his reasons to the vicar as soon as possible, and made a point of catching the cleric at the start of his morning walk one day. Sir John cleverly trapped him in the church porch and the vicar stood agitatedly as the knight gently said, '... and one must remember Mary Magdalene, her way of life ... '

The vicar interrupted, 'Yes of course but ...'

Sir John continued, 'And Jesus did not condemn.'

'Except the money lenders,' the vicar got in slyly.

'But their way of life was unacceptable.'

'True.' The vicar felt he had validated his cloth so he conceded. He was in no position to challenge a Knight of the Realm, and did not press the debatable point that maybe the unacceptable money lenders were so different from an unacceptable prostitute. As if in celebration of the accord between the two men a dove gently took off from the dovecote in a group of farm buildings in the glebe.

Sir John may even have been aware of this vulnerable argument and disregarded it because he knew his objective had been achieved - the vicar would now deal with any chit-chat in order to keep the subtle social layers unaffected within the parish. By one means and another the matter was almost forgotten, helped because the whole business was intermingled with the distraction, and growing prominence of the wider, unsettling situation of civil unrest in the country at large.

Had the squire known who the father was, things would certainly have been different, but Mary kept the matter secret. She had come into the household with Sir John's wife whose family, the Upton Greys, had employed several of the Gunner family over the years, and Lady Germain had taken a special liking for Mary, being appreciative of her responsible character and initiative. Mary knew John Junior could not come clean and his response was to try to help her hold on to her position and so he spoke of her approvingly at every useful opportunity. Indeed it was his comments that had helped to form his father's moderate response, but he was careful not to seem over enthusiastic. The house staff were more knowing, and the gossip amongst the young females was informed by their knowledge of John Junior's inclinations. But because Mary said not a word to any of them, there was speculation that maybe one of the male staff, on the farm side, was responsible after all - just as the Squire seemed to think. In spite of all this they all later played their part when delivery time came.

The fact of the matter was that Mary was indeed an

independent, intelligent young woman, and her more responsible earlier experience with Lady Germain's family had given her a great understanding of the needs of a large landed establishment. She knew that almost the main characteristic of to a servant was her utter discretion. Thus not one iota of gossip of family affairs or finances got to the village from Mary's lips. She was one of these people who, regardless of their station in life, had an amalgam of qualities that were of high order and they had been transferred to Germain Manor. It would have functioned much less well without her. There were so many tasks to be done in the house and estate that a corner stone taken from the staffing edifice would have made the whole less stable ... or so thought Sir John, especially at this point in time, having more than enough duties to perform because of his rank. To lose such a member of his carefully selected staff would have created major difficulties. The positive remarks from John Junior from time to time, on top of his late wife's approval of Mary, served only to reaffirm Sir John's own good judgement.

Sir John's personal responsibilities were huge - the farm acreage and the unused land, as well as a house that had numerous bedrooms, library, lounging rooms, dining rooms, all connected by seemingly endless corridors, plus an almost palatial kitchen and a miscellany of little utility rooms, box rooms, cubby holes, all of which had to be managed, and maintained. On top of that clothing was needed for all staff, horses for work and pleasure and animals for milk and meat. Then there was the saw mill, the garden, brewing, baking, preserving, butter required making. The list went on and on. But perhaps the major consideration for Sir John at this particular time, was the unrest in the country, the antagonism between the King, and Parliament, between the Catholic leaning monarch with his strong views on absolutism, and the Commons with its Puritan streak, and Sir John was stuck in the middle of the continuing and unresolved struggle that had been set in train by Henry VIII. There was recent gossip amongst the servants that Parliamentarian troops had been seen not far from Crondall, and some members of the staff even claimed to have seen Oliver Cromwell in the village.

TWO ... Civil War.

AFTER a series of, on the whole, unresolved battles following the equally unsettled initial battle at Naseby, the Royalists were in Hampshire and Sir John had finally felt obliged to reveal his muster for the king, but only after some pressure directly from the Lord Lieutenant of the county. So in December 1643 he set out to make contact with the Royalist forces, commanded by Lord Hopton, which were quartering for the winter in Winchester. He arrived to witness a bedraggled Lord Crawford, breathing heavily from his frantic ride from Alton to report that the Royalist forces had suffered a reverse. They had engaged with the forceful parliamentarians in the streets and between them had left the church scarred with firearm holes.

It appeared that the two Germain supporters had come in time with their small muster of men gathered from staff and obligated villagers, who had been cajoled to join by means of manipulative arguments of the magistrate. They had to wait around for a few weeks but they were eventually involved in the battle to the east of the city, at Cheriton. It seemed an inappropriate time to be contesting life and death when spring life was evident in the young green, unfurling leaves of the trees and bushes. Sir John was thinking more of whether the ploughing had been done, and whether the harrow had been repaired, and whether old Ben Finch would be able to broadcast seeds properly with his lame leg, broken a few years before when it became entangled whilst trying to stop a couple of frisky young oxen. If he lost rhythm, got out of step, he could leave areas of a land unsown, and waste seed. Then there was Mary, would she be able to manage with a young baby to care for as well? After a moment Sir John dismissed the idea, he *knew* she would manage. She would probably have the staff baby sit whilst she made the place function.

North of Cheriton Woods, the Royalist army, reinforced by the Earl of Forth, moved forward, the Germains having cautiously manipulated their muster to a position behind the imminent action. Parliamentarian forces advanced from their position less a couple of miles away, north of Hinton Ampner. The two armies engaged in Cheriton Woods. Royalist musketeers and artillery under Colonel

Matthew Appleyard, forced a Parliamentary retreat and gained control of the woods, and the Germains were able to make use of the confusion of battle, and uncertainty of which-side-was-doing-what, to keep safe. Carried away by Cavalier achievement, Sir Henry Bard, without authority, tried to press the advantage but exposed a thin defence line. The response from the very well equipped Parliamentarian cavalry of Sir Arthur Hesilrige was immediate, and resulted in eventual Royalist defeat. The raucous sound of carrion crows during the action was an ominous signal. The Cavaliers were unable to recover advantage and the final outcome was complete Parliamentarian victory for Sir William Waller. The Royalists fell back to pause at Arlesford. The Germains, with their muster, had come through safely, but a tattered Cavalier Army had to tidy up the rebuff, the dead, the injured, and the lost and broken weapons. It was an altogether dispiriting activity.

Lord Hopton and his forces regrouped themselves for later action and retreated north to Old Basing, Sir John Germain and his militia amongst them. As the army travelled the tracks close by Crondall, Sir John could not overcome his yearning for his home and property. When they actually went close to the borders of his estate, he rode forward to join Lord Hopton, a pre-occupied and lonely figure at the front of the troop. The noble lord was distractedly pondering on the recurring pain in his leg caused by the injury he had received when a powder wagon had exploded after the battle at Lansdowne. 'If I had just been six feet further back … and had more men available when the Cornish pikemen charged up the hill …'

'This is fate my Lord,' Sir John said.

'What's that?' the commander replied, arrested from his introspections. He had enough things to think about. On top of the Lansdowne business, the recent defeats had been lying on his mind and he felt as if he had the troubles of the world on his shoulders.

'I think the Lord …' the Knight pointed upwards, '… directed this journey to send me home.'

'How do you mean?'

'We are on the west boundary of my estate, the house is just a few hundred yards from here. I have many urgent matters with which to deal, there is much confusion with all that has been going on.'

'I can imagine.'

'You could have gone on a route further to the west, but chose this route.'

'There is the question of supplies.'

'Was there? Or was it as the Lord dictated? So that I can go back and organise a defence strategy.'

Some of Sir John's old muster were within ear-shot and looked at each other approvingly. A couple smiled, they guessed their master's tactic. One mumbled quietly, 'He should be acting in one of those court masque things.'

'Comedy or tragedy?'

'Good question.'

Lord Hopton's mind had been abruptly turned from military matters to those of civil life. 'Well, I think what our forces ...'

He was interrupted by the arrival of John junior who had trotted up to the commander's entourage. 'If you'll pardon me for a moment my Lord ...'

Lord Hopton blinked – his injury, thoughts about deployment of his army, the domestic concerns of this Germain fellow and now some other problem, it was becoming unmanageable. He was not known to be a man of easy going temperament.

John Junior was knowledgeable enough of his father's character to have kept within ear-shot. He expanded on his intrusion. 'I'll continue with most of the Germain men, they are keen and proud to be a part of Lord Hopton's army.' Indeed, there were many from the muster, young men who were seeking adventure, or excitement, or escape from the drudge of their poverty stricken life, who wanted to stay with the army, and were happy to risk potentially debilitating injury, or even death. 'We'll compensate for any small depletion with the spirit of our commitment,' John Junior said winningly.

At that moment Lord Hopton felt so swamped with demands, he would have agreed to anything, providing he could be left in peace. The caw of a group of arguing rooks in the nearby wood seemed to exactly replicate what he had to deal with. He just grunted, and that was interpreted as agreement.

Thus whilst Sir John and some of his muster (the older ones it must be said) returned to the country estate, John Junior was able to take advantage of a propitious opportunity and escape the result of his romantic liaison with Mary and stay with the army. The Cavalier party finally moved further northwards to the king's base at Oxford,

John Junior with them. Young John thought he cut a rather dashing figure amongst the officers of King Charles' army. He sported flowing, curly locks of hair which rested on his starched, broad collar, sitting on a pristine white blouse, with buff leather jerkin over. Below he had deep blue, padded breeches down to his buckled, high heeled boots. The whole was adorned with a bold ochre sash and sword. This sartorial image was not the most eye-catching amongst the upper ranks, but seemed to make an impact, and enabled John Junior to later form a close friendship with young Prince Charles, who was a similar age. His attractive, playful character appealed to the young Prince. When it was felt desirable to send the heir abroad to safety, John Junior was asked to accompany him on what became a prolonged stay away from England with visits to assorted places – Scilly Isles, Jersey, Paris to the Prince's mother who was living in exile in the country of her birth, and finally to The Hague, to the Prince's sister who was married to William II of Orange. Thus, John Junior completely separated himself from his past and eventually lost himself after the Restoration in the excesses and indulgencies of the court of King Charles II.

A couple of the older men from Sir John's muster rejoined the staff at Germain Manor and the news of John Junior was soon disseminated. All eyes were on Mary but she showed not a flicker of a reaction. There was much chatter about this calm response amongst the staff and, arising from this, came the idea that Mary *must* have had a relationship with a man in the village. Encouraging this idea was a woman from Crondall village, Selina, who knew all the gossip and was a compendium of miscellaneous news. She was a comfortably proportioned, untidy but bossy woman who always had her head wear well tied under her chin. Gossips in the village claimed that she kept it on in bed because she had lost the hair on the crown of her head. The woman would drop in from time to time in wetter weather because the half dismembered oak by the rebuilt wing was a good place for collecting the black snails that she needed for her wart cures. She achieved her results by cutting them up and using the substance that bubbled from the resultant mess, as a salve, and had had many successes. Following her observations on Mary there was a pooling of ideas and it was deduced that there was a secret lover whom she met furtively on free days. With the added information of Selina the snail woman the discussion reached the conclusion that the man would have been the one nearest to the manor, thus making a secret meeting more readily possible. He was virile and handsome, and one of the organizers of the annual village fair, but not over friendly. He lived quietly with his parents which fitted well with the idea of furtive goings-on. It was agreed that he was the ideal candidate, confirmed by the fact that both he and Mary had the balanced humours necessary for a good relationship, thus their coming together was more or less inevitable. More importantly, the snail woman had seen Mary talking to him, many times, and always masked by a tree or barn.

Mary would have known such talk was been going on. She even calculated who the staff would decide had been her lover and mischievously mentioned his name once or twice to feed the speculation. Given the opportunity, she may well even have said, 'Yes,' to the man Mary also realised that as far as John Junior was concerned she would have simply been a passing conquest. It was widely known that John Junior was … well, a lecher. So Mary just got on with her life. Such a situation had happened many times before, it would happen many times again.

Sir John Germain was happy to know his son was moving into royal circles but he had to deal with more pressing problems. He may have had an undistinguished role at the battle of Cheriton but the victorious Parliamentarians now knew that he was a Royalist sympathiser with a large property close to the strategic road to the south west. Cromwell chose not to be lenient and Sir John was one of those singled out for punitive taxes. He had to sell many portions of his land to deal with the demand, including one to a rising family called Moseby that had a discreet connection to the Parliamentarian cause which they had exploited with subtle skill. The whole of that turbulent period, the war and the Interregnum, was an opportunity for any resourceful and alert property holder, whether merchant or landed farmer. Ambitious men, aiming to add to their wealth and holdings, sought to take advantage of the increased annual rent available for land at that time, and to manoeuvre a marital liaison by which to achieve a rise in social status, the idea of connection to a title being a teasing ambition.

After the Restoration, Sir John, unlike others, did not receive full reparation, despite John's royal connections, and he felt his comfortable world was being lost, undermined and changed forever.

Sir John's changing fortunes caused him to be less staunch in his loyalty to the crown and his broader sympathies enabled him to tolerate the growing number of dissenting non-conformists, including his mason, Hubert, who had done such good work on the new wing. The result was a team of willing workers. The staff were aware that if the Master went under, they all did, so the whole of the Germain estate workforce, with Mary to the fore, worked extra diligently, and though the establishment was reduced, the Manor and Estate survived. Sir John subsequently discovered that, on the whole, that the smaller acreage of the estate meant everything went more smoothly.

Though Mary had settled for her situation and was content in her role as a single mother and a highly regarded member of the estate staff, she found not all staff members saw her in the same light. The more adventurous and shameless males thought only of opportunity. Mary had to deal with a range of sexual advances and in assorted places, all of which she handled with feminine guile. But eventually she needed to deal with the issue once and for all. When the most lustful of the men followed her lasciviously into the stable, she flirted with him and then suggested that he wait while she, 'got ready', and slipped outside. The man was left to his imagination, which were only thoughts of delights to come. They did not. He was reported missing to Sir John before being discovered in the barred stable. The man protested his puzzlement, but Mary told her story to one of the staff and all, with their knowledge of the male predator, understood the encounter. Indeed Selina the snail woman had observed that his humours were not well balanced having been born with too much black bile. A short while later the dissolute man sought work elsewhere.

THREE ... Moseby/Mosebury.

ALL this drama history had been facilitated through the medium of an inert patient in a twenty first century converted workhouse-hospital. His, my, breathing eased with the success of forbear Mary's stratagem, my heart beat slowed, and the busy activity of electrical signals in my head changed tack. In my dreaming state ... or remembering, or reconstructing, or whatever it was that was going on, I now homed in on the name Mosebury, someone who apparently had property or land in my family ... maybe it was a connection? A name I knew from a distant cousin, and from my father, John, who had heard it from his uncle. 'A messuage with land and livestock,' in Essex, held by a Godfrey Mosebury. Given old spellings, old documents, old writing, maybe Latin, then real ancestor Mosebury must be Civil War Moseby, eighteenth century Moseby, hospital bed Moseby ... and the name must have had a past, in Tudor times and centuries before that. My condition seemed to have linked something together. It was like some inventors and students reckon – you go to bed at night and wake up in the morning with your problem solved ... one of life's little mysteries.

My mystery result was engendered by an uncertain physical state, a recuperative hospital bed and a facility of care. It offered an opportunity for idle, wandering thoughts in a historic Victorian building, with modern add-ons evident in the miscellany of specialist wards, offices, cubby holes and curtained off areas. Boards of information showed departments, notices and charts. Long, decorated corridors and shrub gardens were ornamented by local artists. It was not Victorian, and overall had the touch of a hotel about it ... just the place to relax and cut loose.

But I remained an untroubling patient, just lying there, all the working parts doing what they are supposed to do, whilst nurses came and went, patients came and went, a bit more slowly, but inside my head the comings and goings were traversing a bigger time span ... and national drama.

FOUR ... Thomas.

WITH the dual distractions of Civil War in the 1640s and the Cromwellian era in the 1650s, Mary Gunner had succeeded in holding her place in a period of momentous change. During which time, the baby Thomas was been spoilt for mothering. The rest of the young female staff at Germain Manor had cooed him and held him and dandled him, and they encouraged walking and talking and learning. The Germain family establishment were hardly aware that a baby ... then a boy ... then a teenager, had been kept unobtrusively in the house. Thomas had a life of changing experiences. He was cold in the winter, hot in the summer. He slept in lean-to outbuildings and shared bedrooms with other staff. He had rope-bottomed truckle beds made by the sawyer, hemp sack blankets and mattresses of rushes with the occasional flea. He knew of periods fending for himself, and undertook many out-door estate activities that made him fit. In the background there was a busy but caring mother that together made for a character forming upbringing. Mary revealed the secret of his birth to him and this instilled deeper self-confidence. Thomas became a mature and capable person, with long hair and a beard as was the fashion, wearing a wide collared shirt with jerkin, and breeches of the day.

The rounded package that was Thomas Gunner gave him a bearing that invited instant respect of anyone, something noticed by the female staff in the Germain household, and Crondall village itself, especially a certain Alice Meadows, attractive rather than beautiful and appealing because of a positive, outgoing nature. It seemed the steady eyes in her vivacious face may have been at variance with her manner which was considered and considerate ... a matching description of Mary. Alice Meadows' noticing of Thomas was ... noticed, and encouraged a response.

Mary thought her life was very tolerable - a home (of sorts), a job (of low status, but employment), and a family ... of a kind. Strangely, the thing that gave her much satisfaction was the recognition of her good work by the gift of a most comfortable bed for her lying-in, the single one that Lady Germain had used when she was considered unwell. Mary had all this, and the knowledge that her son Thomas had a good upbringing, and growth experience to fit him for the life ahead. It seemed her potentially unfortunate situation had turned out well.

By the 1660s England had peaceably resettled into monarchical life, and the rounded, adult Thomas had the enterprise and ability to consider setting up a squat beyond the house and gardens, well away from the manor. A more relaxed and tolerant Sir John allowed him to select a place on non-grazing ground, clear of trees, exposed to the sun and protected from cold eastern winds by a convenient slope.

Thomas set about the project with resolution, foraging for stones to form a foundation string for his walls and timbers for the frame and reinforcing staves. The basic building material was soil which was available in the area with the right mix of clay having a small amount of chalk, which he collected with a discarded deer antler he found in one of the manor tool sheds. Thomas added a smattering of straw and grits, as he had seen done in repairs to the manor utility buildings, and worked on the mix before leaving it over winter. He never seemed to be short of company when he turned over the soil, robins were always on hand to sing and forage. His efforts were also noticed by his best friend, Hubert the stone mason who had worked on the rebuilt wing of the manor and volunteered to help.

Hubert was an easy going hulk of a man, a Dissenter tolerated by Sir John. It was a sentiment Hubert embrace fully, he bore no grudge against anyone who once harassed him for his beliefs. Looking and feeling the building material Thomas had mixed the previous year, he said, 'You've been watching renovation work at the manor Thomas, haven't you, this is good stuff. Making mud bricks was how I started.'

'It'll be better when we've knocked it into shape Hubert.'

Hubert placed his steeple crown hat carefully on a log at a safe distance and the two men pounded the material with repetitious effort, like bakers working dough. The routine activity allowed Hubert the opportunity to think and he came up with an idea. 'I'll have a word with Michael in the stable, get one of the horses over, we could get this compacted in no time.'

'Hubert, God bless you. That would be a huge help. I didn't think this through properly, I hadn't realised how long it would take.'

Hubert was a good work-mate, a warm God-fearing individual,

'I'll tell you another thing about getting the horse over, having some droppings in the cob will improve it. In fact we could bring a bit more muck over anyway. Everything is provided by Him above for our needs ... we just have to know how to use His gifts.'

As if to compete with the intrusion to come, a pleasing whiff of wild honeysuckle reached Thomas' nose. 'Must have *muck* in the house walls,' Thomas said and laughed, 'All the best houses have that.' Hubert didn't notice that Thomas was being facetious, he was too excited by his own idea. 'And … if we get Michael we can get some more help from other workers. Michael spends half his time down in the forge'

Meanwhile Old Matthew had arrived to watch Hubert work, as he did from time to time. It was deduced to be an unspoken acknowledgement of the Dissenter's kindness. He stood a little way off, his deeply lined, aged, blank face, just staring. It was what he did. No one quite knew what went on in his head. He was quite decently turned out, brushed hair resting on wide shirt collar, leather jerkin buttoned up, breeches tolerable, stockings well fitted, only one his shoes was without a buckle. The estate staff kept him fed and clothed encouraged by Hubert and Sir John, who had known him all his life. Old Matthew had been young Matthew when he rescued the boy John Germain when he fell into the large stew pond and Matthew had knocked his head on a large stone in the process. After what must have been fully half-an-hour, Old Matthew wandered off in the direction of the house. He had said not a word.

The following spring and summer Thomas, Hubert and others attacked the erection job at frequent but erratic intervals, patiently laying one mud-brick course after another. Being used to the outdoor life and familiar with the weather and its behaviour, they were able to calculate the drying time of each course quite well. Before the arrival of another winter, the walls were up, a door and windows of sorts were in place, a thatch roof laid and the whole protected from inclement weather. It was finished just as winter approached. The very, very great many hours of patient work they had all done brought Thomas a feeling of complete and utter satisfaction … as if they had built the Pyramids in a day. Thus did the Gunner family acquire their hovel.

FIVE ... The Germains.

A LONG period of employment by Lady Germain, single
motherhood, a natural sense of responsibility and intelligence, made
the mature Mary a noticeable character within the household. But,
she was not gregarious, so other staff instinctively treated her
differently, with a respect touched with a little deference. She had
the quality of Vermeer's 'Milkmaid', lowly and yet projecting an
aura of natural self confidence. Her role within the household was
significant, but informally so. Mary was perceptive enough to be
aware of this but not exploit it, and in some ways she became the
effective house steward with access to the Estate Steward, Rupert,
Sir John's right hand man. Mary frequently elected to do more than
her share of the mundane jobs to demonstrate that she was not
behaving above her station. It was thus that Sir John caught her one
day in working mode, singing a butter churning song in an empty
kitchen - churning relentlessly at the butter tub.

'Ah Mary, caught you doing the chores.'

As soon as he appeared Mary stopped singing, smoothed her
apron, rolled down her sleeves and tucked a strand of loose hair
under her cloth bonnet.

He seemed to feel a need to explain himself. 'I was taking a
short cut through here. It's a long trek round to the garden doors to
the house.'

Mary waited for something to which she could respond.

Sir John carried on, 'Actually it's lucky I've caught you on your
own.'

She wondered if his short cut was a device to see her alone for
some reason.

'There's something I've wanted to say to you for a long time.'

Mary felt she had to say something and tried to make a neutral
noise, but wasn't sure whether it sounded like, 'Oh? (What are you
up to?)', or 'Ah,' (You want me to clean the latrine?).

'You know you are a very unusual woman. We've known each
other a long time and I can say with certainty that you are one of
those people who, for whatever reason, have an amalgam of qualities
that stand out.'

Whatever neutral noise Mary felt she had made before Sir John spoke now seemed inappropriate. Her shoulders heaved as she just breathed in deeply.

'I'm grateful for your work over the years, you've been a pillar. It was Lady Germain who first noticed your dedication and diligence long before we were married ...'

'That was some time ago,' Mary said.

'And her judgement has been born out over all this time. Of course one shouldn't be surprised by outstanding women with the example of our own Queen Elizabeth and, dare one say it, 'The Maid of Orleans'. Both were national figures, but Joan of Arc was born a peasant, so outstanding character can fall in any place.'

Mary was silent, she could not imagine what to say. The quiet seemed to be amplified in that bare, functional room, and the atmosphere strained even though, now that affairs in the country had settled, Sir John had become more relaxed, and he dressed accordingly. He had forgone the fussy and frilly cuffs and wide collars for simple ones, with status evident only in the quality of the red-brown satin of his loose shirt and rich dark blue velvet of the waist-coat beneath his top-coat. But he didn't appear to be comfortable, and hurried on.

'We had such a woman here in Crondall some years ago, Bessy the innkeeper. Have you heard of her?'

'Yes there is some gossip about ...' Mary didn't finish, Sir John was in full flow.

'Her husband died and she was penniless but fortunately she had previously been clever enough to develop beer making skills. Through her guile, organisation and management she made a success of our village inn and then moved on to London where she became a successful wine-merchant. With her well placed contacts she discreetly also became something of a costume adviser ... or something, I never quite understood how she operated, but came to lead a life of some status.

Mary nodded. 'Yes, in the village they talk of ... '

But there was no stopping Sir John. 'The estate steward finds you difficult ...' he said through carefully combed beard and moustache.

Mary was shocked by this sudden change of tone, she breathed in to protest but didn't get a chance to say anything.

'… difficult because he uses your abilities beyond what is expected of you, and he feels undermined by doing so.'

Mary recovered. 'I just do what's necessary, what needs to be done.'

'Exactly. He's lucky. And so am I. Thank you Mary.' He broke away, his topcoat flowing out behind him, then turned back to say, 'I had to say that Mary.' And went, out past the cumbersome cheese press, courtesy of the blacksmith and the sawyer, beside which was the by-product, a large bowl of whey. Partly hiding in the corner, was a barrel of beer. By the time of this exchange Sir John was quite old and it seemed he was, as it were, tidying up his life as it got towards its end, and he did indeed have to make his parting remark because he had so wanted to for a long time … but it came out in a rather spiky sort of way because he didn't quite know how to carry out the task. Mary stood almost in shock.

She was aware that she did indeed have valuable abilities and experience, and that they were recognised by Sir John. But she also, at times, wondered whether she had been singled out for special consideration because Sir John really knew of her dalliance with John Junior, his son, many years before. The idea was never far from her thoughts.

With Mary in this state of mind, her cherished boy (she never saw him as a man even though he very evidently was), Thomas, came into the kitchen. It was a regular early afternoon routine timed to fit round the staff habit of finding assorted other places to recover their own first half of the working day. Mary and Thomas raided the half hidden barrel in the corner and sat down at the kitchen table with jugs of ale. Their faces seemed to shimmer as the bright sunlight bounced off the well scrubbed table surface onto their faces.

'It's interesting how a family like the Germains …' Mary gestured above to the house, '… have gone on for so long.' The estate brew seemed to be of interest to a searching bee. Thomas flicked the creature away. Mary preferred any private chats between them to be in the kitchen which she felt, reluctantly, was more comfortable than Thomas' wasteland squat.

'Have they always been nobility?'

'I only know the last hundred years or so, back to about Henry VIII, and Sir Geoffrey de Germain, who had the place built, or rebuilt should I say, given it was once a monastery. I remember my aunt Isabel telling me her mother used go on about how Sir Geoffrey was always trailing around as if he was some Italian prince from Florence.'

'They have to, to show where they are on the ladder.'

'Same fate in the end though.' Mary points to the floor.

'What about Lady Germain? When she was Constance de Upton Grey, what do you know about them?'

'One property marries another.'

'Always seems to be the case.'

'Unwritten law, almost,' said Mary.

'Nine tenths of it,' Thomas responded.

Mary smiled ruefully. 'Where ever you are on the social ladder … it's how I came to work for Lady Constance. Your uncle Robert got our place when granddad died and I ended up having to work out at Upton Grey manor.'

'And so now, cousin George is in the village and I am here.'

There was a momentary pause in their conversation. Mary, with a mother's careful curiosity, took the opportunity to raise a personal matter. '… and Alice Meadows is in the village too …'

Thomas smiled at his mother's circumlocution, 'Yes,' he said simply, but Mary was the more experienced player of subtle conversational games, she waited for the silence to be punctured, '… and yes, she does mean something to me,' Thomas added.

'Good, I like her,' Mary said and returned to the subject, '… getting back to lineage, you have a good mix - Germain blood mixed with Gunner blood,' she said with a laugh, 'It *must* be good stuff.'

'Did you get to know what it was like in your aunt Isobel's day?' Thomas asked.

'King Charles, James, Queen Elizabeth, King Henry, what's the difference?'

'Nothing but trouble it seems.'

'Bad blood maybe,' Mary said, grinning.

Thomas joked back, 'Blue blood, the wrong colour.'

'Not like us eh?'

'Good blood?' Thomas asked with a grin.

'Exactly, going right back to Adam and Eve.'

'And now going on … to what I wonder?'

Mary seemed content with her lot at Germain Manor.

SIX ... George discharged.

I seemed asleep in hospital, but was in another world and had the suggestion of a smile on my face. What was going on inside my head was not unpleasant. Pam was sitting on a chair beside the bed in the ward, and smiling gently through her concern in response to the apparently pleasing experience I was having. The warmth on her face sat well on her nicely groomed features. She didn't try to hide the passing years but rather, chose to lead an active, easy going and happy life thus enabling time to settle pleasantly on her face. Her light make-up was used with artifice.

A nurse walked by at that moment. 'Should I wake him?' Pam said.

The nurse looked at me. 'Looking at his face, I'd say that would be a pity, he seems to be enjoying himself.'

'True,' Pam replied simply.

'I shouldn't think five or ten minutes longer in here would worry him.'

'Also true,' Pam said, 'I suppose I'm thinking more of the five or ten minutes longer on this chair.'

The nurse smiled, 'Everyone says that.'

'Well you don't want people to stay in here longer than is advisable do you?'

'That's true as well.' The nurse walked off down the ward.

My eyes flickered open and my brain got a handle on where I was. I saw Pam. 'Hello', I said softly.

'Hello,' she replied, 'It seems they've had enough of you then?'

'Yeah, they said to me ...' (I did me funny voice.) ..."Yoov dun yaw porrige like a good boy Mr Gunner, yoo can go."

Pam smiled a response. 'Was it nice where you were whilst you were asleep?'

'I suppose it was really ... interesting.'

'Your head has always been able to conjure up something a bit different.'

'... it was the clarity of it all ... the Restoration ... a big house in the country, an old monastery ... sitting in the kitchen with sunlight through the leaded window, and a shining, bare table surface with its dark shadow on the flagstone floor underneath … it was so detailed, I could even see splashes of water on the floor by a leather bucket.'

'I always find dreams confusing.'

'They can be. But this was pretty straightforward. At least I think it was. But was it fact or fiction, that's the question.'

'You can't trust what's going on when you're asleep.'

'Maybe we should.'

'I don't believe so.'

I put on my God-like voice, "There are more things in heaven and earth Horatio …"

'Maybe...' Pam stood up in business-like mode. 'Come on, we've got to get you back home.'

I continued, '… and if things have actually happened, they exist, somewhere in time … they are, stroke were, physical, the point is can they can be found?'

Pam was in good bossy-boots form. 'Come on.'

'Yeah, I know, they want the bed for the next victim. I'd better get dressed and get all my things together.'

'Such as they are,' Pam added. 'I've spoken to the medics, got all the info., I know where we're at and how we go on.'

'That's my girl. Got 'em all organised.'

'I've fixed a follow up appointment with our doc. He'll do BP and change your medication I imagine. Then I expect you'll have a blood test.'

'Are you going to organise me?'

'That's a secret.' Pam looked serious.

I made light of it. 'Whatever … it looks as though the future is going to be interesting.'

Pam looked puzzled. 'I don't know what that means but I shall be keeping an eye on you.'

"… keeping an eye …", I thought, and smiled to myself. I'd had quite an adventure in hospital keeping my eyes closed. I wondered whether it would now finish. I sat on a chair, as Pam insisted, and she bustled around, putting bits and pieces into a shopping bag - wallet, newspaper, half a bar of chocolate, glasses case, a bunch of keys, a rumpled paper receipt, a little container of peppermints … I didn't realise I had gathered so much junk. I closed my eyes for a moment, and listened to Pam's rummaging noises. They seemed to have a soporific quality. Before long I was elsewhere.

A STORY of HENRY & JANE
in the time of HENRY VIII.
(George going home)

ONE ... Henry and family.

... seeing an unfocussed image of flickering grey with ragged shapes in pastel shades. In a grey fog, swirling dust could be discerned, then falling debris ... and a heavy thump, regular and controlled. There was further noise with squabbling rooks in nearby woods, but still the constant thump. It took a moment for the vision to clear to reveal what looked like the late stages of the demolishing of a building, a clerical building, a monastery. A group of grimy faced men, in the dust covered and ageless, peasant garb of dirty tunics and torn leggings were dismembering the wing of a three hundred year old structure.

Standing by, and apart, dominating the scene simply by the contrasting quality of his dress was the resplendently bearded, florid cheeked, Sir Geoffrey de Germain – silk clothes in a pallet of primary colours, firs, chains of office and jewel-encrusted ornaments, topped with a fur brimmed cap at a jaunty angle – he had been a strategically obsequious attendant at court, and rewarded the with monastery and estate by the King, Henry VIII. Sir Geoffrey, held the manor of Crondall on behalf of the Monks of Winchester Cathedral and had plans for a fine country manor house. When he was satisfied that the men were doing his job as required, Sir Geoffrey rode away on his Barb stallion, another acquisition of his manoeuvrings at court. He was anxious not to have any dust settling on his splendid apparel before entertaining a fellow noble.

The King felt similarly caring about England and contested the idea of having any decisions about rule in the country being made in Catholic Rome. In addition, when he was not blessed with a male heir, he felt it was due to the judgement of God for wrongly marrying his brother's widow ... or so he said. So, for one reason and another, he sought divorce, but the Pope would not allow it and

Henry, a strong headed man, wanted his own way. So he separated the church establishment of the country from Rome ... and monasteries from inhabitants. The result of actions taken at the royal court was an unsettled country.

The destructive noise of a monastery being remodelled into a personal display of wealth and status travelled aggressively through the soft country air across some scrubby fields of ash and blackthorn to a busy field of barley which was, in turn, a few fields away from 1540s Crondall village. In one of the demesne fields an early harvest was being gathered. A good proportion of the villagers were in the field, including Henry Gunner and his family. The urgency of harvesting demanded a collective effort and careful timing to defeat the uncertain English climate. Each family formed a 'team' unless a 'team' had a spare worker or was a person short, in which case swaps were made, sometimes with eruptive effect when families had fractious relationships. In spite of that, the task at hand went efficiently ahead because to do otherwise could have been detrimental to each family's food stock and may have been punished at the manor court. A period in the stocks could have been the sentence meted out for unacceptable behaviour.

The sound of swishing and rustling of the sickle mingled with the distant demolition racket, until that soft, rhythmic noise was broken by a sudden outburst of anger, an expression of discontent from a tired peasant. 'Mind my foot.'

'You shouldn't stand so near.'

'You should watch what you're doing.'

'You've got your bit and I've got mine.'

'Exactly, and you've strayed into mine, look.'

There was a pause before, 'Oh.'

The exchanges went quiet, one of the peasants, with his head down, surrounded by nothing but barley and disengaged by a long repetitive day, had indeed drifted off his patch.

Harvesting by hand was a very time consuming job. And physically demanding - a single cut meant a slight crouch for a tall man and co-ordination of the left hand to hold back the grain with the reaper's baton, followed by an accurate swing of the sickle (a tool used by Crondall Manor at the time) with the right. Two cutters were followed by the collectors, raking and gathering the cut grain into manageable piles, a job only completed when tied with straw to form sheaves, ears of grain upright … all repeated and repeated, all day long. Even a small field could take two or three days, another couple would be needed for collection, stacking the wagon, transporting to barn and unloading. Then, after a period of storage there was the laborious threshing to do in order to separate the ear from the husk. The tool for this, the flail, was basically two jointed sticks, handle and swingel, and all threshers had tales of backs with welts and lacerations acquired in their apprentice days. Luke Wood, the village thresher, told the story of a couple of strangers who appeared at the mill demanding food. They tried threats, and ended up limping out of the village with jeers of abuse, rather than the usual noisy hue and cry, having learned something of the art of flail wielding.

Henry Gunner was one of those virile, blooming country specimens of 40 or so. Some might have called him spare framed but activity on the land, close to nature, gave him the energy and air of an animal, with an expressionless face and hazel eyes that seemed empty, offering nothing clear but suggesting a mind of cool calculation. His wife, Jane, was a good partner, supportive and rarely complaining, dressed in lightweight summer garments, usefully straw coloured shift with a red bodice fastened to show her womanliness. In her well structured face one could read assurance in her alert eyes, and generosity in her full lips. All the women had their cloth headwear tied under their chin to address the demands of the extensive movement of the work. The family, with five children of assorted ages, worked uncomplainingly in their allotted part of the field.

The efforts of the Gunner family continued with little communication, only what was necessary to deal with the task at hand. Added noise was from magpies a few feet behind - the harsh, staccato, cha, cha, as they scratched around for insects and seeds, any sort of pickings. 'Don't cut it too low Edward leave some stubble for the animals to feed on.' 'Can you tidy up that stoop for your mum you two?' 'Keep the ties tight Isabella … you remember how Knotty Withers showed you.' 'You must make sure the stooks are upright you two.' 'Can I have a rest dad?' 'Only five minutes then Phillip.' Henry knew he would have to relent for the youngest as it was one of those hot, sticky summer days, threatening wet and stormy weather. Six year old Phillip was the family mascot and had been taken in by the Gunners after Jane's sister had died in childbirth and the boy's father left the village. He had been allowed to do a bit of gleaning by the bailiff as a means of preparing him for field work when he was older. Jane encourage him to feel he was contributing to family life, but she monitored him carefully in case he became too successful and, by gathering too much, made the bailiff think the Gunners were exploiting the concession. Jane gave Phillip an encouraging hug, and the smile that she used frequently to encourage effort and overcome difficulties.

Against the distant noise of demolition, field work and magpies, could be heard the occasional thin, penetrating cry of a red kite overhead, its long wings and distinctive swallow-tail tacking the winds, looking out for any small creatures injured or killed during the work below. Then an approaching clip-clop of a horse was added to the mess of sounds, getting louder until it stopped. Henry looked up and across the field over the heads of all the other workers, and saw Sir Geoffrey de Germain, straight backed, colourful and resplendent on his horse, had stopped to talk to the bailiff. Henry could see that the field was now cut and the next job was transportation. Sir Geoffrey was making a last minute check – he'd seen the building labourers, he was now seeing the farm labourers. He was not one of the barons who left his estate management to underlings - steward, bailiff or reeve, his estate control was as fastidious as his dress. It was his privilege to be richly dressed, and those socially below him were expected to dress according to the social level they occupied. Henry wore a skirted, half-sleeved tied jerkin, over a loose plain shirt and a domed, brimmed hat in readiness for whatever the weather might bring, rain or sun. The bailiff exchanged a few words with Sir Geoffrey before he rode off. The bailiff shouted towards Henry and, though he didn't hear what was said, those workers closer to him almost immediately started to lift the sheaves and stack the waiting wagon at the edge of the, so Henry and his family did likewise.

'Sir Geoffrey looked pleased with himself, in his finery,' Jane said.

'He's a picture of our new life – and of the downfall of our proud and overweening church,' Henry said.

'A confused church, a Latin or English one?'

'Whatever the King says,' Henry replied.

'As the rector mumbles most of the service I don't know what language he's using anyway.' Jane was not disconcerted by Henry's animal eyes, her male management skills were well exercised by the experience of lots of brothers.

'That's a sensible rector. With the mind changing about what language to have, mumbling's the best idea.'

'Margaret the Widow thinks it's the Cardinal, not the King,' Jane retorted.

'Who knows, all the king wants is to get Rome off his back.'

'… I expect they're all dithering.'

'And that makes for uncertainty, look what's happening at the court, deaths left right and centre. All on top of the church business, it's bound to affect our lives sooner or later.'

Jane was reluctant to think about the matter, the activities of the privileged always intruded on the lives of the lowly. She pointed to the west. The dark clouds indicated an approaching downpour and she simply replied, 'Let's get this stacking done quickly before we get a soaking.'

Henry called out 'I'll take this one and if Edward and Isabella take those two we'll be done, off you go the rest of you.' The bailiff was at the wagon checking the loading. The three Gunners made their final contribution and joined the rest of the waiting family at the corner of the field. The smell of newly cut grain hung heavily in the air. Henry took charge of the tools, the sickle, a sharp-stone, and a knife, and put them all into a back-pack that Jane had made from a couple of pig-skin off-cuts, and led the straggle off to the village.

TWO ... Monologue.

THE twenty first century Gunner was also on a journey. Pam was driving me home in her careful way and the radio offered entertainment with, 'Songs from Musicals'. I dozed comfortably on the seat beside her. It was soft, I was warm. She was chattering away whilst I reacquainted myself with car seat relaxation as country town surroundings flicked past the car. I was not entirely engaged. 'Yes,' I said instinctively when Pam offered an inflection that invited response. I even added, 'I agree,' and, 'That's true,' from time to time if it seemed appropriate. Even after the hospital drama she still had a lot to speak about ... regarding Peter.

'I know you are very involved in his badminton and he is really coming on, but I sometimes wonder if he can handle the pressure. He's worked very hard and created such an expectation in himself.'

'That's true.'

'Mind you we're lucky with our Paul, not being really sporty, he can see things from a different perspective, and it makes him objective.' Pam slowed as a car a few head in her stream prepared to turn off to the right. She smoothly dropped down a gear. Someone flashed a headlight at someone else. Was that a, 'Hello you!' or a, 'Get out of my way!' Pam took no notice.

'Funny our son isn't keen on sport but his son is. Peter is more like you, that sporty characteristic must have jumped a generation.' The traffic speeded up a little and Pam slowly accelerated and changed up a gear. 'But Hugh, with his organisational and management skills is constantly on the look out – in case you get too involved, or if Peter pushes himself too hard. One way and another, it's a good set up.'

'Yes.'

'You have to be really special to be a big success at anything but I sometimes think it's harder with sport because it's so tied to one particular time ... the Football Cup Final, Wimbledon Tennis Final.' Pam paused, another thought struck her. 'Mind you it's the same for any performer – pianist, actor, whatever ... do you think Peter is ... or could be, special? I think it's possible.'

'I agree.'

'It would be wonderful if he really achieved something wouldn't it?'

'It was all a long time ago.'

Pam turned briefly to look at me.

'Have you heard anything I've been saying?!'

'I know.'

She didn't speak anymore and listened to 'Songs from Musicals'.

I was in a dream world.

THREE ... Simple life.

THE peasant Gunners were on their routine, tired, daily dawdle along the well used track from field to village. It was a, 'there's-no-hurry', because, 'time-goes-by', sort of amble. On one side was another worked field, on the other was a string of untidy bushes that marked the transition to the woods, territory for pig foraging, kindle gleaning and building wood for the lord.

Jane said, 'When the rain's over the stream will be running nicely. We can have a clothes wash, it's been a while since the last one.' She brushed some clinging bind-weed seeds off her shift.

'I'll get all the buckets filled up again then,' said Henry.

'Thanks,' Jane said.

They walked quietly for few paces before Henry suddenly said loudly, 'Look out!'

Jane was alarmed, 'What?'

'A snake!'

'Oh no, where?!' Jane screamed.

'There,' Henry said and pointed … at nothing.

Jane looked. 'You!' she said, 'You gave me a scare.'

They both enjoyed the moment of nonsense and were glad the working day was over. A variant of such exchanges had been enacted many times. Other child-like diversions were played out to mitigate the tedium of the daily grind, and unchanging village surroundings. Henry and Jane simply made the best of it. He linked her arm, smiling happily. 'I'll make up some soap then,' he said, 'I've got a bit of fat I put by for rushes and candles.'

'We won't need them this time of year.'

'Good point, and after a day in the fields we'll only need to sleep.'

'If we wait for a few weeks, I'll have time to dry some lavender. It makes all the difference in with the fat, the smell without is foul.'

'Look at that,' Henry said.

'I'm not going to get caught out again,' Jane replied.

'No, the tree, the beech.' Henry pointed. 'Do you remember, I marked the place.'

'Ah … where you jumped out and kissed me.'

He stepped over to inspect it. 'It wasn't a very good mark. But it's still there.'

'You're an old softie on the quiet aren't you?' Jane smiled. Henry grinned back. She look away to check that a full complement of children was still in sight on the track. They were passing the manor gibbet post, thankfully unused for a few years. The children were disinterested as they skipped and played chasing games in and around the adjacent bushes of hawthorns and hazels. Little Phillip was chased by Edward 18, tall, thin and ungainly, reluctant but really able when in the mood, and Isabella 17, a fresh youthful beauty who was a good fowl minder at other times, and matched her mother's character, accepting life's good and bad times. 'Keep Phillip clear of that hole over by the fallen oak you two,' Jane called. Phillip was frequently over-taken, picked up, swung round, put down, and another chase began. The middle girls, 'the Giggly Gunners', 14 and 15, were in animated conversation, teenage fingers stabbing here and there, accompanied by low voiced, confidential noises, interrupted by loud, dramatic squeals. The very essence of youth. They were totally unaware of their surroundings. Some very vital young person's issue was being expounded – who was making eyes at whom?

Henry said, 'I think we must have been good little workers today.'

'No, the lord just knows how to get the best results - from people, the weather, even the king,' Jane observed.

'But his family are just jumped up peasants,' Henry said sourly.

'They worked hard, long days, got their own tools, hired them out … it's a tough way of jumping up.'

'They only did that after all the death of the great pestilence, then getting hold of plots of land.'

'The Germains just made the most of the chances that followed, and carried on doing so.'

Henry didn't want to let it go. 'Born out in the field they were back then. Out in the field!'

'We've all heard the story.'

'Waverley Abbey lost half their monks, did they care?'

Jane didn't reply but Henry's comment triggered a thought.

'Two hundred years ago … I wonder what our families were doing?'

A moment of pensive quiet allowed the buzz of bees to mark the pleasant but close heat of the day before Henry backed down, 'It's all a long time ago. Come on you lot.'

They gathered the children together as they reached the large horse chestnut tree that marked the edge of the village. It was a feature in the community, in the spring it wore spectacular bloom, like a tree of candles.

The origins of habitation at Crondall must have been due to the availability of water, long before the Romans came. The winding shape of the village followed a meandering stream with plentiful water agrimony, comfrey, reeds and sedge enjoying the moist environment. The burgeoning manor house was some distance away, the dominant building in the village was the church with its Norman tower, and inside, the powerful Norman/Romanesque pillars of the nave. Also at a distance one or two more recent homes had been made on patches of unused waste land.

The village itself was a collection of indifferent buildings, a mixture of round and oblong, several with little more than sack hangings at windows and doors to keep out the winter cold. The structures were of sparse timber frames with paling and mud infill, and thatched roofs. Some had mud walls falling away, and roofs which were a patchwork of thatch, straw, moss and turf. Not the best way of dealing with uncertain English elements. Lack of time to do repairs *may* have been a valid excuse, work obligations could be onerous, and some peasants had to carry a bigger work-load than others. The manor court tried to enforce repairs by fines but generally the bailiff found people were simply too poor to pay for either repair or fine. Where-ever the homes were, they were of inferior building material, the best having gone to the manor or church.

Any animals that a family were lucky enough to have, were in an adjacent yard, penned in by a scraggy hedge reinforced with hazel sticks, and willow ties. It was roughly done because a bad winter meant that repairs were not been fitted in before the spring field work was required. Animal pens were downhill to avoid any effluence permeating living space. Some places also had a vegetable patch as part of their holding. The hotchpotch village had almost fifty homes, including any animal pens and vegetable plots and, with the church and glebe, it measured less than a furlong.

When the Gunner family walked clear of the chestnut tree and onto the village green, they were in effect embraced by a place that could almost be said to be the whole of their life. It was noisy too - babies crying, parents squabbling, young people shouting. Dogs, sheep, pigs, chickens, geese, wood chopping, hammering and a miscellany of other activities made a never ending clatter and hum in the air. The hubbub sometimes included church bells and, if the wind was in the right direction, the splash of the mill waterwheel.

The expected rain started to fall and Henry called out, 'Last one to get home has to get logs for the fire.' They all set off at a lick and Henry, whilst leading, had an accidently-on-purpose stumble ... and took in the logs.

FOUR ... Church.

FOLLOWING the harvest, Henry told the family that, given the unpropitious year's weather, the wheat would be down and bread was likely to be short in the winter. In anticipation of this he had made a point of having the family attend church regularly in the hope that it would be noticed and maybe, just maybe, the rector would be kind and forego, or at least reduce his right to the ten per-cent tithe of the family's share of the harvest crop. Fortunately, the 'Giggly Gunners' didn't mind attending church as they enjoyed it almost as entertainment. The girls were diverted by the ludicrous fantasy decoration on the church walls, the brightly coloured paintings of the saints, the monstrous figures and demons, the grotesques carved on bench ends, it all seemed to only stir up amusement and muffled sniggers. Jane's, 'Control yourselves,' evoked a response of a pulled face ... but quiet. The Crondall church had not at that time succumbed to the desecration resulting from the King VIII's split with Rome. The reaction of the older ones was entirely different, they were disturbed by the depiction of hell, of devils, because they were of an age to understand their eventual demise and, being well tutored by the church and ideas of the time, had a horror of that uncertain future. They spent almost the whole service looking at the floor.

Late in the day the next Sunday, Henry was on the lookout for the rector and caught him at the lychgate as he was coming from the church, followed by some of his chickens. He wanted to discuss the tithe payment in the unfavourable financial circumstances and had a surprise response.

'Yes, the bad harvest will create a problem for a lot of people,' the rector said, 'Indeed, several have already spoken to me about their payment obligation.'

Henry's spirit sunk. It was true, some of the other serfs had already said the same to him. He looked appealingly to the rector. There was a food stain at his breast, evident on his clerical garb. The rector was known to be partial to soft boiled egg. His tonsure needed a bit of attention as well the crown was being encroached upon by hair growth.

The rector went on, 'But in your case, I think the church can be lenient. Only pay half, yes? I think that's fair. The humility and fervour shown by your older children was exemplary.'

Henry was taken aback, he didn't know where to look, a scattered of feathers was only vaguely noticed on well trodden animal path through the pattern of graves. He hadn't quite understood the rector's comment but did appreciate the tenor of what he was saying, so he simply said, 'Yes,' hoping to sound approving, even holy, thus giving the impression of a father who had schooled his offspring properly.

The rector continued. 'They were looking down humbly throughout the service, it showed true devotion. Only old Margaret the Lame, is as devout as that.' The rector always carefully identified which of the three Crondall church-going Margarets he was referring to – the Nurse, the Widow, or the Lame.

Henry was quick to acknowledge the pious character of his two children. 'That's right,' he said.

'Your children showed a good example to others in the village, well done,' the rector said and swept off down the track, his long heavy over-gown puffing up the dust, the chickens running behind, necks thrusting energetically backwards and forwards.

As Henry turned away from the rector he looked back momentarily at the church and his face wore a smirk, but it disappeared when he saw that Margaret the Widow was emerging from the building, as was frequently the case. She would have noticed him between the row of young yews and he knew that Widow Margaret would not approve of his smirking. She was an aging, lonely soul given to almost nun-like clothing and finding things to do in and around the church. It was appreciated by the religious fraternity but most people did little more than exchange greetings of the day with her. It was no deterrent, she walked forcefully everywhere with her stoop, head thrust forward, like the prow of a ship pushing through the sea. She adjusted her stiff cloth bonnet as she homed in on Henry. 'Was that the rector Henry?'

'It was indeed.' He tried to give a response that didn't encourage further conversation.

'I don't think he's caught up with the changes that are going on everywhere …'

162

'No indeed.' And Henry started to walk towards the village green.

Widow Margaret caught his sleeve, pulled him close and became confidential. 'I reckon it's not to his liking.'

'How did you work that out?' Henry responded instantly but regretted saying the words almost as soon as they were formed. He'd invited conversation.

'I keep my eyes open, I speak to people. My sister's seen him struggling over the good book, the new one translated into English. She told me there was something unhappy, even despairing, in his eyes. And my cousin over in Crookham saw him talking to the rector there, he's a Latinist too.'

'Interesting …' a nice neutral reply Henry hoped.

'All this chopping and changing is unsettling, and it's at times like these, that bad things happen.' Widow Margaret became distant, perhaps recalling some disturbing experience. Henry debated whether it would be appropriate to say anything, but she came back to herself, 'No, it doesn't feel right not hearing Latin in church.'

'I'll see what Jane thinks,' Henry said. It was the best he could think of as a means of escape.

'Good idea,' Widow Margaret said, 'I'll catch up with her later on.'

'Right.' Henry then really did get on his way to the village green.

The fact of the matter was that Widow Margaret really preferred talking to other women and so the end of their exchange suited all round … except maybe for Jane. Henry felt he may have been a bit unkind to Jane ... but he also knew his wife was more than adequate for any uncertain situation.

FIVE ... Dialogue.

WIVES have dealt with uncertain situations created by their husbands down the ages ... including heart attacks. Pam was a good chauffeur, careful, unlike me always in a bit of a hurry. She kept a good look out for all the road signs and did what they said, never drove or spoke on the mobile, had her car serviced regularly, her car lights on at the right time, her wipers going when they should, and she never did a three point turn in a main road. She might have made a good driving instructor. When Pam commented on my work at the steering wheel, I growled back, 'Oh sure, goody two shoes.' But it was a decent marriage. Early hard work with each other and careful management of tolerable careers; two children fitted in, and each of those children now with their own teenage children. Overall, we felt that the life we had was more than satisfactory ... until lifting paving slabs dramatically interfered.

Pam now had her Monteverdi CD on to accompany her driving.

I began to disengage from forbear Henry's dilemma about how an impoverished ordinary man can avoid oncoming national religious turbulence. How can a mere peasant deal with the machinations of powerful political forces? As I came to, I took in where I was, and realised I should try to be companionable. 'Did the flower meeting go all right?'

'Ah, you're with us again. It was the usual, Sidonie talked too much. Norman got hot under the collar about pesticides. Maureen went on about the government.'

'And the local authority?' I chipped in.

'No not this time actually. By that time we were into the wine drinking bit.'

'That's why you go to those meetings – cup of tea to start, some of those presentation tins of biscuits, a bit of a chat, then into the vino. Not bad.'

'We do discuss business you know.'

'Yes, and end with a couple of bottles of wine. Very nice.'

Pam began to regale me with what actually went on in the week's flower show meeting. "It was Maureen who set Sidonie off, she introduced the subject of reality television shows and ...'

I was looking out of the window at the passing view - lamp-posts, cyclists, shops, lights, buses, cars and people keeping up consumption … the variety fluttered by. It was like the flickering of an old thirties film. Pam spoke engagingly, but competed with changing engine revs., gear moves and tyres swishing as traffic was negotiated, corners turned, and gradually all the sounds seemed to merge, to become a medley of abstract noises as if it was the flapping projector of a run-out film. It all served only to dull my senses, and I wondered how my forbears were getting on with the village church people in those fractious and uncertain times. It was my family, my connection, with a lifestyle in which social order was imposed, superstition could thrive, life was cheap, death frequent. All that must have affected how my forbears thought and undermined their aspirations.

Pam noticed I had gone quiet and turned briefly to look at me.

'Oh, you're off again,' she said, 'That didn't take long.' She decided to listen more carefully to her Monteverdi, and drive on in her watchful way.

SIX ... The inn.

IN the run up to the sixteenth century the people of Crondall were living at a time when the power and unity of the Roman Catholic Church was being confronted by increasingly disenchanted devotees, outraged by the growing misbehaviour of a number of the clerical community. The matter came to a head with the forceful statements of a German priest. Nearly twenty years before Henry VIII's rejection of Rome, in 1517, in Wittenburg, along the river Elbe, Martin Luther pinned to All Saints Castle Church door, his Ninety-Five Theses against the selling of Indulgences. It was a matter he insisted be embraced by the Church to make it a respected and respectable establishment once again. He argued that the selling of Indulgences to sinners to buy forgiveness and redemption was not acceptable. Whilst there were indeed many clerics throughout Christian Europe who led simple, caring lives, giving themselves to God and their religion, there were also others who were taking advantage of their privileged situation. The church owned and controlled one third of all property and land in England and was supported by tithes, a ten percent payment by everyone of their annual benefit from food, crops, business and money. This paid for the upkeep of feeding, housing and administering an expanding church ... but was a tempting opportunity for those clerics with an eye to the main chance, and not many scruples. Selling of Indulgences had no place for Luther, forgiveness was in the gift of God, it had nothing to do with money. England was not unaffected, indeed King Henry VIII had used the development for his own ends, and in the small, remote village of Crondall, 60 miles from Court, the situation created only uncertainty, confusion and apprehension. The rector and church wardens were unsure whether church adornments were permissible or not.

After the chat with the rector, Henry and Jane were careful to offer a show of religiosity in church before rector and Jesus Christ, though in reality their commitment wavered due to the uncertain, changing climate created by the King. For Henry Gunner church was an opportunity for him to ponder, he even commented to Jane that it was exactly the place to ponder. In the presence of God and Jesus, Henry thought about his life, the village, the Lord of the Manor, the Royal Court. In just a few short years the Pope had, as it were, been dismissed, Chancellor Thomas More executed, the Lesser Monasteries dissolved. Queen Catherine had died, Queen Anne executed soon after, and then religious rebels marched on London (and were executed for their pains). Within a year a new queen, Jane, died. It seemed the whole court was damned … and maybe the king, even though it was said he was devout and religious. It was confusing, and ominous. Some villagers said that King Henry VIII's father had only emerged as king after settling differences amongst the nobles at court with battles in many, many parts of England. Could the unsettled court of Henry Gunner's time affect Crondall?

Henry looked around at the congregation, for some sign, some help, but there was just a hundred or so silent people all with heads turned attentively to the pulpit, the main body packed closely together with those few at the top of the village hierarchy comfortably seated at the front. They seemed like sheep feeding in the meadow, or crows on a field after ploughing.

His eyes flitted around the church, to the monuments of the great and good. Expensive images of remembrance which marked the engagement of the church in praying for the commemorated, to provide a blessed after life for their departed souls. Henry knew he was one of those who wouldn't have a monument. The wealthy could buy their way to salvation but the poor had only work-effort to achieve that end. Had Henry, and his family, worked hard enough? His eyes drifted pensively up to the cruck roof timbers and he saw the pleasing geometry of graceful curves and complex angles which created dramatic light and shadow, bounced here and there by sun shining through the side aisle windows. The creativity he saw brought calm to his mind, offering satisfaction, fulfilment, and Henry wondered whether it had some God given abstract meaning. As if to celebrate the moment, a wonderfully coloured moth fluttered into a shaft of sunlight from the window behind the altar. Its meandering flight seemed to seal a mystical moment of fulfilment.

After church it was routine that most of the labourers and their families would tip out to the village inn, the complementary landmark at the other end of the village track from the noted chestnut 'candle' tree. In the distant past it had been a stone and thatch building that had once housed the church's animals for the winter. As the church developed its estate, it was converted into a somewhat isolated house for visiting friars then, as time brought further change, the church lost interest and the village embraced what had become a dilapidated building. When King Henry took things over it was dismissed altogether as beyond recovery ... except to a more enterprising person.

At the now renovated inn, Bessy, an outgoing young widow, and a small ball of contented energy, had moved in some years before, following the death of her young husband from tuberculosis. It was no surprise that she had previously started a successful small brewing operation in an outbuilding of their old home, it was in the blood, her grandmother had been voted in as the ale taster because she was a stickler on measures and quality. For generations the family had held the village ale taster role. So, at the old church animal pen, Bessy bartered beer for building work and materials, with men who were unsuspecting of another of her talents, wheeling and dealing, and Bessy developed an outlet in the village that denied any potential competition, and had difficulty in keeping up with demand. It looked very inviting in a clearing beside the small beech wood where Henry and Jane had managed to get a log-seat.

Henry pronounced on his church reflection. 'As I was looking up, I was wondering why it is said in the bible, that we are the flock.' He raised his hand to gesture at the people scattered around, some standing, some sitting on the ground, others on yet more logs, or fallen trees. All of them had come from the church a couple of hundred yards away.

'We are the flock, the sheep,' he said, 'We put our head down, feed, look for food, like them ...'

Jane waited for him to expand on what he had said, but nothing came. It was apparently supposed to be a fundamental truth.

Their two older children, Edward and Isabella, with small jugs of ale, were sitting on straggly, overgrown grass at the edge of the approach path and playing dice with small cubes of wood, scrounged from the village carpenter. The 'Giggly Gunners' were playing with dye-coloured cherry stones with their friends, watched by young Philip. They were all well behaved in spite of (maybe because of)

Henry's lugubrious disposition. Interaction between the parents was based on understanding each of the other, which gave the family a consolidating strength, a model for the children and resilience for an ongoing family. The villagers said the reason Henry and Jane got on was because they were opposites and complemented each other. Whatever, the children managed the ups and downs of life without being too fractious. The loss of three further children soon after their births, before they had acquired the resources to survive, did not undermine the general contentment of the family, deaths being accepted as acts of God, a part of the pattern of life.

Jane looked at Henry. She'd heard the sheep sort of comment more than once. 'Maybe we are the sheep, but have to go on.'

'Why.'

'Because.'

'That's not an answer.'

Jane's face broke into a mischievous smile, 'So that we don't end up as smoked lamb.'

Henry smiled back, 'That is as good an answer as any.'

Jane hooked her arm into his. 'Exactly.' She looked nice and relaxed without her work apron, wearing a small plum coloured bodice over her kirtle, which she had adorned with an ochre waist band that showed off her womanly shape. 'And we can be well pleased, we had a little victory with the rector and the tithes.'

'...little.'

'It goes with all the other little blessings, look at them.' Jane pointed to all the children, now running, hiding, talking ... just being happy. Then Isabella did her familiar, wicked impersonation of Widow Margaret's walk – stooping, with neck thrust forward and moving at speed, unstoppable, knocking dice and hats aside. The dice players protested and 'Widow Margaret' waved a dismissive hand before, dead eyed, she made the sign of the cross over the group.

Henry smilingly took in the activity, it was life affirming, and he tugged Jane's arm more closely into his. 'And you're a little blessing too,' he said.

'There you are then,' Jane said, 'Nothing to get moody about.'

Almost as if to underline the lighter tone, one of the crowd started playing the pipe and tabor, the pipe with left hand, and the tabor, strapped over his shoulder, with right. He wore a tightly sleeved shirt to prevent interference with his instruments, and a stocking hat which was nodded clear of the eyes to essay a little jig. He couldn't avoid responding to the beat of his own music. His appropriately lively, weather-beaten face had a shaggy, untidy beard that looked as if it would hide a meal of bread crumbs.

A couple of late-comers from the church, a man and woman, were just arriving down the track and on hearing the music started to skip towards the main group.

They had a call from Bessy, 'Two jugs?'

'I thought you'd never ask,' replied the man.

'I'll have a big jug,' said the woman.

At the edge of the crowd a couple of happy old men, torn stockings, stained breeches, patched jerkins, battered hats, were sitting on what the village knew as Arthur and Stephen's log. They were being observed through the chatting drinkers by a pair of gaunt faced women, a well known village duo. One said, 'Arthur's not that old, I don't see why he should be on parish relief, he should work.'

The pair were given to much smug head nodding as they dissected the character of their fellow villagers. One given to complaining a lot and known as Nag, the other tended to wag her fingers a lot so the pair were known, behind their backs, as Naggy and Waggy. 'He gets up to all sorts to get his ale,' Waggy said softly, pointing to the jug she was holding for emphasis.

'I can't blame him for that, our river water gave my stomach a real turn out last week.' Naggy had a pained face.

'It's still not right,' Waggy said.

The women were enjoying their own jugs of ale, and breathing well fuelled fumes over each other as they leant forward to whisper confidentially.

'He's a slippery customer, that Arthur. Gets round those church people,' Naggy said with edge.

Unaware that their characters were being gently down-graded, Arthur and Stephen were taping their gnarled walking sticks on the ground to the music when they were approached by a couple of young men, also responding to the music. The sequence had happened before, many times. The old men offered their sticks, bystanders cleared a space, and the young men cracked the sticks together just once. They untied their ragged neckerchiefs, and assembled for a Morris dance. An ageing onlooker gathered her shawl around herself, and twitched her branch-crutch rhythmically. Her companion held on to the arm of her tunic to feel the movement, smiling sightlessly towards the musician who, his three fingers flying over the pipe holes, had increased the beat. The skipping couple jigged through the inn crowd to join the young men and the four achieved some semblance of a Morris dance routine, cheered and clapped on by the well oiled Arthur and Stephen and the other villagers ... except for Naggy and Waggy.

'Not sheep,' Jane said as she nodded at the performers.

'That's right, but it's only a little change, for a little while.'

'Ohhh ... you!' Jane exclaimed.

'... and so it goes on,' Henry added.

'It does', Jane thought, but didn't reply, she didn't want to invite conversation about an endless subject. 'And will continue to go on,' she thought, 'So what? But things do change. We had a Roman Church once, now we have an English one, things change, but we go on.' Jane put her arm on his shoulder, like she must have done many times with her children. 'What am I going to do with you?' she said.

'Help with the harvest again tomorrow.'

'Ha!' Jane expostulated.

Henry wasn't one of the world's happiest of spirits, but he cared and could turn his hand to almost anything. 'Come on, let's go, I've still got to make the basket I promised the rector for Lammas Day and we've got another long day tomorrow.' Henry downed his ale.

Jane followed suit. 'I suppose so.'

'I dread first light and hustling to get to the fields,' Henry said.

Jane had other worries. 'I dread having to wake up the children these early mornings, they find it hard to rouse themselves.'

'Yes,' said Henry reflectively, 'But they'll get used to it, like we did.'

Henry gestured to the children, time to go. They started their trek back and left an English village scene of Breugel-like festivity, with its boisterous dancing and the odd consequential coupling in nearby bushes to follow.

SEVEN ... The village.

THE Gunner family was straggling past the green heading for the delights of home - a one room wattle and daub place, with hearth in the middle and just four rush beds, thus topping and tailing was essential. Seating was provided by a bench, stacked with three legged stools, the only way to manage the minimal space being to keep things out of the way until needed. A single rough-hewn table provided the facility for food preparation and storage, with space taken for pots of berries, beans, nuts and a larger unit used for preserving meat and/or fish when some scarce salt became available. Each item was covered to protect from rats and mice, especially the pot covering any rare home-made cheese. A wooden bucket of water was underneath for general usage. The dangling chain directly above the central hearth provided the means for smoking a joint of meat or fish, when it became available. Sacking curtain round the parent's bed aimed to provide privacy. The manor had recently allowed Henry to negotiate a copyhold tenancy, and make repairs to a hovel that had been unoccupied after a death without an inheritance claim, when it had reverted to the lord. Henry's overcrowded previous abode had been a permitted add-on to his parent's place and when he moved out, other siblings immediately moved in. But the overcrowding was only eased, not solved. With grown children, Henry and Jane would need to confront another housing issue before long.

Across the green Grumpy Eleanor, an aging, harassed woman, threw a bucket of water outside her hovel, splat. An enlarged puddle was evidence of similar previous actions. She put the bucket outside the entrance, took hold of her besom standing by the entrance and went inside, 'I've told you more than once I've got to do the floor,' the voice faded and was lost. 'Don't put that on, you'll make it smokey, use the beechwood,' suddenly erupted and a mumble followed before, 'And you can clear the mess outside.' It was quiet for a moment. Then a young boy was ejected from the hovel, 'Make it look decent or the village will be after us.' The boy stumbled to a stop, looked impassively at the water, and stood debating how to avoid any course of action. Grumpy Eleanor's hovel was built on an ancient sunken hut site and whilst the floor cavity helped to provide wall strength, that had to be set against the difficulty of floor cleaning. Grumpy Eleanor was famous for her sharp tongue, but her adherence to village strictures was appreciated.

Beyond the green could be seen a network of paths and the extensive raggle taggle of assorted surrounding fields, worked and un-worked, with crops or fallow, in an incomprehensible pattern. A view in any direction provided Henry and Jane with a daily reminder of the labour intensive life they led. Alongside Grumpy Eleanor's continued complaining could be heard Arthur's and Stephen's disordered singing on their way home from the inn. The sound carried beyond the fields to entertain the animals in the wastes, some with hedges or wattle fences. In the track that meandered past the green was no shortage of gouges filled with water that had not evaporated. The bailiff had assigned the thresher, Luke Wood, to make good the holes but he had had an accident with the flail, so hovel slops and other dubious substances fed the stagnant water, to provide a breeding ground for mosquitoes and fly maggots.

All villages were self-contained communities with almost all needs to sustain basic life provided local craftsmen. They all had a manor court for village management and Crondall meetings were held in the Tithe Barn, with elected freeholders to supervise decisions. Here items like crop rotation, fallow field choices and the like, were voted on by the whole village. Henry tended to support the majority because it was seldom that much was gained by changing established routines. The court was chaired by the lord or his steward, with bailiff and reeve as village officers. The main controlling agency however was the self contained village itself because poor tracks and minimal means of transport discouraged travel. It was like an open prison. But in fact a trek up to the top of the local landmark, Dora's Mount, offered a view of the outside world – the market town of Farnham and its imposing castle, where unavailable items in the village could be found, and those having holdings with spare capacity could sell their superfluous produce. Henry never thought it worth the trouble to visit Farnham because it was four miles way. Crondall was just one of hundreds of equally self-sustaining habitations, each a functioning co-operative, without which effort the community foundered.

Jane and Henry walked further on in silence, broken only by the sound of village life – crying babies, banging (some sort of repair activity), cocks squawking, distant sheep, and Arthur singing incoherently as he tottered past. Stephen had disappeared. Arthur belatedly noticed the couple and attempted a bow, 'My Lord. My Lady.' Henry raised a hand in acknowledgement and said simply, 'Arthur.' Jane had been wondering about meals at the manor hall when she noticed, as mums do, that young Phillip had started to head towards some bushes beyond the hovels.

Jane called, 'Phillip!'

The young boy stopped and turned and Jane walked over to him bent down and said quietly, 'If you're going for a squat, can you wait until we get right back? We've got some nice fresh grass dad brought back, it's much better for cleaning yourself.'

He was pleased to hear the news, 'He's good at finding soft stuff.'

'He is,' Jane said simply.

'Do you know where he goes?'

Jane rustled his hair. 'No. You know your dad.'

Phillip dashed off clear of them and Jane hooked her arm into Henry's as she rejoined him at the entrance to their hovel just in time to see a mouse scatter near the hearth. It was a good place to scavenge for fallen food, or had the creature had a whiff of the cheese hiding under the rough earthenware bowl, Jane wondered. Outside, the jollification at the inn could still be heard clearly in the quiet country air. It would go on for some time. It was probable that other musicians would turn up, a recorder player, and the village fiddler. They knew of the limited tonal range of the pipe and tabor and that the player would be in need of their support. The village, like any other, was self-sufficient in all talents and the variegated life of Crondall would continue, as in other places … and at other times.

EIGHT ... George gets home.

FAINT music could be heard coming from the house, music that falls gently on the ears, Miles Davis circa 1950s. In leaving an MP3 running when she went to pick me up from the hospital, Pam planned that nice relaxed music would greet the returning patient. And I appreciated the gesture.

'The man, Mister Cool' I said as I opened the front door.

'I thought you'd like it.'

'Home. No place like it.' I made a bee-line down the hall into the sitting room and my armchair. Nice familiar surroundings after my hospital experience. I wondered about my forbears who preceded Henry and Jane. There had been so much political in-fighting before King Henry VIII. Could it have involved my Gunners in Crondall? There had been the Wars of the Roses and wars with the French. The family had so much to contend with - mud-brick housing, a poor unvaried diet, inadequate clothing, the usual changeable weather, and as for health … lucky me again, in a couple of days I'll have a check-up and be prescribed medication.

Pam called out. 'You sit down, and I'll bring you a nice cup of tea.' She had put the kettle on and was taking off her coat off to throw temporarily over the newel post.

I called back. 'Do I want tea? This is a celebration.'

'And we'll celebrate with a cup of tea,' Pam said firmly.

'Yes boss,' I replied and threw my coat onto the sofa.

Pam was in the kitchen and I settled into my nice, well upholstered armchair in the sitting room. There was something reassuring about the comfort which it offered. That single seat was a symbol of the security and protection provided by the whole house. I was doubly sensitive to my surroundings after my experiences of the last two or three days. The house really did seem to offer relaxation and reassurance, helped by the colour tones of curtains and upholstery which were subtly muted, not confronting. The timber beams were a grain-lined and dusty black, contrasted by casement windows offering aging off-white. Whilst it was true that the house could be rather dark without bright sun, well placed lighting actually encouraged a feeling of warmth and homeliness. Small rooms, rather low ceilings and good draft control, also helped make our home cosy and comfortable.

Pam returned with a tray of tea things, including baklava. She poured the tea for both of us and offered me half a baklava. 'This is what you celebrate with, your favourite,' she said.

'That's more naughty than alcohol,' I expostulated.

'Only half, and half for me. Just this once. Then you'll have to be a good boy. It seems we'll have to be very careful about diet and exercise from now on.'

'We'll see,' I said challengingly.

Pam was serious and firm. 'We will if I have anything to do with it.'

I held up my arms before my face protectively, 'Oooo, that's very dominant. Do you do bossy mistress?'

'I'm serious George, I spoke to the doctor at length. It's time to ease off a bit.'

'Don't worry, I've been into sport for a long time. I know about how to keep the body in good shape … in good times and bad.'

'It's your head I worry about not your body, it sometimes leads you astray.'

'That I admit, it can lead me in the wrong direction, but … at the same time it can send me in the right direction to good advantage.'

'That, _I_ have to admit.' Pam started off to the kitchen again. 'Need napkins for the baklava.'

'It's probably why I had a good time in hospital … no, interesting time, would be a better description.'

But Pam had gone.

Later, when I had re-established my affection for the whole house, I stepped into the conservatory to get a good look at the whole garden. Clematis and roses were tied back onto the trellis attached to the house walls, and flowers were coming through here and there. Pam had had the grass mowed, the borders were neat, and the weeding up-to-date. I calculated that she must have made a point of getting everything top notch to prevent me from tackling any physical work. I could see the bottom of the garden - there were the offending paving slabs lying across a pile of others, broken. I must have lifted them up, and dropped them. Well, it looked as though I'd have to get in a handy man, or a gardener, or both. Looking on the bright side, it could even be a chance to exchange some ideas and maybe get a better looking garden. It wasn't bad as it was, especially when the sun was out in the summer. Even at a distance, I could see that there was something that was not quite spot on … a chat with an expert could be just the job. And then - sitting and relaxing in the nice garden in the sun, with blue sky, soft breeze, birds twittering, a glass of wine … heaven. If it was allowed! That was definitely the course to take, lifting heavy things, getting hands dirty, not to mention, cut, bruised, bitten by insects, spiked by thorns, stung be nettles … who wants it? The paid gardener!

A gentle voice wafted from the sitting room, 'I've got my eye on you!'

I turned back to look into the sitting room, 'Of course. You can't trust that husband of yours anywhere.'

'I was tempted to get all paving mess done and out of the way but I don't know what layout you've planned ...' and she added with firmness as she joined me, '… to tell your gardener when he comes.'

'I don't think that I know the final layout. I keep changing my mind.'

'So get an expert in.'

'Sounds sensible.'

Pam pointed to the bottom of the garden, 'Not allowed,' she said.

'What is allowed?'

'Taking wives out for a nice dinner - of the salad variety.'

'Sounds good to me.' And I added, 'The husband will put on his going-out-to-dinner togs.'

A STORY of RICHARD & JOAN
in LATE MEDIEVAL DAYS.
(George is pensive.)

ONE ... Richard.

Richard Gunner, or le Grannar, thought himself to be a lucky man, even though he lived alone in a fourteenth century hovel. It was on the edge of a hamlet called Ewshot, within the parish and Hundred of Crundell. To go to church he had to make a trek of a mile or so to Crundell village, but the demand was not onerous on an active young man who kept himself to himself. The hundred was a Saxon administrative area that contained many villages and was assessed as being able to support a hundred hides, a hundred family units. Crundell was the word for chalk pit, a word which over time had a make-over and became Crondall.

Richard's hovel was a simple round hut dominated by a large sloping straw roof, a cone framework of rafters meeting centrally and sitting on a complex arrangement of stake walls, all in turn worked with wattle and hazel poles. The structure had resulted from repairs and patches over a long period of time. But it provided tolerable and effective shelter for Richard after he found himself alone when the last of his fading parents had died. He had made further repairs of the walls with hazel, mud, dung and straw, and the roof with a rush and turf mix. But this was only after making late payment of the heriot, the transfer of ownership tax to the lord, and the recording of the bond in the manor rolls. In these negotiations his undemanding character had encouraged the sympathetic support of the Ewshott village leaders. The hovel soon resembled others when it gained matching moss and lichen.

Richard hadn't had much time to get really close to his parents, or to any of his siblings, because his parents were dead by the time he was eleven years old, and any potential surrogate parents within the extended family had their own problems to deal with and work obligation to fulfil. So after his older sister got married and his younger brother succumbed to typhoid, Richard had been left to fend for himself. He learned at an early age that only by hard work could he get the things that he needed.

His family was known to be good and reliable workers and their reputation opened doors for Richard to get work experience, and he discovered a special talent as a carpenter. His reliable and efficient work became noted by the lord's steward, via the miller, then further afield within the Crundell Hundred. He became known for his woodworking skills but spent a great deal of time at the Ewshott manor mill. The whole wheel function really needed replacing and Richard was constantly required to keep the float boards, the cog work, indeed the whole lot in good working order.

'You'd think, with the money the lord makes from us all, he'd get a new wheel,' said the miller in forthright mood. The pair of them had been standing under the sail looking at the latest repair. They had to raise their voices above the slurp and splash of the mill waters.

'I've done the float boards, you'll be all right,' Richard replied, with his raggy work apron on. It was an item the miller had given him when Richard had once torn his tunic working at the mill and the garment was essential protection for his only tunic and leggings. His straw hat was something he could more easily make himself.

The miller remained worried. 'Will it be up to a fast flowing river in the winter rains?'

'Have I ever let you down?' Richard smiled reassuringly.

'No. We're lucky, having you.'

Richard waved him away as if to say, 'It's nothing.'

'I sometimes feel that the lord takes advantage of you.'

'I don't mind,' said Richard, 'All these repairs give me work.'

'It really needs a complete rebuild. How would you like to make a whole new one?!'

'What a thought. What a job.' Richard was almost overwhelmed by the very idea.

The miller moved away from the noise of the splashing waters.

'No chance. The lord spends all his money on eating, feasting and floods of visitors. I'm surprised there's any animals left around here, they eat anything that moves that lot. They'd eat us if they didn't need us for work ...' He paused, but hadn't quite done justice to his discontent, '... and they all dress up as if they are at the king's court.'

'They have to don't they?'

'... and they don't speak like us ... all going on in French, don't understand what they're talking about half the time.'

'Don't worry, I'll keep your mill going, we can make the coffers tick over for the steward, and we can have a happy lord of the manor.'

'It's not the steward that makes me tetchy, it's the Crundell mill. They're trying to pinch our customers.'

'I thought they <u>had</u> to come here,' Richard said, '... manor custom.'

'You'd think so. They've got Crundell, we've got Ewshott. But their miller is up to something. I think he's got some sort of fiddle going.'

'How? You're not supposed to change the manor payments system.'

'Maybe not ... unless the steward is in on it.'

Richard was surprised. 'The steward, well ...'

'There's not that many straight ones around.'

'But our steward ...'

'Stewards, bailiffs, reeves, they're all at it.'

'I didn't think ... '

The miller remained in blunt mood. 'I hope their float boards break down in the winter and then we'll see.' He kicked a loose stone from the track into the water, plop. 'They'll slip up sooner or later, and get caught out.' The miller put a comradely arm round Richard's shoulder. 'And we've got the best carpenter.' The slurp and splash of the mill gurgled on.

Richard's compliant character made him easy to work with and he did well out of the relationship with the miller who spread the word of his good work amongst his contacts. At certain seasons of the year he had too much work, with mattocks, axes, hammers, hoes and ploughs needing replacement parts of the right size and shape of wood. The miller seemed to feel that Richard had some God given, innate ability and was impressed by his dexterity and care, and noticed especially his commitment, even obsession, with the need to have good 'cross grain joints', because of 'wood movement'. When Richard explained about the 'tongues', 'shoulders', 'cheeks' of the

180

joints that were apparently all over the mill, the miller was agog. His commitment to his craft carried over to the matter of appearance. He had an equal pre-occupation with grain pattern, because he felt his work had to look good as well as work well, qualities that came to the notice of the church which sometimes commissioned him to take on work and even do some ornamental carving. The overall result was that Richard's talent enabled him to get by without the need to fulfil all his day-labour demesne obligations, which he could swap with some villagers for his carpentry skills, because repairs to tools and hovels were an on-going need. His father, Simon, had been forced to do much extra day-work to make ends meet and Richard often thought that this was a factor in his father's demise, coming on top of long exhausting days of physical labour in the fields as part of his villein obligation.

Richard's life, like all peasant labourers, was from boyhood to the end dictated by the seasons. It was little different from animals that only altered their actions and habits to suit the changing conditions of the year. The season, the month, brought changes in the atmosphere, and the earth and the vegetation which dictated the working life. Thus was the whole life of the villein, a routine year of root and seed crops, hoeing, haymaking, harvesting, then another, and another. A simple life, a healthy life and a happy life for some souls.

It was the miller who jokingly called him Richard le Grannar because of his pre-occupation with wood grain, and the name stuck to register in the mind at large. In time the villagers came to know him simply as Richard Gunner because of the lazy misspelling of the reeve or his clerk when totting up the tithes of the lord of the manor.

Although Richard had an innate ability, his working life was really an activity to fill loneliness. As a diversion he made the odd implement and ornament, and even sold some things, but he also had an unfinished project, an idea that came to him when idly looking at church windows during Sunday church. Richard decided to make windows and a door for his hovel and he spent more time inspecting window construction at church than attending to the service. Good fitting ones would offer better weather protection than rush screens or animal skins. However he still spent much of his non-working time in his hovel asleep, either because he was tired or, in the winter after sunset, there was generally nothing else to do in his doubtful rush-light. Occasionally, in the utter darkness and quiet of a lonely winter night he would welcome the sight of a thatch roof fire, in Farnham a few miles away. There was something in the punctured blackness that offered companionship, though Richard felt bad about the damage caused to, or even loss of someone's life.

In fact it was in the darkness of night, that his loneliness acquired a different character. He could enjoy night life - to the company of nocturnal sounds. When the activities of the day reduced almost to silence, he could listen to the urgently flapping wings of bats, which roosted in the ruins of the old castle a short distance away. There was also the rustle of animals in the undergrowth, and all the grunts and squeaks of night life, especially the puffing and scratching of lumbering badgers, which left behind deep holes as evidence of their frequent visits. Even the gentle hiss of wind in the trees seemed like music, and storm winds were drama. But most of all Richard listened out for the barn owls, his favourite, who did a good job keeping down the rodent population. He found the bold call of the creature on a crisp night pleasing, even life-reaffirming in a way. Maybe the owl's tendency to be a bit of a loner matched Richard's inclinations. It did not make a furtive sound, but something friendly, wanting to communicate, maybe like Richard really behind his outward reticence. He wished he could respond to the owl ... hear about living in a little nest, keeping it nice, working to get food, and finding a partner to get more little owls.

In some ways it seemed that Richard le Grannar, or Gunner, wanted nothing from life, and just went unthinkingly about it, like the animals he lived alongside - birds, deer, bees, rabbits, butterflies, boars. Richard was just like them, except that he didn't spend so much time scavenging and chasing for meals, and he enjoyed their company. He had a particular daytime delight in the scratchy chatter of the yellow hammer which used to greet him almost as soon as he appeared at his hovel doorway early in the day. Richard always said, 'Good morning,' as he started his walk to work, but the little chap would stop his song, only to then start up again when he had flown to what he calculated was a safe distance.

As with the need to work to provide for himself, through his experiences growing up, Richard had learned how to feed from all that he found in abundance around him, cooking as and when required. His hovel always had a fire at the ready with a battered old iron pot that had come to him from some dead family member or other when he had first settled in.

'This really belongs to you by rights,' a distant relative had said, suddenly appearing outside the hovel one day struggling with the item.

Richard was surprised. 'Does it?'

As soon as he had put the pot down, the relative, a dishevelled boy of maybe thirteen or fourteen, was able to have a good wipe of his productive nostrils with the back of his hand and transfer the deposit onto the bottom of his tunic. He was somewhat under-fed, but obviously a lively character, he kept shuffling from one leg to the other. 'Made by our blacksmith my mum said,' he said.

'Thanks. How are we connected?

'I think your mum's a cousin of my mum, or something. I don't know, I just get on with things.'

Richard hadn't quite known how to respond to that so he just said, 'Thanks, I'm really grateful.'

The relative seemed reluctant to go. 'My mum told me to bring it over.' He shuffled from one foot to the other.

'Well, say thanks to her too please.'

'She said that you have to do things like that to get to heaven.'

'Oh did she?' Richard couldn't think of what else to say.

'Yeah.' The boy gave a huge sniff. 'And everyone wants to get to heaven.'

'I think they do.'

The pair stood looking at each other, neither saying anything for a moment, then Richard said, 'Where are you from?'

'Farnham way.' He had yet another wipe of his nose and another wipe of his tunic.

'Bit of a distance.'

'No. I like walking ... you see things.'

Richard realised he was talking to another loner, one who had something he wanted to say, 'Oh yes?' he said.

'Saw a man in Crondall on a horse, trying to buy wool and sell tunics. And yesterday, in Farnham, I saw players by the castle, there were monks and guilds and a procession and a juggler and singing ...' his eyes shone brightly.

'That was good.'

'I didn't see it all 'cos I had to get back to help my dad, but the bit I saw was about the three wise men going to see baby Jesus.'

'You were lucky.'

'I was. It was serious and made you worried, and then funny bits made people laugh, everyone was looking.'

'Where did they come from, these players?'

'I don't know. Some of them talked funny, but it didn't matter because the sounds of the words matched. Made you listen.'

'That's poetry I think,' Richard suggested.

There was another pause and then the boy said, 'It was good,' and ambled off, satisfied he had been able to tell of his adventures. Richard, back to his usual lonely self, wondered whether the boy's shuffling and final exit was because he wanted to relieve himself.

He was looking reflectively at the old iron pot, which he filled daily with useable leftovers, and, given his good relations with the miller and access to the manor oven, he was never short of bread. His decent diet went alongside the well exercised and fit life of a man with a predilection for work and so he presented to the world a strong and well shaped individual in his mid-twenties. His face was, unsurprisingly, an inscrutable mask, and even his greetings with the miller were such that they did not invite a long exchange about the state of the world ... or even the state of the weather. Staring at the old iron pot made Richard think about the broken old skillet he kept hanging from the roof. He remembered what his father had said to him as a very little boy, something that stuck in his mind, so it must have been important.

'Remember to get, and look after, all your iron things because only the blacksmith can make them. Anything else you need you can do for yourself.'

It was good advice, it seemed to direct him to his life as a carpenter because the basic material he needed, wood, he could easily get.

TWO ... Home change.

THE annihilating crisis known as the Great Pestilence turned out to be the making of Richard. His years of self-sufficiency had developed in him a good idea of personal safety, and his lifestyle kept him clear of potential danger ... by keeping his distance. As a growing number of people in Ewshot died in 1348 following the appearance of sores or boils under arms and under groins, Richard thought it would be wise to get away. He bumped into the steward outside the mill one day and his concern was so great that he, for once, acted out of character, and blurted out his concern. In some ways they were similar characters, the steward was not a gregarious person and also kept his distance, but he was terse rather than gentle, and spat words rather than spoke them.

'I want to get away from here,' Richard said.

'How can you do that?' The steward asked.

'The village is cursed.'

'You've got your work obligation on the desmesne.'

The remark brought Richard up and in the quiet the slosh and splatter of the mill seemed to hiss at him.

'But if I go to somewhere like Crundell I can still come back here and do it.'

'A hundred days a year!? And maybe another hundred days over there ...'

'Yes but I can do some swaps, and ...' Richard didn't get that far.

'And how will you find another place to live?' His beady eyes seemed to pierce Richard like an arrow.

'I've been able to get along all my life so ...'

'No, it can't be done. I've got my contract with the lord. All you people have to do your quota, that's how things are done.' The tone of his voice was challenging, he matched the rush of water through the mill.

Richard became more conciliatory. 'I heard the miller over there said they were not cursed like here.'

'Lucky them,' the steward said and strode off. It seemed he was in a grumpy mood ... or maybe Richard's miller friend was right, there was something going on.

The matter nagged at his sleep at night so he made an exploratory trip to Crondall, where he found an empty hovel in a state of disrepair. He was now in a quandary, should he respond to the fatal mayhem back in Ewshott and go? Would it be possible, when the lord's manor covered both villages, and the steward's authority with it?

Back in Ewshot the Great Pestilence plague had taken many of those in the centre of the village, especially the old and the young. There was a feeling that the village been sent the disease as punishment for having offended God by not fulfilling an ordained civil obligation – the prompt payment of ransom to free the lord of the manor when he was captured by the French during the campaign of King Edward III. Their late collection of taxes had procured His wrath. On top of that was the idea that the aggregate of non-church goers had increased before the plague and had been noticed by Him. Others felt it was because of the number of unsanctified couplings on the lists for the church courts. There was also the thought that the coincidence of all these transgressions at the same time may have been unlucky, and became noticeable by Him, and He thought it was the last straw. The village leaders calculated that the unfortunate simultaneous occurrence of these misdeeds meant they must devise some sort monitoring system that could forewarn of such a looming juxtaposition.

(The miller had overheard the lord of the manor, Sir Michel du Bec, say he had not been happy about his ransomed return to England because he had so enjoyed French knightly hospitality. He thought the French had such a better understanding of the chivalric code.)

Richard himself wondered whether God knew that his church visits coincided with cold, rain, and windy weather ... and even hot weather when the cool of the church was welcome respite. But as he hadn't contracted the illness he assumed that either God had somehow missed this, or maybe He was so busy dealing with all the sin ... or maybe Richard's diligent working life had compensated for the church thing.

Shortly after his exchange with the steward, Richard had cause to wonder the complete opposite ... that maybe God had sent him a different message. The steward was one of those who fell to the Plague and Richard thought the timing must have been significant. He debated whether it meant he should be doing something, but he dithered about exactly what. However, when the toll of deaths in Ewshott became so worrisome, and a that number of villagers started to leave, Richard decided to go too, and take a chance.

All he took with him was his bed sacking and a coarse blanket, spun and woven by an old widow woman in exchange for a pair of stools he had made for her. He took his rough earthenware drinking pots, wooden platters and cutlery, his repaired throw-outs. He stuffed those items into the bed sacking. His treasured iron skillet, and cooking pot containing sundry small items, he put carefully into a hole under some discouraging hawthorns, covering with leaves. Leaving his home was a wrench, he knew it wasn't much but it was a part of him, it completed him. The feeling was so strong that he provided protection for 'his' home - a lovingly carved, closely grained, lime wood image of St. Thomas the Apostle, the patron saint of builders. Richard looked at it tenderly as he recalled the difficulty he had carving the arm which was raised in blessing before he placed it securely to look down and do its guarding job from an adjacent ivy covered oak tree. Even if overgrown, protection would be given. Richard started the trek to Crondall wondering if his things, his possessions, his friends, would have the same re-affirming effect in a new place.

He went to the empty hovel he had found in Crondall village. It was on a small decent plot of land on the edge of some wastes, and had a proper timber frame, unlike the rickety basic structure that he had left in Ewshott. It was in a bad state of repair but had potential. There was a robin chirruping busily around the structure and its liveliness lifted his spirits. A few young trees had taken advantage of recent inactivity, oaks, hazels, ash, beech, hawthorn had all found ground on which to establish themselves. On arrival he checked that the place was clear of any rat holes, knowing well about the menace of rats as did anyone who was familiar with a mill. Richard noticed it had an unused, dank smell but, he thought with a smile, 'I'll soon give it my own smells'. Satisfied with what he saw, he tentatively moved in.

When he was reasonably straight, Richard quickly made a point of speaking to a man he had seen foraging in the area several times, sometimes for food, sometimes for fuel. Richard called out to him across the scrubby ground outside because he needed information but he kept his distance as he'd overheard a conversation the previous week in which it was said that some chicks had died when a plague-affected person had breathed on them.

'Know anything about this place?' he said.

All the man did was gesture, thumb pointing down to the ground.

Richard acknowledged that he understood. 'Ah.'

'They all died. Plague.' The man was a drab, hunched, put-upon sort of man and looked ill which was worrisome. Richard had thought Crondall was not subject to God's blight.

The man went on, 'Take it. I would.'

The place suddenly seemed to represent a threat in that time of falling population,

'It was weeks ago, with sick and dying, no one knew what was going on.' Richard felt that the tone of the man's voice sounded dispiriting, as if he felt doomed, but Richard was a practical man and saw the hovel as a roof over his head. He also recalled that his move seemed to have been backed by God's design. 'There was no family with any rights to it so the lord claimed it,' the man added, not sounding doomed after all.

Richard turned away to pensively look into the inside. He knew the lord of the manor would hear of his actions, and he would have to answer for his boldness. But with the steward now out of the way ... Richard immediately stopped debating with himself, the very idea shocked him and he regretted such an uncharitable thought. He now looked penetratingly into the dark then turned back to speak to the man but he had disappeared further into the scrub with his latest pickings. Richard recalled, with a grimace, that the man had kept his distance too. He must have thought that maybe Richard, coming from plague-affected Ewshott, could have the disease.

The layout around the hovel suggested that at one time there had been a garden. A couple of lichen covered apple trees were evident, and a leaking barrel indicated that rain water had once been collected. The basic structure was still strong and the floor was well trodden and hard. There was even a slightly raised area on the northwest side for sleeping. On the east side, the noticeable indentations in the mud floor indicated the site of the kitchen table. The clay hearth remained intact in the centre, with stones in place to contain burning logs, and invitingly hung above was still a chain dangling for the cooking pot. A few hooks and hemp strings hung from the rafters. It was bigger than his previous place and Richard reckoned it to be un-necessarily large but after further thought he realised he could have his own making-things space inside, instead of being outside exposed to whatever weather was on offer. What's more the open space was opposite the south facing doorway, the best light source. He'd also have room for the assorted pieces of naturally shaped wood he collected for work.

Richard quickly set about the necessary repair work. There was no shortage of hazel sticks, clay, moss, straw, sandy soil, all nearby. For the roof he used more straw, some heather and a few sticks of wicker that he had found by the stream north of the village. It was a place he liked. Sometimes he spent time there in early spring watching a pair of kingfishers come and go when feeding their young in the nest on the muddy bank. Soon the interior of his new hovel could hardly be distinguished from the old, as he had gone back for his broken skillet, scavenged from the original site of the flooded Waverley Abbey, and his trusty battered iron cooking pot which he filled with sundry bits. He later collected the couple of stools he had hidden in a ditch that had provided him with clay used for mud bricks; one had been made for Widow Elizabeth who changed her mind.

On one visit back to his old Ewshott home, Richard waited for an hour for a man who was gathering sticks for firewood to go from near his old place, because he wasn't sure about how the Great Pestilence worked but thought it was safer to give it space. He was reassured when he saw disturbed ground near his old hovel, and noticed that squirrels had been hiding their winter hoard. They were obviously well and active. The locals in Crondall also gave him space, and allowed an interval to pass in order to see that he was clear of the Great Pestilence plague before he was, as it were, 'let in'. Then he was readily able to find work in the new circumstances of reduced availability of workmen. Obligatory work for the lord no longer supplied the working man-hours needed to fully work the land. To make up for the shortfall in man-power, the lord needed additional, paid, workers to fulfil his demesne farming needs.

THREE ... The Black Death.

EWSHOTT and Crondall were more or less on the route to London from the source of the plague, Weymouth, where ships from the English province of Gascony docked carrying flea infested black ship rats. The disease had made the long journey west from the Far East via trade routes to the Eastern Mediterranean and then across the continent. The contagion spread throughout the country, and in less than two years it had even started to bring death to people in Scotland. It seemed however that such a cataclysmic development did not impinge upon those supposedly running the country, they remained pre-occupied with other activities, those involving - ransom of captured noble prisoners and plunder, in both France and Scotland. All this was led by the king, Edward III, whose status as monarch at that time was reliant upon success in the battlefield, mainly in France through disputed claims to large territories. The tortuous dynastic situation between England and France, went back a long way, to William the Conqueror, with changing alliances and unresolved disagreements on both sides.

At that time, 1348, with so many deaths resulting from what became known as the Black Death, the land was in danger of being unproductive because of a shortage of workers. Those who survived, like Richard, were becoming less beholden to the lord whose position was weakened by the need for workers, and peasants found jobs easier to get and much better rewarded. The more opportunistic amongst the working community were able to manipulate concessions from manor lords, small concessions for them, but a huge gain for the newly employed who, in some enterprising cases, would go on in later years to become landowners themselves. Most stopped short of buying out of the feudal contract because whilst the work on the lord's manor lands was an irritating obligation, the lord had legal obligations, which included protection from marauders, and certain paternalistic care. One family manoeuvred their opportunities with great skill, the le Germin family, who began their growth in status with additional holdings, and sheep, at a time when English wool became the foundation of wealth of many landed families. Richard's self-interest was demonstrated in a less ambitious way. He knew the manor court officers had knowledge of him but were pre-occupied with manpower problems, and negotiated a freehold bond aided by confusion in the court rolls over whether the plot itself was in the lord's tied lands or his waste lands.

FOUR ... Night out.

MY negotiation was for booking dinner with Pam in the restaurant room of our village pub., seven and half centuries after the time of my forbear Richard's feudal dealing. It had once been the home of a late Victorian novelist, now forgotten, but in his time very successful. Thus, the structure had space for bars, restaurant and all ancillary rooms. When the writer died the property had lain untouched for a long time whilst ownership was contested. Eventually a brewing company got hold of house and contents, and used its original look to build a venue that had a wide appeal. Walls were almost lost for sepia photos of Victorian worthies, and black and white pictures of a football team c.1908, a cricket team c.1933, a tapestry group c.1954, shelves of books, heavy Victorian drapes, and here and there a glimpse of William Morris, flock wallpaper, plus the appropriate copy-lighting units of the period. The idea of the man, his time and his craft was conveyed without detracting from the potential of money earning floor space.

Our pleasant evening was one of surprisingly careful exchanges as if we were in the early stages of 'going out'. The fright of me being carted off to hospital in an ambulance as an emergency seemed to make us more sensitive to each other, as if imposing a need to re-establish our relationship. Perhaps a reaction to the fragility of life had impacted in a more meaningful way than any other event in our lives. We were both in a state of delicate sensitivity.

As Pam drove us both home, she said, 'That was really nice.'

'I agree,' I said with the satisfied look of a person fulfilled.

'A chance to get back to normal.'

'What's normal?'

'… after all the drama.'

'You could call it that.'

'Did your whole life flash before you?'

'It did, after a fashion.'

'Interesting?'

'Very.'

'I tried to find myself.'

'And did you?'

'I suppose I did … sort of.'

'Sort of potted family history was it?'

'More sort of, 'The history of Joe Bloggs'.'

We drove along with just music for while, a repeat of an old Prom. Concert before Pam resurrected the conversation. 'Yes, a happy evening I'd call that.'

'Have to have a heart attack again,' I said jokingly.

'You most certainly will not.' There was an edge in the words that suggested an undercurrent of tension. Pam had once again presented herself with exemplary taste, dressing in clothes of muted, complementary colours, her face having the attractive appeal of knowing calm resulting from acceptance of life.

'Lock me up will you?'

'If necessary.'

'Sounds interesting ...' Pam knew better than to respond to that, but I was feeling mischievous, '... is it going to be interesting?'

Pam's face gave nothing away and there was a pause before she uttered, 'What was so fascinating when your whole life flashed before you?'

'It's all locked away in my head,' I said tapping my cranium.

Our car, a C180 Mercedes, was driven into the driveway of our old timber framed house which had all the gentle curves, the lack of straight lines of a rather aged place settling onto land constantly reshaped by centuries of English weather patterns. Headlights were switched off, the engine died, and our footsteps punctured the crisp country quiet.

Later, it was still dark and the silhouette of the house could be discerned against the slightly clouded sky of gentle moonlight. At the first floor level windows emitted alight. Inside, Pam and I were in our bedroom lying back in bed, heads on pillows. We were both staring up at the ceiling in pensive mood and not speaking. It seems a night out to celebrate my return home after a dramatic rush to hospital had drained us of that day's ration of energies. We lay in one of our companionable silences. Pam waited for some physical contact, sexual or even non-sexual, but we remained utterly quiet, each with our own thoughts. Pam eventually drifted into sleep, well earned after what had been an energy sapping day. I remained wide awake, staring at the ceiling. I was at home, in my base ... once the home, the base also of others, in twentieth century, the nineteenth, the eighteenth, and back to ... someone like one of the Mosebys maybe ... someone who didn't have a car outside, central heating, and all the benefits of our time. Other forbears would have had a day out in the fields working - aching muscles, tired, hungry, cold ... or hot; to be rewarded with a draughty home, an uncomfortable bed and a repetitive diet, followed by another day of the same. Yes, I reckoned I was a lucky boy. I felt complete, at one, in tune. I'd been there, and back. There? Where? Back? Back from where? In spite of all my positive feelings there was something unsettling ... I usually thought of myself as being half-full, but now I felt as if I may have been over-full ... or even over-empty.

FIVE ... The gabblers.

RICHARD was a docile person and his uneventful life included irregular visits to Sunday church at Crondall, which he calculated he must have attended about the right number of times because he had not been brought down by the plague ... unlike more than just a few others. One fine summer's day he walked through the churchyard and looked sadly across at the number of new graves. The disturbed plot was surrounded by trees and buzzing with other excited life - beyond the trees stood a boggy pond and insects could be seen flying above, caught in the mid-day sun. Dragonflies were looking for a meal and above, swallows were diving and wheeling over the whole area. The activity did not impinge on the stately progress of mallards, mother and six chicks, through the algae free areas of the pond.

Richard in his undemanding way, asked little of the fourteenth century, but had tried to dress up a bit for church and wore his best clothes, a simple, loose hay-coloured shirt with a faded pink tunic tied with thin rope at the waist. It was the first time he'd had a second set of clothes, the result of better rewards available to a decreased workforce. The colour of his brown leggings almost hid the smudges of dirt on the garment. He'd used some old pig hide for his home-made footwear and brimmed hat.

As he got beyond the graveyard, clear of the unkempt boundary wall, Richard reached the isolated old stone building at the edge of the village that had been neglected by the priory. A narrow short cut to the village green had been made through the remains, and had become a meeting place for a group of young malcontents, day labourers, who had gathered to discuss the matter of serf servitude. They always settled in this 'no-man's land' site to start their gabble, it became routine as the lengthening days and better weather gave opportunity for more social activity. There wasn't much else to do. They draped themselves around, on the large stones and logs that littered the approach to the entrance.

A mendicant Franciscan friar had told a lad with a bruised eye, when he was a boy, of a king three hundred years before who had come across the sea to impose ruthless laws on England, and made all his mates into lords. This was the basis of their gabble. Not for the first time the young fellows discussed that their lives were hard because of this king, called William the Bastard. Apparently he had gone quite near Crondall before he went on to the west, where the wild people were. The tone of their conversation, with its intermittent laughter, had a youthful ebullience that would have given any listening bystander the idea that the issue was not taken seriously. But the young hot-heads were serious enough to have stopped the enemy and have dealt with them properly had they been around at the time.

'I would have got a big army and swords, spears and shields ...' bruised eye said loudly whilst he shuffled on the remains of a wall. He hesitated because, having equipped his army, he realised he needed tactics. '... and because I know the country, I'd come up behind them.'

Some of the midges from the nearby pond had found their way to the group of rarely washed, invitingly young bodies, an attribute which protected them from the Black Death. The boys swatted urgently as swallows were arcing elegantly above biding their time.

Variants of the attack part of their conversation had been offered week after week by different young men, who presented their own version of the defence plan as if new, before being interrupted by the odd interjection where one or other had forgotten some detail. It was all done excitedly as if they were in battle, but eventually they ran out of ideas, and moved on to the matter of post-victory.

'Kill them all!' said a rather small but blood lusty sort of fellow, a suitable comment from someone covered in midge bites.

'That would be a waste, turn them all into slaves, get them to do all the work. And we could have a celebration dinner at the castle,' bruised eye said.

'But if you killed them all, what would you do with the bodies?' One was a bit more of a thinker, a more calculating individual. It was Anthony, son of the village bailiff, Ralph le Germin.

He was backed up by his friend, son of the village reeve. 'If you make them into slaves they'd have to be fed,' he said as he lifted a loose stone. He discovered that watching woodlice scattering for cover offered more interest.

Anthony, leaning languidly against an exposed, solid upright timber, said, 'And they'd have to have somewhere to live.'

'Why?!' said bloodlust.

'Because they tried to take over our country!' Bloodlust had some support from bruised eye.

'They deserved to be treated hard.' Bloodlust was a vengeful man.

On this occasion, when Richard was squeezing through them, he had to indicate that there was need to make some space for a young woman who had followed behind him down the church path and along the track. 'Oh, yes,' they said and quickly made space with unexpected grace.

Once Richard and the woman had walked clear of the group, she said, 'I don't know why they can't talk about something else. You'd think the impact of the Great Pestilence was more important.'

Richard was his usual monosyllabic self, 'Yes.'

'You're from Ewshott aren't you?'

'Yes.'

'I've got relatives over there. But I haven't been there because of the plague.'

'Sensible.'

'Did you see much of it?'

'No. I kept out of the way.'

'Sensible,' she said looking at him with a smile.

He couldn't stop himself having the trace of a smile. 'I think so.'

'Did you lose anyone?'

'No, there's just me.'

'I thought so. You did a good job that place over near the wastes on the edge of Trefle Field. It was Thomas de Becheur's place.'

'Did you know him?'

'No. Thomas died a few years ago now. Lived there for about twenty or thirty years. All the family did.'

Richard didn't know what to say next, because he had not been long in Crondall, and did not really know the woman, who was a noted village figure because she successfully protested at the manorial court when the steward had enclosed village pasture land to graze his sheep, a right he did not have. She cited manor custom and precedent, and gathered so much support within the community, that the lord and leading villagers had been forced to condemn the steward's action. As a result of this event she had become the person to seek out for all sorts of village problems.

Richard realised that he needed to say something, especially as he was talking to a woman.

'Trefle Field, is that what the place is called?'

'It seems to be.'

'What happened to them … the family?'

The young woman indicated that he was about to tread in some droppings. Richard hadn't noticed, he was concentrating on entertaining her. He stepped aside and she answered, 'The parents were old of course, one was killed by a tree one night in a storm, fell on her. They found her the next day. The man starved I think. Don't know what happened to the boy, went off I think.'

'Sad,' Richard said.

'Not unusual … '

'I suppose ...'

'What do you do when you're not working?'

'Not much.'

'Shall I come and visit you?'

'Well, er …' Richard had difficulty with the question, '… all right.'

The conversation happened so quickly and at such a speed that Richard could not really get hold of it and found, it seemed, that a woman was going to visit him … in his new home. He was confused, his thoughts were scattered, in fact there were so many they were crashing in to each other.

They walked on a few more paces whilst the woman waited for further words but nothing happened so she simply said, 'When?'

'Oh … whenever you like.'

'Well, you'll be at work tomorrow. I've seen you at the mill on Mondays, so I'll come later this afternoon shall I?'

'Yes,' he said in his inimitable way.

'I'll bring over some of our ale, we brew up from time to time and we've got some to celebrate mid-summer eve.' She had a winning smile. 'I don't expect you do much brewing yourself?'

'No, not really.'

'We've been trying dandelion leaves in with the malt, it's good. But we need to see what other people think of it.'

'I'd like to try that,' said Richard, now interested. He enjoyed a drop of ale, his access to the mill giving him the opportunity to get some barley for malt making, then brewing. If he didn't have any wood jobs to work on he had a sup, especially when there was nothing to do in the winter dark. He could then happily fall asleep and be set up for the next day's work.'

'God be with you,' she said and walked to the other end of the village.

'You as well.' Richard called and walked back towards his hovel. His face for once was not impenetrable, it was soft, relaxed. Was it possible there was a glimmer of a smile of self-satisfaction?

SIX ... Joan.

RICHARD was in his hovel in a dither. It was only when he got back from the church he realised the enormity of the situation he had placed himself in. He knew you had to offer food when someone visited, like they did at the monastery when travellers dropped by. He'd have to forego his normal breakfast and manage with some beans and peas, and his drop of ale ... maybe the woman would leave him some of the dandelion stuff? The woman ... he realised he didn't know her name ... she might want more than a bit of bread and the hunk of the cheese he'd got from the reeve for a job of work. So Richard put some more cabbage in his ever-ready pot over the hearth, and added a few herbs he'd dried from springtime and he'd still got some apples in the basket dangling up in the roof. As a standby he also had hazel nuts in a covered wooden bowl. Richard moved the flour pot clear of the entrance area and looked around for anything else, then came across a treat, a pot of pickle, with onion, radishes and cabbage stem, his favourite. Finally he checked that here was no evidence of ants in the food area. When he thought the matter through, Richard reckoned he could offer quite a feast so he started tidying up the place. He hung everything from the rafters - a working smock, some strings of yarn spun by the miller's wife, some sprigs of lavender, plus an old worn sickle, a souvenir of his father used for boon-work - and he cleared cob-webs at the same time. *Everything* was clear of scavenging rats. Then tidied his shaped wood store, including the component parts of his new shutter/ window, and put his tools in a neat bundle - axe and his collections of saws, hammers and chisels. In amongst these items he had his bucket, made from a couple of hoops from the unusable barrel he'd found outside, a few staves from his wood collection. It contained water for handy usage. It was lucky Widow Elizabeth hadn't wanted the stool he'd made so they would both be able to sit down. Lastly, he could clear the rushes from the floor as conditions had been dry of late.

So, all things considered, the situation wasn't so awful after all. But what did she mean, 'Come later this afternoon'? What time was that?! Richard was in a state of anxiety, there was the fire to watch, the wood platters and drinking jugs to get ready, the lay out to do, sitting places to fix … so much. Then he thought maybe his apple wood logs would be better, making a nice smell. But the smoke wouldn't find its way through the rush roof, just stay inside. And the table was a bit wobbly because of the uneven earth floor. Richard tried it in several positions but it wouldn't go right, and he couldn't solve the problem so his thoughts became scattered, like they were outside the church. He was dithering.

With Richard in this state, the woman arrived in the doorway, a pitcher slung over her shoulder, and looking rather fetching in her ankle length flowing wine-coloured gown over a mushroom toned chemise that reached up to her neck. She wore a cloth head-dress tucked into this. 'Hello Richard,' she said. He had difficulty in stopping himself from knocking into the wobbly table … she knew his name. He blinked and gaped, and she saw. 'The miller told me. Apparently the miller in Ewshott was always saying how good your work was. Richard Gunner. You know how things get around, even the whole manor.'

'Yes,' he said in his monosyllabic way.

'Here's the ale.' She held up a pitcher. 'Got any jugs?'

'Yes,' he said again, and went to inside of the hovel. She followed, 'My name is Joan.'

'Joan.'

Inside, Richard gestured to the newer, steady stool, the one Widow Elizabeth had failed to take, and he went to one of the many items dangling from his roof. He did have a couple of little horn jugs he had managed to get hold of at the mill. They'd been washed with water from the stream he'd put into the repaired bucket. Richard placed the jugs carefully on the wobbly table and Joan poured the ale.

'Sorry about this,' he said waving his arm around the place, 'And all the smoke, it's ...'

'That's alright,' she interrupted, 'You only need somewhere out of the weather and place to sleep at night. That's what you've got.'

'Yes.'

'You've said that before.'

'Sorry.'

'That too.'

Richard smiled, he couldn't help himself. It was a means of

releasing his embarrassment at his lack of conversation. He took a sip of the ale.

'Good eh?' Joan said.

'Yes.'

'Your favourite word.'

Richard laughed at her, and himself. He was beginning to get an after-taste of the ale, which was indeed rather good. Better than the stuff he sometimes made, and would be drinking the next day.

'We live near the east end of the village, you can see us working on our strips over towards Farnham when we're not on manor lands. It's not too bad because we don't have to go so far as some of the others.' Joan gave Richard a relaxed smile. 'You were lucky to already be in with the miller over in Ewshott. He even had the bailiff here in Crundell talking about your work.'

'Yes,' Richard said.

'I suppose we'll have to get used to, 'Yes'?'

'Y… I don't know what else to say.'

'Don't worry about it. Not everyone's like me, I gabble on.'

'Yes, it's nice.'

'… yes.' She said teasingly. 'As I said, the miller told the bailiff about you and the bailiff told the steward, I even think he told the lord. It's not only the villagers that gabble on.' Joan laughed with abandon and enjoyment.

Richard didn't think the remark merited such delight and was not sure how to respond. After a slight pause he said, 'Your ale really is good.'

'Have some more.' She topped up his jug, and gave herself another one.

'How many dandelion leaves do you put in?' Richard asked.

'Well you can put in what you like, but you've got to give them a bit of a boil to take some of the bitterness out. Then it's a matter of the taste, how sweet you want it, I like it to be equal … a bit of sweetness, a bit of bitterness.'

And very soon even Richard was actually talking a bit more. Their chatter was matched by the blackbirds which were making their familiar noises as the day wore on. Richard and Joan made a good pair. She did most of the talking, he did most of the listening. Complementary it could be called. It was nature at work. It became the medieval link in the Gunner story.

202

A STORY of GEORGE at HOME.

ONE ... A thousand years or so.

IN my aged house the next morning, I was just able to engage with the twilight world of sporadic reflection that my heart attack journey had somehow provided. I sat dozing in the armchair of our comfortable sitting room with an un-drunk cup of coffee on the side table. Not only had I been through two hundred years of stories of my known forbears, but a version of their lives in the critical, major events that my earlier generations had lived through - the eighteenth century and enclosures, the seventeenth century Civil War and social change, the sixteenth century and religious change, the fourteenth century of decimated population and economic change. They were events and times that shaped a nation, my family. Before then, back to the previous big event, 1066, some forbear must have been entered in the Domesday inventory for Crondall, as a villein, maybe a serf.

A thousand years ago, the real mists of time, was a time of few references, a time of comparatively little social detail. A time of scarcely disseminated ancient writings about pre-history, and scratched tombs or cave pictures, wooden churches, wall paintings and ornamental writings of scribe-monks. Useful references didn't really impact until the Renaissance, a development that was quickly followed by the arrival of printing due to the work of the German, Johannes Gutenburg, and when this invention was brought to London by William Caxton in the late fifteenth century, information could then be readily disseminated.

That period of a few hundred years between the Black Death and back to the Battle of Hastings, with the victory of William the Conqueror, was a period of Norman oppression, and serfdom for any lowly Anglo-Saxons. It is flicked through like a flip-book or a what-the-butler saw machine. And those earlier versions of Richard and Joan le Gunners, each post Hastings generation of them, led an unchanging life, repeated many times over. Many, many times.

Richard and Joan le Gunner versions one to twelve ('le serf Richard et la serf Joan') toiling in the fields, ploughing with oxen in Hampshire, clearing back acres of woodland with crude instruments, and in total thrall to the lord of the manor … doing the bidding of their many overlords, for three hundred years. They were, by the laws of the day, virtually the lord's possession. They had indifferent shelter, and food was hard to come by. It was best not to be ill or have an accident, treatment was by (un)wise men and women. Perhaps it was fortunate that life was so short. And I was at the end of it all, as were others, at the culmination of their long line - Pam, fellow patients, all at the end of their own story.

Though I was not really the end, there were others to follow, for me, the next was Hugh, then Peter with his hope of badminton success … how would his children fare in the twenty second century?

During the period of my mental sojourn, monarchical power had begun to be diluted, and the idea of easing social controls had been established. An incremental pattern of change was set in train to develop slowly down the centuries, maybe kick started by the improved employment opportunities that followed the Black Death. Twenty seven or eight generations of collective actions and ongoing change had continued down to me in hospital in the twenty first century.

But from me to the William the Conqueror was forty generations, and there were hundreds more before his time - Anglo-Saxons, Romans, Celts, Iron-Age people, Stone-Age people, the Neolithics and even more 'ithics. I, or my sub-conscious, or semi-conscious, had given up on my, sick/drug induced/hospital journey with Richard le Gunner. I could not get beyond a repeating life of deprivation and slavery. As for hunting in a gang, grunting and carrying a spear, wearing animal-skin clothing, well …

TWO ... A new life.

TWENTY four hours later I was catching up on life, taking it easy, as prescribed by everyone. I was in my sitting room, the mid morning coffee position, holding Dan Brown's 'The Da Vinci Code,' which I was belatedly reading on the day before the garden paving slab excitement. The heavy critics thought it lacked quality, but I found it a good read and it had excellent sales. Objective achieved, job done surely? I had told Pam I had a lot to do - catching up, because of the sudden pause in my life, and so many things to do, I didn't know how I could fit it all in. So Pam went to a coffee get together to discuss what to do about one of the flower show members who made dubious cakes for their functions. It was thought that maybe the woman should be dissuaded from baking the cakes. It seemed she was getting on and she was, well maybe … well, one just didn't know. The idea was to explain that they been offered a special concession by the relative of a committee member who had appeared on a TV cooking show, and it would be silly to turn her down with club funds so low. Whilst that was the idea, the problem was how to make it happen, present it, embellish it, sell it. I told Pam that her experience in these matters was critical, and she should go. It worked like a charm. The truth was that after the busy hospital ward, the busy family history journey, I just felt the need to be alone in own place for a couple of hours or so.

On my own in the quiet of the house, the racing blood in my head would not be quelled, the compulsion could not be resisted. I made my way across the soft carpet to the back door, stepped out onto the patio, and walked down the steps, continuing slowly, even nervously, down the garden to see the offending area, and offending items. And there it all was, or more exactly there they were, three paving slabs, lying askew beside a very shallow trench in the lawn, which was intended to neatly hold the paving. I now remembered in detail - I had tried to move the job along a bit more quickly because the light level had dropped and I thought it was going to rain. So I had decided to lift three slabs instead of the one as planned. Then - ouch, ow, bang, out! Next … head whirling … I'm out … dreaming, is it Holby City?! More head work ... and then a sort of life history, big time. I stood there, stock still, staring at my incomplete handiwork. If I couldn't lift paving slabs, what could I do? And if I couldn't do even undemanding tasks around house and garden, what? What next? Open a bottle or two? But even a little bit of what you fancy was now a health risk apparently, along with butter, salt, cheese, chips, crisps, cream, chocolate, cakes, coffee, sugar and of course anything with saturates, which seemed to get into everything. Wheat products could be tricky. And vegetables were dodgy, carrots seemed OK but one mustn't have too many, and cabbage was flatulence inducing. Even some fruits had too much acidity. Some research department somewhere would next discover that any last untainted food would be unhealthy, and the only thing that would then be left would be starvation, or some drug over-dose concoction for a final exit.

After a week out of hospital, I found I couldn't handle the sedentary lifestyle. I'd finished Dan Brown's 'The Da Vinci Code', and seen some day time TV - a few post WWII documentaries, and black and white British films. They brought home to me the changes that I had lived through. I got into a routine of a daily walk round the village. I'd checked in with Peter who was doing well in the junior badminton county championship. I'd fixed for various jobs to be done by a range of people - gardener, handymen and decorator. And I talked to Pam about going away on a trip, a chance to do nothing, and just be indulged. I teased her - could she manage to go without assorted village meetings for a couple of weeks or so?

She came back strongly, 'To keep you away from the garden, out of your tool shed, climbing ladders, chopping logs, and clear of the possibility that you might do something stupid, in that man-like way, I'd willingly go on a tour with you. We could do something a bit different, 'do' a whole country, what about Poland?'

I realised I'd touched a raw nerve and recalled an ad. in a glossy Nat. Trust mag. 'What about a trip down the Rhine? A gentle drift down the river peering at castles that looked as if they were built by the Walt Disney design department ... arrival at a historic city ... meet people. That could be a really good, very slow relaxing journey. A snail Orient Express all the way ... to Switzerland.'

Pam paused. 'Sounds good, providing we don't over eat. There always seems to be too much food on those cruises.'

'I'll do some more checking up,' I said, 'Look at a few web-sites.'

THREE ... The path of paving.

LIFE jogged along. Pam got back to her busy going here and there lifestyle. I read more books, watched more telly, whilst at the same time scratching around trying to set up our leisure trip. Peter had made it to the final of the junior badminton county championship. And one day, I felt really good, and decided to walk round the garden. I even put on my gardening clothes, secateurs at the ready in my pocket, pulled up a few weeds, pruned a bit of overgrowth here and there. It's what one does, routine pottering. After I'd made a few piles of stuff for the compost, I walked down to the bottom and confronted the paving slabs. They seemed to accuse me, transfix me, remind me of the drama they'd created. Once completed, the paving path was supposed to provide a pleasant route to a shady arbour set in a small pergola covered in clematis. I could have a glass of wine there whilst the sun shone and the flowers bloomed. When I first had the idea I thought it too coy for words, it would have been like something out of, 'House and Garden' ... and it would be coy. 'So what?!' I thought.

Finishing the path was not a job that I'd listed to be done by assorted workers, because I had still not made the final decision about how the path should look. But the matter was simple, no decision equals no path, no arbour, no idyllic spot. The thought that now confronted me was not a gardening matter, it was like one of the table tennis matches I'd played all those years ago – it was me ... or the other guy. It was me ... or the paving stones. I decided to go back to the house and check all my sketch-plans of the project, and settle on the best one, then find a landscape gardener ... in between seeing about the trip down the Rhine.

FINALE.

ELSEWHERE more boisterous activity was occurring. It was match point in the final of the junior county open badminton championship.

Peter was not expected to win, but he had been working doubly hard, he was fitter and stronger than just six months ago. He was confident, and grateful that his grandfather had been so hard on him, pushing him - exercises in the gym, arms, legs; stamina on the track, heart and breathing; and a programme of footwork routines, over and over again. And constant court practice in addition, Peter recalled that his grandfather had said it didn't mean anything without getting the head right. To be so practiced in body and mind that the game performance flowed spontaneously and independently, and yet, strangely, one was still able to monitor the effort – the footwork, the arm swing, the loose wrist, the eyesight sharp with eyes never off the shuttlecock. To be in the moment, not concerned about the loss or winning of the last point, not concerned about the moment to come, the possibility of defeat or victory. His grandfather had been almost obsessive about this playing ingredient. Feeling a complete lack of it in his own game all those years ago had made all the difference to his performances. He had repeatedly mentioned that his arms had too much tension, his wrist was tense, his footwork heavy, his breathing stertorous, all because he didn't have the right mental attitude. And because he was worried that he was about to lose a point, or over excited in anticipation of winning the next point. He was never _in_ the moment.

Peter's face looked impassive, it was difficult to tell whether he cared at all about what was going on. His opponent had to deal with expectation that he was the favourite, and now in danger of losing to someone considered to be a lesser player. There was a tension in his face, the jaws were clenched, the eyes bright with excitement, maybe too much excitement.

Peter jogged a little to keep himself loose, so did his opponent. They both settled for the imminent serve, but Peter still rocked a little to have his all his muscles toned in preparation for whatever direction the shuttlecock would take. He locked his eyes on the shuttlecock in his opponent's hand, cleared his mind for action. The shuttlecock floated over the net almost touching it, and short, Peter judged it to be just within the serving area. With precise care he returned it shorter and closer to the net on the server's forehand, really requiring him to lift the shuttlecock very high up into the roof and open out the game. As the shuttlecock fell the server ran back anticipating a smash to his forehand but Peter chose the critical deep backhand far corner to make a more difficult return for his opponent to make. And so it proved, the problem of accurately hitting back with body turned away from the net and less control with the wrist, was decisive, the returning shuttle-cock went into the net.

There was an ear shattering howl of delight. A punch in the air. Much jumping. 'Yes! Yes! Yes!' Peter shouted. Feelings of elation were allowed when the game was won, and success achieved.

CODA.

THE Gunner household was, in contrast, quiet, the garden looked bright on a fine English summer day - grass cut and lush, the flowers colourful, birds chirping in appreciation. It was settled, just the gentle sounds of nature, but it was suddenly shattered by an elated Pam calling from the back door. She had returned from another meeting to a ringing telephone. Pam could see George sitting contentedly, looking at his completed project. He was a picture at the bottom of the garden in the cherished arbour, the pergola-arch set within a beech hedge and entwined with established clematis and an attractive stepping stone path snaking its way back to the house .

Pam walked down hurriedly … but in a lady-like way.

'George! George! Didn't you hear the phone go? Good news. Good news. It's Peter.'

George didn't move. There was no reaction. Nothing. His eyes were directed continuously, twinklingly one might say, at his new stepping stone path in the lawn. He had dirt all over his hands.

POST SCRIPT.

Later, Peter and Pam were clearing through the miscellany of George's desk … Pam found a thick file on the desktop on which he had written … 'Notes on a Joe Bloggs.'

THE END.

<u>Notes ... for interested parties.</u>   The use of the name Gunner replaces Craddock, because the Craddock family line really IS Gunner, the story being that the family name was Craddock Gunner into the 20c and dating back to at least the end of 18c.   The Gunner element was lost in the (now) Craddock line, in the 1880s, for some unknown reason which, one is tempted to think, might be 'interesting'.   George was the Christian name used down generations of Gunners for centuries.   A Crondall, Hampshire, parish record notes the burial of a George Gunner in 1680.

(Poss. b. during civil war when parliamentary forces were in the village.)

(George - Greek, farmer or earth worker – a name rarely used in England before the 18c. Hanoverian Georges, though the name dates back to third century and St. George.)

For the record – the early material is a decent representation of facts. The Lucy (Zavvy) + John (Leslie John) stuff is my version of their lives, but with little embellished details.   The Fred, Ethel Edith, Bridget, James material is an interpretation derived from the <u>facts</u> of their lives, with more embellishment, but a fair version I should think.   The journeys within Ireland, and England, are imagined as is the Penny Gaff ingredient which is invented from Mayhew.   When we get to 'early' George, we are in to crossover time – material based on <u>some</u> facts, with a lot of embellishment. Thus what actually happened in The Globe pub is imagined (with some help from Mayhew).   All the material chronologically before this is almost all fiction based on historical events.

The ***brief*** mention of Walter Gunner is a disservice, he lost both feet trying to stop a runaway tram.   In 1919 he was awarded the Albert Medal for bravery.

(George's 'Public Relations Manager at Wayside Friary Hotel Chain' = TV drama Producer/Director at BBC.)

212

After-thought - an ingredient in the idea behind this project was the twenty first century pre-occupation with the present, thus the story strand of a present (in hospital) connected with its past.   Additional, was the idea to, '... inform, educate and entertain' (to use to a familiar phrase) using the novel form.   It may be, that in places, the, 'inform' element intrudes but I hope the, 'entertain' element remains sufficiently satisfying.

Sources consulted – Frances & Joseph Gies (14c.), John Chandler (Salisbury,) Henry Mayhew (mid. 19c,) plus Marion Gibbs, Liza Picard, Roy Porter, Wlm. Henry Hudson, J.H.Bettey, J.P.Thompson, Richard Cobbett, Charles Dickens, Peter Ackroyd, wikpedia, BHF, and other authoritative writings.   The end product will I hope, be considered a reasonable idea of the history of the Gunners, a Joe Bloggs family.

Notes on the ANCESTRY LINE :-

The first half takes place in and around London, approximately back to about the time of the Industrial Revolution, and is informed mostly by available material.   The sequence of characters appear in the following reverse chronological order :-

George Gunner.   (mid 20c.)
John & Lucy Gunner.   (early to mid 20c.)
Fred(erick) & Ethel Edith Gunner.   (19 into 20c.)
James & Bridget Gunner.   (19c.)
('Early') George & Ann Gunner.   (very late 18 into early 19c.)

The second half moves into rural territory, to Crondall, Hampshire, and continues back, based on historical material, in reverse chronological order, and the character sequence is :-

Jump to ... William Gunner and Lizzie.   (mid 18c.)
Jump to ... Mary and son Thomas Gunner.   (mid 17c)
Jump to ... Henry & Jane Gunner + family.   (mid 16c.)
Jump to ... Richard (le) Gunner and Joan.   (mid 14c.)
... and the rest.